beauty

beauty

Foreword by Diane Ackerman

An Anthology by John Miller

CHRONICLE BOOKS
SAN FRANCISCO

To maintain the authentic style of each writer
included herein, quirks of spelling and grammar
remain unchanged from their original state.

Library of Congress Cataloging-in-Publication Data:

Beauty / an anthology by John Miller; foreword by Diane Ackerman.
p.   cm.
ISBN 0-8118-1340-1 (pbk.)
1. Beauty—Literary collections. I. Miller, John, 1959-
PN6071.B36B33 1997
808.8'0353—dc21   96-44525
CIP

Front cover image: photographer unknown, circa 1921
Book and cover design: Big Fish Books
Composition: Eleanor A. Reagh, Big Fish Books

Distributed in Canada by Raincoast Books,
8680 Cambie Street,
Vancouver, B.C. V6P 6M9

10 9 8 7 6 5 4 3 2 1

Chronicle Books
85 Second Street
San Francisco, CA 94105

Web Site: www.chronbooks.com

SPECIAL THANKS TO JENNIFER PETERSEN

BEAUTY

Diane Ackerman

Foreword

⌣

C LOSE YOUR EYES and picture the face of someone you love. Without meaning to, you will begin to smile, your eyes will squint just a little as you savor the image, and a warmth will flood your heart. As poets have said, a face can launch a thousand ships, or stock a private armada of rejection and woe. Lovers can sit and stare at one another for hours, soldering their hearts together with a whitehot gaze, finding in the other's face a view of paradise. The only other time this happens is when a mother looks at her child. Hypnotized by the baby's face, gladdened by the narcotic of her love, she could happily sit and stare at it for days on end. The baby smiles at her, and she melts. A child is the most powerful pitchman on earth, and that really is the secret to facial beauty. What physical features of a woman's face does every era find attractive? Society reads childlike, even infantile, facial features as "cute." Small children naturally

DIANE ACKERMAN *is the author of* The Moon by Whale Light, A Natural History of Love, *and the best-selling* A Natural History of the Senses *(1990), where she shares her ideas of beauty.*

develop plump bulging cheeks, a large forehead, big eyes, a small round chin and, often, dimples.

But fortunately, beauty's power isn't absolute in every case. The equation of looks and personality runs in both directions: We credit attractive people with being superior in other ways: but we also credit good/talented/superior people with being more attractive. Consider the sometimes dissonant features of many famous and talented women thought to be beautiful—Marlene Dietrich, for example, an icon of the Thirties. She was a beautiful woman with an angular face and quite sunken cheeks. To achieve that caved-in look, she had her upper rear molars removed when she was a young starlet. To look wide-eyed and innocent, she plucked her eyebrows into very high, thin, rounded arches that made her look like she was always on the verge of asking a question. Many of the signals she gave off were of a tough, hard-boiled, cigarette-smoking vixen. But her look confused the effect nicely—could a sweet, innocent child really be so tough?

As Dietrich understood, we often judge someone's character by their looks. Attractive people do land jobs more easily, get promoted faster, have more sweethearts, and, if they're criminals, even receive lighter jail sentences. So it's no surprise when John Woodforde reminds us that reconstructive surgery is simply an ancient practice that's thriving once again. And if the era is decadent, as Dietrich's was, the innocence becomes the novelty, the real *frisson*. Tweezed eyebrows came back in the 1990s for a similar reason—because there wasn't much left to surprise us. What with AIDS, crack cocaine, "ethnic cleansing," gruesome

mini-series, high corruption, and tabloid blood-fests, real innocence was in short supply. But we remembered what it was, we
knew what innocence felt like in our eyes, in our cheekbones. We
wore it like an antique gem. And we knew instinctively it was a
selling card.

After all, the face is the first thing we notice about someone. A face reminds us of our parents, or an old lover, or someone who hurt us. Faces tell us how people feel, if they're anxious,
playful, confident, or sullen. Sometimes a face records, in its fine
lines, a lifetime of easy laughter or stubbornness. Character may
come from within, but a face gives one a sense of identity. While
other animals can recognize and greet their kin and friends by
smell, we recognize a person by the face. When a new baby is
born, one of the first questions we ask is: "Whom does he or she
resemble?" We have to be able to recognize faces quickly to weave
through all the relationships in our complex society, and we're
especially good at spotting a face in a sea of warring stimuli, or
recognizing a familiar face from just a few lines of caricature,
especially a beautiful face.

We study and admire Sophia Loren's or Paul Newman's
beautiful face, just as we do the face of a loved one. Humans have
always been fascinated by the face, whether it's familiar, exotic,
or famous. Portraiture goes back at least as far as sixteen thousand years, to the days of the Cro-Magnons, who carved the profile of one of their people on a limestone plaque, which was
discovered in a cave at La Marche, France. Throughout history,
humans have associated identity with the face—the face we find
on ancient coins, in Ice Age carvings, in death masks, on the

shrunken heads of enemies, outlined in ochre on Paleolithic walls, painted in three-quarter view (known as "eye and a half") by 15th-century Venetians, carved in gems as cameos, etched on copper to make cheap daguerreotypes, collected in photo albums. In his portraits, Leonardo strove to reveal what he referred to as "the motions of the mind." We find faces on ancient coins, in death masks, on the shrunken heads of enemies, carved into jewelry, painted on musical instruments, outlined in ochre on Paleolithic walls. We collect photographs of faces. We face off, face the music, interface, lose face, do an about-face, face up to, fall flat on our faces, talk face to face. We consult the face of the clock, stand facing a lake, notice how the face of the city has changed, and lament how life may one day vanish from the face of the earth. A mother can be hypnotized by the scrunched-up marvel of her baby's face, happily watching it for hours. Couples, magnetized by love, can stare at each other's face for what seems an eternity. On the face of it, we are obsessed with faces. And why not? A beautiful face is enough to start the engines of love.

Edmund Burke

The Qualities of Beauty

O N T H E W H O L E, the qualities of beauty, as they are merely sensible qualities, are the following: First, to be comparatively small. Secondly, to be smooth. Thirdly, to have a variety in the direction of the parts; but, fourthly, to have those parts not angular, but melted as it were into each other. Fifthly, to be of a delicate frame, without any remarkable appearance of strength. Sixthly, to have its colors clear and bright, but not very strong and glaring. Seventhly, or if it should have any glaring color, to have it diversified with others. These are, I believe, the properties on which beauty depends; properties that operate by nature, and are less liable to be altered by caprice, or confounded by a diversity of tastes, than any other.

Heralded British statesman **EDMUND BURKE** *wrote on a dizzying array of topics:* On American Taxation, Reflections on the French Revolution, *and* A Philosophical Inquiry into the Origin of Our Ideas of the Sublime and Beautiful (*1776*).

W o m e n   a n d   B e a u t y

·◞

W

HEN WE THINK about beauty, we usually dwell on the mechanics—skin creams, hairdos, how to apply mascara. This is an important approach because, after all, most of us are always ready to learn some new trick that will make us more attractive. And these techniques do work. Nonetheless, what I propose to do in this book is to give a different approach to beauty, one that will serve women of all ages and of different natural gifts. My approach to beauty begins not with the face or figure but with the mind. If you can learn to use your mind as well as you use a powderpuff, you will become more truly beautiful.

As teenagers most of us are enthralled with makeup and hairstyles. This is a new world to us and a badge of our femininity and we spend hours at the mirror experimenting. But as time goes by, we limit our beauty explorations to a new color of lip-

---

Actress **SOPHIA LOREN** *detailed her thoughts (and tips) on her most impressive attribute in the 1984 book,* Women and Beauty.

stick or a new hairstyle. We become set in our ways. Our ideas about beauty have become formed and we move on to other pursuits. When we are shopping for a new dress or at the hairdresser, we might give some thought to the way we look, but we do so in a sporadic and disorganized way. This means that as adults we are left with ideas about beauty that haven't really changed since we were adolescents. As mature women, we still think that beauty is technique and too few of us progress beyond that notion.

I suggest that once the fervent explorations of our youth are past, it is time to take a new look at beauty. For mature beauty is very different from youthful beauty. It demands a different approach. Where youthful beauty is unconscious, mature beauty is knowing and sophisticated. It admits to effort. It is also richer and more complex.

Beauty is valuable. There is no doubt of that. We live in a world that prizes beauty and rewards those who are believed to be beautiful. This can seem most unfair until you come to understand what beauty really is and what part it plays in your life.

A journalist once said of me that my mouth is too large, my nose is too long, my chin and lips are too broad and yet the sum of the parts is somehow beautiful. I tell you this not to praise myself but simply to demonstrate that beauty doesn't exist as an ideal. There is a great deal you can learn about beauty that has nothing to do with cosmetics or hairdos or diet or exercise. If I can convince you of this, the techniques of beauty, important as they are, will fall into their proper place as enhancements, not essentials.

If you were to ask a half dozen people what they think makes a woman beautiful, you would probably get a list of specific features: a big smile, long, glossy hair, a firm, slim figure, perfect, glowing skin and so on. All these attributes are certainly beautiful and any woman would be glad to have them. Yet I believe that beauty is something more than this.

Perhaps you have heard it said that "beauty is only skin deep," or some such proverb, and you may not believe it. It sounds like a stuffy moral judgment or the sort of comfort a mother gives her plain daughter. But from my experience in a business obsessed with beauty I can tell you that this notion of beauty being something more than a list of features is true.

I am sure you can see it in your own life. Consider for a minute the women you know and see frequently and one or two will probably come to mind as being especially beautiful. But if you think about it, they are probably more attractive than beautiful. Because if you stop and examine these "beautiful" women you will almost surely see that something more than hair, eyes, skin and figure made them spring to mind. In fact, they may have some defects like a big nose or small eyes or a less-than-perfect complexion. Yet somehow they have convinced you, and probably most of the people in their lives, that they are beautiful.

You have to remember that the beauty business today is large and lucrative. It is a business that is forced to assume that ideal beauty is a reality, otherwise it couldn't possibly come to grips with the many different ways in which women are beautiful. To handle such diversity would be an overwhelming task and would rob the fashion world of the "freshness" of each season that adopts and promotes a new "ideal" beauty. It is easier—and more profitable—to tell people that all lips should be pale this year than to tell them that pale lipstick is being sold but not to buy it unless it is right for them and their old lipstick is worn out. It is largely for business reasons that fashions change so much from year to year, and the woman who is deemed "beautiful" this year is outdated the next.

But ideal beauty is a mirage. Altering your hairstyle to the "perfect" style for your face or discovering an extraordinary new night cream or eye shadow or this season's popular new dress designer will certainly alter your appearance, but real beauty is not just a matter of looking up-to-date. There is an element of beauty that has nothing to do with what you will see in most books and magazines. Once you have accepted this, you are ready to understand what makes a woman beautiful and to learn how you can cultivate your own beauty in the most effective way.

In my opinion, there are two things you must recognize about beauty in order to achieve it: first, that it is within your reach, and second, that it is worth working for.

I think it is helpful to take a close look at the word "vanity" in order to convince yourself that beauty is within your reach.

Vanity and Beauty

I read not long ago that to be vain is to have too high an opinion of one's looks. This seemed correct to me and of no particular interest. But later the definition came back to mind, and the more I thought about it the more it seemed to me that it contained an important error. We know that vanity is foolish and therefore, according to this definition, if we are to avoid vanity we must have an accurate opinion of our appearance. But do we take the world's opinion of how we look and assume it is the truth? Do we count on others to let us know where we fit on the scale of perfection? I believe that this would be a great mistake.

You must be realistic about many things in life. If you are a bad driver, you shouldn't borrow someone's new Rolls-Royce. If you can't sing, you shouldn't inflict your arias on others. But no matter what others think, you must be convinced that, in your way, you are beautiful. What this amounts to is that in order to be beautiful, a woman must be vain. At first, the idea seems repulsive. Who, after all, would wish to be considered unrealistically pleased with her own looks? But give the idea a little more attention and I think you will understand what I mean and will come to agree with me.

As I said before, a collection of perfect features does not make for beauty. Perfect features, perfectly assembled, call to mind the cold proportions of a Greek statue, not a warm, desirable, beautiful woman. So if it is not conforming to an ideal of what is beautiful that makes a woman attractive, what is it? And what does this have to do with vanity?

Again, if you turn to your friends or even to women who appear in the media, you will see that the beautiful ones, those who catch your eye and make you delight in them and perhaps envy them, are the ones who believe that they are beautiful. Somehow they have discovered that they are beautiful, and they radiate the pleasure of their discovery, even though their features or their figures or their makeup are not perfect. You recognize immediately their confidence in their own appearance. Indeed, I am convinced that nothing makes a woman more beautiful than the belief that she is so.

When I began my career, my nickname was "Giraffe" because I was so tall and awkward. No one thought I was especially beautiful, but everyone knew right away that I was proud. In the beginning people were impressed with my confidence, and gradually they came to see it as beauty. On the other hand, I know a woman who is convinced that she is too tall; she is so self-conscious about her height that most of the time she looks as if she would like to disappear. All she thinks about is her height and that is all you notice about her. Unless her attitude changes, the sad fact is that although she is very pretty, she has no chance of being thought attractive.

And so we return to the idea of vanity. If to be vain is to have too high an opinion of your looks, then you all should learn to be vain—not in the vulgar, competitive sense, but with the healthy, positive conviction that you are beautiful. You must all, somewhere deep in your hearts, believe that you have a special beauty that is like no other and that is so valuable that you must not abandon it. Indeed, you must learn to cherish it. Later I will talk about some of the qualities that you need to think about if you are to have a healthy vanity, such as charm, self-confidence and style. But first I want to convince you of the importance of vanity for your own sense of beauty.

Though I, like everyone else, have made mistakes in discovering my own beauty, I can tell you of an instance early in my career when the vanity of a young girl served me well. When I first had the opportunity for a screen test, I was just a girl from nowhere eager for a chance to begin a career. After every screen test it was always the same story from the technicians: there is no way to make this girl look good—her nose is too long and her hips too broad. And would I think about trimming off just a bit of my nose?

In retrospect, I am surprised and proud of the vanity of the girl I was then. Though poor and anxious to begin work, I refused to alter anything. They would take me as I looked or not at all. I was very lucky that I didn't ruin my career at that moment. Eventually I profited by looking only like myself and not like what was fashionable years ago with certain film technicians in Rome. Though I made that decision instinctively, I realize now that a woman who believes with great conviction in her attractiveness will ultimately convince others that she is correct. And like my tall friend, a woman convinced of her ugliness will also convince others of it.

It is a lack of vanity that leads women in so many wrong directions in their quest for beauty. If you have a low opinion of your appearance, you are at the mercy of every salesperson and every hairdresser who wants to give you bad, if "fashionable," advice about how you should look. We have all seen women changing their look from season to season, trying to discover their beauty but always vulnerable to the world's opinion of their appearance. They, and we, need vanity in order to discover our genuine beauty.

Working Toward Beauty

Perhaps you are saying, "It is all very well, Sophia, for you to say that I must be vain and then, believing I am beautiful, I will be so. But it's not that easy for me." Of course, you are right if you hesitate at this point and tell yourself that beauty is more than belief. Yes, there is a mundane side to this, which brings me to my second point about beauty: that it is worth working for.

At first this seems obvious—what woman would deny it? And yet . . . and yet . . . there seems to be a side to most women that refuses to recognize that it is worth the time and effort it takes to be beautiful. As I have said already, only the very young girl is effortlessly beautiful. She has a freshness and potential that are uniquely appealing. But don't envy her. It is immature to think that you can be beautiful forever without trying, that a freshly washed face and the most handy clothes will carry you through a lifetime.

I am afraid that the media help promote the idea of effortless beauty. We watch a film in which a woman wakes up in the early morning, her hair tousled but somehow perfect, her face dewy and radiant, her lashes dark seemingly without mascara, her lips naturally rosy. We are supposed to believe that a woman really looks this way in the first minutes of her day.

I know I don't look like that and you probably don't either. But we are made to feel that there is something wrong if we have to put effort into achieving our best look. Many woman, understandably enough, rebel against this. They tell themselves that they won't bow to fashion and the dictates of beauty, that it is all impossible and frivolous and not worth the effort. They give up. They wear any old thing and see lipstick as a political weapon. Though I can understand this reaction, I think they are making a mistake. With a positive attitude, beauty is within the reach of every woman.

Don't be ashamed to take the necessary time to maintain your appearance: it is important to your own feelings of self-esteem and therefore will affect how the world reacts to you. I don't mean that spending hours on makeup and shopping and hairstyling is essential to beauty. I know many women who have brief and simple beauty routines that serve them very well. In this book you will learn about my beauty routines, and they are certainly not complicated or time-consuming. But no one arrives at such routines without effort.

I hope that I have convinced you to take your beauty seriously. I hope that you will, perhaps with the help of this book, discover what is beautiful about yourself. And then I hope that you will commit yourself to the effort that real beauty requires.

And finally, before I become too serious and ponderous, let me remind you that the pursuit of beauty is one of the great joys of being a woman. It should give you pleasure and it should be fun. When you try on a hat or an eyeliner, you see yourself in a new light. Knowing yourself a little better gives you confidence and even power. Working toward beauty should bring both joy and fulfillment.

Self-Confidence

In 1959, I was making a film called *Heller in Pink Tights*. George Cukor was directing, and I was eager to work with him because he had a reputation as a "woman's director." Everyone said he had a special instinct about developing a woman's potential and had an eye for beauty. I expected him to spend a lot of time fussing with makeup and costume, and he certainly was demanding about these things. But gradually I came to learn that for him the soul of beauty was elsewhere. One day, in the course of explaining how a character should emphasize her attractiveness, he said something that I have never forgotten: "Beauty without self-confidence is less attractive than ugliness with self-confidence. If you are confident, you are beautiful."

Since then, time and time again I have seen Cukor's words demonstrated at parties, on film sets, or on the street: a woman without self-confidence will never be beautiful in a way that attracts others. I can't tell you exactly why this is so, but it is. Perhaps because we are all to some degree doubtful about ourselves, we look to others for certainty. This is as true for a woman who wants to be beautiful as it is for a politician who wants to lead men. If a woman seems convinced of her allure, we believe her and we are drawn to her.

Confidence is difficult to define, but we all know it when we see it. Sometimes it can be a woman who walks proudly down the street and attracts our eye even though she is not particularly pretty. Sometimes it is a man who, though very famous or important, is genuinely kind to those around him. In my opinion, self-confidence implies a balance between courage and self-control. True confidence is always marked by simplicity and sincerity. Confidence grows when you try to be yourself at your best.

You can build self-confidence by knowing yourself. That is not just a matter of counting your strengths. You must know your weaknesses as well. Self-confidence doesn't grow from perfection; that is out of the question. If you know your weaknesses, you can control them, not vice versa.

Confidence begins with experience. You act in a certain way and you meet with success, and the next time you are confident about how to act. I have found this to be true in so many cases. When faced with my first interview or my first television talk-show appearance, I was far from confident. But I tried to act as if I were completely calm and in control, and that helped me. The next time, I was truly confident even though I was still nervous; I had been through it before and I knew what to do.

As far as beauty is concerned, in order to be confident we must accept that the way we look and feel is our own responsibility. It can be hard to accept this today in a world which encourages us to put the blame for all our problems elsewhere—on our parents, friends, jobs. But unless you decide to take a positive attitude toward your appearance, there is little hope of success. You can never be confident because you don't believe the matter is in your hands. Once you are convinced you have reason to be confident, the potential to be truly beautiful is yours.

A Large Bosom or a Small

T HE AMERICAN IS *happy to bring his wife to the surgeon, thinking that she will regain all her beauty. It is with joy and insistence that he encourages her to have an operation. He often asks to be present in order to lavish encouragement on her and to discuss with me the best location for operating. The Englishman shares this point of view but is rarely present at the operation . . . In the northern countries the most complete mascu- line indifference prevails.*

DR. SUZANNE NOËL, CELEBRATED FRENCH

COSMETIC SURGEON, 1926.

Most cosmetic surgery in England is done by general surgeons as a part-occupation. Yet some may carry out in the course of a year 100 face lifts, 150 nose alterations and 50 operations on breasts— so it is suggested by London's Harley Medical Group.

JOHN WOODFORDE'S *salient question, "A Large Bosom or a Small," is answered in the pages of his amusing 1992 study,* The History of Vanity.

Cosmetic surgery grows more sought after and twenty per cent of applicants are men. Some submit to it to keep a spouse or because they are in the public eye; but vanity in its most commonly accepted sense is the usual spur. For a woman (and equally for a man) the trauma of just getting older can prompt action; cosmetic surgery seems the means to a fresh start. It can, in a way, put the clock back. But in due course nature will take over and a return trip to the cosmetic surgeon will be necessary.

People have been having facial operations since civilizations began. Noses, for example, were being restored and repaired in India thousands of years ago. The Roman doctor Cornelius Celsus drew on Indian experience for his work and for his book *De Medicina* of A.D. 30, in which he wrote about plastic surgery for noses, lips and ears (the first writings about such operations in surgical literature). It must be said, though, that these operations were to deal with injuries and gross defects of nature and not just to concoct good looks. Terrors, needless to say, were involved for the patients.

Modern cosmetic surgery dates from around 1885 when various local anaesthetics were invented as improvements on laughing gas. In 1887 the surgeon John Roe of Rochester, New York, published an essay called "The Deformity Termed Pug Nose," which described treatment. The first abdominal operation for overweight was performed by Howard Kelly of Baltimore in 1889. He relieved a man of 15 pounds of fat. The first face lift was carried out by Eugene Hollander of Berlin in 1901, for a Polish aristocrat who offered detailed sketches of what he wanted done.

An actress underwent this operation in 1906 at the hands of Erich Lexer, a German, who was talented as a sculptor and painter as well as a surgeon.

Results in those days looked tight, mask-like and only good in parts. Photographs survive. Hollander believed it was necessary for a patient to feel very uncomfortable tension for up to three days. Robert Gersumy of Vienna thought he had the answer to the tight look: injecting paraffin wax instead of any scalpel work. But he did harm to the reputation of cosmetic surgery after writing enthusiastically about this in 1903. The injections did indeed remove wrinkles, but only for a short time; they caused much discomfort and before long the cosmetic results were dreadful.

Such well-known doctors as Joseph Safian of New York recall patients begging them in the 1920s to deal with the effects of paraffin injected into the face. Hundreds of cosmetic surgeons struggled almost hopelessly to remove masses of facial tissue infiltrated by solidified paraffin wax: the whole permeated part had to be taken away. Indeed, work on paraffinomas, as they were called, constituted a major part of the early cosmetic surgeon's practice.

A large number of the cosmetic operations in the early twentieth century seem to have been performed by people stigmatized by the medical profession as charlatans, often because they advertised incautiously. And certainly there was some irresponsible advertising in the Press. The Princess Bust Developer was said to do wonders and a certain Bust Cream and Food was unrivalled for developing not only the bust but also the neck and arms.

Bust developers, abdominal supports, chin straps and wrinkle removers were manufactured mainly in Chicago, America's center for folk songs, folk nostrums and folk medicines. It was in Chicago that Dr. Charles Conrad Miller, graduate of Louisville College of Medicine, wisely opened a cosmetic surgery in 1903. Soon the public flocked to it, partly because of the many articles he wrote—such is the power of the printed word. Dr. Miller, only partly a quack, wrote a book called *Cosmetic Surgery* which caused a stir in 1907 and is still looked at by surgeons.

> *When a woman consults the family physician regarding a defect of facial outline the family physician is likely to laugh. But cosmetic surgery is a special field worthy of the closest study by the ablest of our profession, for he who operates has at stake the future happiness of the patient. Operations for improving the appearance cannot be botched. The criminal carelessness of advertisers is unbelievable to those who have not seen the results . . . Many who have consulted me have been mutilated . . .*

Dr. Miller described the excision of crow's feet lines, the correction of thick or inverted lips, nose improvement, changing the size of the mouth, removal of facial lines, making prominent ears lie flat and the obliteration of tattoos. He pioneered treatment for bag-like folds of skin around the eyes, issuing photographs of this work which influenced surgical practice. He described the creation for a young girl of a dimple, "located by her smile," remark-

ing that he had to be "forced into the performance of this particular operation."

Dr. Miller did his operations under the local anaesthesia
of a weak cocaine solution—half a grain in an ounce of boiled
water. He used gentle techniques. He sewed with fine cambric
needles and to avoid tiny marks never tied his stitches too tight.

With the pace and glamour that marked the 1920s,
bright predictions for the future of cosmetic surgery came true,
and even more patients arrived at Dr. Miller's new clinic in a
fashionable part of Chicago. Having there the assistance of
four nurses, he performed cosmetic procedures one after
another, sending patients wanting a general anaesthetic to a
nearby hospital.

Dr. Miller's prose style drew attention from many outside
the medical world and no less a writer than S. J. Perelman wrote
of him as follows under the heading "Mid-Winter Facial Trends":

> *The doctor starts off casually enough with instruc-
> tions for correcting outstanding ears, which range
> all the way from tying them flat to the head to some
> pretty violent surgery. Personally, I have found
> that a short length of three-quarter-inch manila
> hemp bound stoutly about the head, the knot pro-
> truding just below one's hat, adds a rakish twist to
> the features and effectively prisons ears inclined to
> flap in the wind.*

Other surgeons often disagreed with Miller, only to take up his inventions as their own years later. It is a fact, though, that his long career was marred by some of his experiments. In 1926 he wrote of curious materials implanted through a tube to correct depressions and lines, these including, in his words, "bits of braided silk, bits of silk floss, particles of celluloid, vegetable ivory and several other foreign materials."

With the depression of the early 1930s, demand for cosmetic surgery was reduced and Dr. Miller became busy with general surgery. He wrote modestly: "As one grows older one finds more satisfaction in doing operations which cure disease rather than those which merely satisfy vanity." For all that, cosmetic surgery remained his great interest and in the words of Dr. B. O. Rogers, his book "*Cosmetic Surgery* justifies our regarding him as the father of modern cosmetic surgery."

Dr. Miller issued forty-four papers as well as the book, and surgeons prepared to do cosmetic work on his better principles became active after the First World War, in which wonders were done restoring wounded men. Further, many face-lifting and other beautifying operations were undertaken on civilians in the period 1918–30.

Raymond Passot wrote in 1919 of the great social value of cosmetic operations, their stimulating effect on morale, urging that women should not leave things until the skin had collapsed. In 1920 Adulbert Bettman was encouraging face-lift patients by assuring them that little discomfort was involved. "One woman," he writes, "after having the operation, proceeded immediately to a local department store where she bought a hat suitable for her now youthful appearance." Jacques Joseph of Berlin was genuinely concerned about the poor and the oppressed, and in 1921 gave accounts of wrinkle-removal to help prematurely-aged working women of forty-five to get employment.

There was in the twenties an unexplained fashion for a flat chest—see any contemporary photograph or drawing—and some women found their effects at strapping down to be inadequate. Women with heavy breasts went to a surgeon in despair: their trouble, they said, was too much to live with. The surgeon was able to effect with difficulty a reduction. Then, within a few years, came a fashion-reversal from America. And bosom culture was mandatory.

Up and down the country English women were now buying special brassières and trying to stimulate reduced breasts to fill them. Some gave up and bought inflatable busts with a short tube for topping up. Others, preferring the real thing, returned to their surgeons for an expensive surgical enlargement.

For the women of Japan an awkwardness arose after 1945 when fashion called for the wearing of bust-conscious Western clothes made for Western figures: Japanese women are flat-chested by nature, a circumstance catered for by the kimono. Cosmetic-surgery clinics began to multiply in Tokyo for the implanting of tissues and bags. The clinics were visited, too, by Japanese men, proving unexpectedly vain about their eyes, noses and ears.

In England nose operations took off. Rhinoplasty soon became a refined art and today surgeons can shorten, lengthen, tilt or straighten exactly as wished. They say the hardest part of the job can be to convince a patient that it may not be the nose which is at fault but the chin, which could need adding to with a slice of silicone; once the face is so augmented, a person's existing nose may look right. A surgeon writes: "The nose is a peninsula, not an island. It makes no sense unless considered in relation to the mainland, the face."

The brilliant demonstration of what cosmetic surgery could do for the wounded of the Second World War has led to an ever increasing demand for facial improvement. Because of the derogatory sense of the word vanity, cosmetic surgeons are anxious to tell prospective patients that they are not being just vain in wanting a change in their appearance. The directors of the Harley Medical Group in London, providing all kinds of cosmetic surgery, are conscious of an unadventurous attitude on the part of general practitioners. "Prospective patients seeking their advice," they write in the brochure, "are likely to meet attitudes dismissing the benefits of treatment as simply vanity. But the medical profession is gradually becoming more aware of the psychological benefits to be gained from self improvement." Even the best plastic surgeons were formerly magisterial about beautifying work. Now they increasingly exchange views and attend seminars all over the world on how best to correct and improve on nature.

People with certain facial defects are indeed fortunate today. At the beginning of the twentieth century, appallingly, little girls might be made to wear the equivalent of tight corsets on their faces. Edith Sitwell, the distinguished poet, underwent torture because of her parents' efforts to make her prettier. A surgeon put her into nose slams; but the treatment was ineffective.

Osbert Sitwell relates in his autobiography: "Her nose was still not the shape for which my father had bargained, so the reign of iron and manacles began. The harm inflicted on her nervous system and her physique proved to be costly, though not irreparable; it took months to break down the adhesions that had formed . . ."

Every third advertisement on American television is for plastic surgery, according to Lisa Armstrong in the *Independent on Sunday Magazine*, 1991. In 1989 Ivana Trump appeared on television after having such an operation. "What have you done to yourself?" asked the interviewer. "You look *wonderful*." Mrs. Trump indulged in understatement. "I just changed my make-up and played with my hair a bit." She did not say that to stave off the depredations affecting a lady of 41 she had undergone extensive and by no means fail-safe surgery; the work took in her lips, cheeks, breasts, thighs, stomach and bottom.

In parts of America, according to the magazine *Blitz*, the sixteen-year-olds of 1991 no longer asked for a car for their birthday, they asked for cosmetic surgery—a request mildly insulting to the couple who gave them birth. The search for physical perfection is at its most urgent in Los Angeles where the display of bodies on the beach inspires a restless pumping-up of figures and faces. Muscle implants are popular. For those not happy with their calves the answer is of course a silicone implant. As for hair transplants, Americans need only flick through the advertisements in *LA Weekly* to hit upon somewhere to go.

Those who may be called the ambassadors of cosmetic surgery, as Mrs. Trump may be, are on full view as performers at the time of writing: Brigitte Nielson and Dolly Parton with their enlarged bosoms, Michael Jackson with his changed skin color, Cher with a type of perfection produced by all possible treatments, the pop star Madonna who had her lips injected with collagen to fill them out, Jane Fonda who admits that the excellence of her form was the result of silicone injections and Kirk Douglas with his pleasing but slightly overstretched face lift. The list is endless.

To Helen

᭡

H ELEN, THY beauty is to me
Like those Nicean barks of yore,
That gently, o'er a perfumed sea,
The weary, way-worn wanderer bore
To his own native shore.

On desperate seas long wont to roam,
Thy hyacinth hair, thy classic face,
Thy Naiad airs have brought me home
To the glory that was Greece
And the grandeur that was Rome.

EDGAR ALLAN POE *wrote numerous non-terrifying poems during his life-time. "To Helen," for his wife, is from his* Collected Works.

Lo! in yon brilliant window-niche
How statue-like I see thee stand!
The agate lamp within thy hand,
Ah! Psyche, from the regions which
Are Holy Land!

Pagan Beauty

◞

T

HE ATHENIAN CULT of beauty had a supreme theme: the beautiful boy. Euripides, the first decadent artist, substitutes a bloody moon for the golden Apollonian sun. Medea is Athens' worst nightmare about women. She is nature's revenge, Euripides' dark answer to the beautiful boy.

Though the homosexuality of Greek high culture has been perfectly obvious since Winckelmann, the facts have been suppressed or magnified, depending on period and point of view. Late nineteenth-century aestheticism, for example, was full of heady effusions about "Greek love." Yet Harvard's green and red Loeb Library translations of classical literature, published early this century, are heavily censored. The pendulum has now swung toward realism. In *Greek Homosexuality* (1978), K. J. Dover wittily reconstructs from the evidence of vase painting the actual

---

CAMILLE PAGLIA *is the author of* Sex, Art and American Culture *and* Vamps and Tramps. *"Pagan Beauty" is from her controversial book of essays*, Sexual Personae (*1991*).

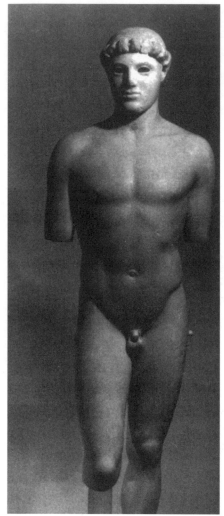

mechanics of sexual practice. But I depart from sociological rationales for Greek love. For me, aesthetics are primary. The Athenian turn away from women toward boys was a brilliant act of conceptualization. Unjust and ultimately self-thwarting, it was nevertheless a crucial movement in the formation of western culture and identity.

The Greek beautiful boy, as I remarked earlier, is one of the west's great sexual personae. Like Artemis, he has no exact equivalent in other cultures. His cult returns whenever Apollonianism rebounds, as in Italian Renaissance art. The beautiful boy is an androgyne, luminously masculine and feminine. He has male muscle structure but a dewy girlishness. In Greece he inhabited the world of hard masculine action. His body was on view, striving nude in the palestra. Greek athletics, like Greek law, were theater, a public agon. They imposed mathematics on nature: how fast? how far? how strong? The beautiful boy was the focus of Apollonian space. All eyes were on him. His broad-shouldered, narrow-waisted body was a masterwork of Apollonian articulation, every muscle group edged and contoured. There was

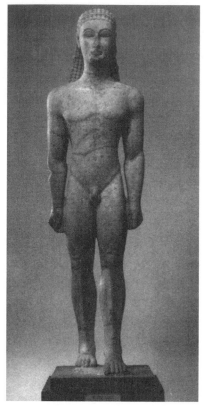

even a ropy new muscle, looping the hips and genitals. Classic Athens found the fatty female body unbeautiful, because it was not a visible instrument of action. The beautiful boy is Adonis, the Great Mother's son-lover, now removed from nature and cleansed of the chthonian. Like Athena, he is reborn through males and clad in the Apollonian armor of his own hard body.

Major Greek art begins in the late seventh century B.C. with the Archaic *kouros* ("youth"), a more than life-size nude statue of a victorious athlete. He is monumental human assertion, imagined in Apollonian stillness. He stands like Pharaoh, fists clenched and one foot forward. But Greek artists wanted their work to breathe and move. What was unchanged for thousands of years in Egypt leaps to life in a single century. The muscles curve and swell; the heavy wiglike hair curls and tufts. The smiling kouros is the first fully free-standing sculpture in art. Strict Egyptian symmetry was preserved until the early classic *Kritios Boy,* who looks one way while shifting his weight to the opposite leg. In the broken record of Greek artifacts, the *Kritios Boy* is the last kouros. He is not a type but a real boy, serious and regal. His smooth, shapely body has a white sensuality. The Archaic kouros was always callipygian, the large buttocks more stressed and valued than the face. But the buttocks of the *Kritios Boy* have a feminine refinement, as erotic as breasts in Venetian painting. The contrapposto flexes one buttock and relaxes the other. The artist imagines them as apple and pear, glowing and compact.

For three hundred years, Greek art is filled with beautiful boys, in stone and bronze. We know the name of none of them. The old-fashioned generic term, "Apollo," had a certain wisdom, for the solitary self-supporting kouros was an Apollonian idea, a liberation of the eye. His nudity was polemical. The Archaic *kore* ("maiden") was always clothed and utilitarian, one hand proffering a votive plate. The kouros stands heroically bare in Apollonian externality and visibility. Unlike two-dimensional pharaonic sculptures, he invites the strolling spectator to admire him in the round. He is not king or god but human youth. Divinity and stardom fall upon the beautiful boy. Epiphany is secularized and personality ritualized. The kouros records the first

cult of personality in western history. It is an icon of the worship of beauty, a hierarchism self-generated rather than dynastic.

The kouros bore strange fruit. From its bold clarity and unity of design came all major Greek sculpture, by the fourth century female as well as male. Hellenic art spread throughout the eastern Mediterranean as Hellenistic art. From that grew medieval Byzantine art in Greece, Turkey, and Italy, with its dour mosaic icons of Christ, Virgin, and saint. The Italian Renaissance begins in the Byzantine style. Thus there is a direct artistic line from Archaic Greek *kouroi* to the standing saints of Italian altarpieces and the stained-glass windows of Gothic cathedrals. Homoerotic iconicism goes full circle in the popular Italian theme, St. Sebastian, a beautiful seminude youth pierced by phallic arrows. Those arrows are glances of the aggressive western eye, solar shafts of Apollo the archer. The Greek kouros, inheriting Egypt's cold Apollonian eye, created the great western fusion of sex, power, and personality.

In Greece the beautiful boy was always beardless, frozen in time. At manhood, he became a lover of boys himself. The Greek boy, like the Christian saint, was a martyr, victim of nature's tyranny. His beauty could not last and so was caught full-flower by Apollonian sculpture. There are hundreds of pots, shards, and graffiti hailing so-and-so *kalos,* "the beautiful," flirtatious public praise of males by males. Dover demonstrates the criteria governing depiction of male genitalia, opposite to ours: a small thin penis was fashionable, a large penis vulgar and animalistic. Even brawny Hercules was shown with boy's genitals. Therefore, despite its political patriarchy, Athens cannot be considered—horrid word—a phallocracy. On the contrary, the Greek penis was edited down from an exclamation point to a dash. The beautiful boy was desired but not desiring. He occupied a presexual or suprasexual dimension, the Greek aesthetic ideal. In convention, his adult admirer could seek orgasm, while he remained unaroused.

The beautiful boy was an adolescent, hovering between a female past and male future. J. H. Van den Berg claims the eighteenth century invented adolescence. It is true children once passed more directly into adult responsibilities than they do now. In Catholicism, for example, seven is the dawn of moral consciousness. After one's First Communion, it's hell or high water. Brooding identity crises were indeed the Romantic creations of Rousseau and Goethe. But Van den Berg is wrong to make adolescence entirely modern. The Greeks saw it and formalized it in art. Greek pederasty honored the erotic magnetism of male adolescents in a way that today brings the police to the door. Children are more conscious and perverse than parents like to think. I agree with Bruce Benderson that children can and do choose. The adolescent male, one step over puberty, is dreamy and removed, oscillating between vigor and languor. He is a girl-boy, masculinity shimmering and blurred, as if seen through a cloudy fragment of ancient glass. J. Z. Eglinton cites images of youthful "bloom" in Greek poetry: "The adolescent in bloom is a synthesis of male and female beauties." The slightly older ephebos gained in gravity but retained a half-feminine glamour. We see it in the pedimental Apollo, the Delphic Charioteer, the bronze Apollo at Chatsworth, the white-lekythos Eretrian warrior seated before a gravestone.

These youths have a distinctly ancient Greek face: high brow, strong straight nose, girlishly fleshy cheeks, full petulant mouth, and short upper lip. It is the face of Elvis Presley, Lord Byron, and Bronzino's glossy Mannerist blue boy. Freud saw the androgyny in the Greek adolescent: "Among the Greeks, where the most manly men were found among inverts, it is quite obvious that it was not the masculine character of the boy which kindled the love of man; it was his physical resemblance to woman as well as his feminine psychic qualities, such as shyness, demureness, and the need of instruction and help." Certain boys, especially blondes, seem to carry adolescent beauty into adulthood. They form an enduring class of homosexual taste that I call the Billy Budd topos, fresh, active, and ephebic.

The beautiful boy is the Greek angel, a celestial visitor from the Apollonian realm. His purity is inadvertently revealed in Joseph Campbell's negative critique of fifth-century Athens:

"Everything that we read of it has a wonderful adolescent atmosphere of opalescent, timeless skies—untouched by the vulgar seriousness of a heterosexual commitment to mere life. The art, too, of the lovely standing nude, for all its grace and charm, is finally neuter—like the voice of a singing boy." Campbell quotes Heinrich Zimmer's praise of the "heterosexual flavor" and yogic awareness of Hindu sculpture: "Greek art was derived from experiences of the eye; Hindu from those of the circulation of the blood." Campbell's "neuter" is a blank, a moral nothing. But the beautiful boy's androgyny is visionary and exalted. Let us take Campbell's own example, "the voice of a singing boy." In a Seraphim recording of Fauré's *Requiem* that substitutes the King's College choir for the usual women, the treble parts are taken by boys from eight to thirteen. Alec Robertson's review seeks a tonality of emotion for which our only language is religious: boys' voices "add an unforgettable radiance and serenity to their part, impossible to sopranos, however good"; the soloist's singing has "an ethereal beauty that no words can describe." The rosy English or Austrian choirboy, disciplined, reserved, and heart-stoppingly beautiful, is a symbol of spiritual and sexual illumination, fused in the idealizing Greek manner. We see the same thing in Botticelli's exquisite long-haired boy-angels. These days, especially in America, boy-love is not only scandalous and criminal but somehow in bad taste. On the evening news, one sees handcuffed teachers, priests, or Boy Scout leaders hustled into police vans. Therapists call them maladjusted, emotionally immature. But beauty has its own laws, inconsistent with Christian morality. As a woman, I feel free to protest that men today are pilloried for something that was rational and honorable in Greece at the height of civilization.

The Greek beautiful boy was a living idol of the Apollonian eye. As a sexual persona, the kouros represents that tense relation between eye and object that I saw in Nefertiti and that was absent in the Venus of Willendorf, with her easy, forgiving, spongy female amplitude. Zimmer correctly opposes heterosexual Hindu "circulation of the blood" to Greek aesthetics of the eye. The beautiful boy is a rebuke to mother nature, an escape from the labyrinth of the body, with its murky womb and bowels. Woman is the Dionysian miasma, the world of fluids, the chthonian swamp of generation. Athens, says Campbell, was "untouched by the vulgar seriousness of a heterosexual commitment to mere life." Yes, mere life is indeed rejected by the idealizing Apollonian mode. It is the divine human privilege to make ideas greater than nature. We are born into the indignities of the body, with its relentless inner movements pushing us moment by moment toward death. Greek Apollonianism, freezing the human form into absolute male externality, is a triumph of mind over matter. Apollo, slaying the Python at Delphi, the navel of the world, halts the flood of time, for the coiled serpent we carry in our abdomen is the eternal wave-motion of female fluidity. Every beautiful boy is an Icarus seeking the Apollonian sun. He escapes the labyrinth only to fall into nature's sea of dissolution.

Cults of beauty have been persistently homosexual from antiquity to today's hair salons and houses of couture. Professional beautification of women by homosexual men is a systematic reconceptualizing of the brute facts of female nature. As at the nineteenth-century fin de siècle, the aesthete is always male, never female. There is no lesbian parallel to Greek worship of the adolescent. The great Sappho may have fallen in love with girls, but to all evidence she internalized rather than externalized her passions. Her most famous poem invents the hostile distance between sexual personae that will have so long a history in western love poetry. Gazing across a room at her beloved sitting with a man, she suffers a physical convulsion of jealousy, humiliation, and helpless resignation. This separation is not the aesthetic distance of Apollonian Athens but a desert of emotional deprivation. It is a gap that can be closed—as Aphrodite laughingly promises Sappho in another poem. Lascivious delectation of the eye is conspicuously missing in female eroticism. Visionary idealism is a male art form. The lesbian aesthete does not exist. But if there were one, she would have learned from the perverse male mind. The eye-intense pursuit of beauty is an Apollonian correction of life in our mother-born bodies.

The beautiful boy, suspended in time, is physicality without physiology. He does not eat, drink, or reproduce. Dionysus is deeply immersed in time—rhythm, music, dance, drunkenness, gluttony, orgy. The beautiful boy as angel floats above the turmoil of nature. Angels, in Judaism too, defy chthonian femaleness. This is why the angel, though sexless, is always a youthful male. Eastern religion does not have our angels of incorporeal purity, for two reasons. A "messenger" (*angelos*) or mediator between the divine and human is unnecessary, since the two realms are coexistent. Second, eastern femaleness is symbolically equivalent to and harmonious with maleness—though this has never improved real women's social status.

The pink-cheeked beautiful boy is emotional vernality, spring only. He is a partial statement about reality. He is exclusive, a product of aristocratic taste. He flees the superfluity of matter, the womb of female nature devouring and spewing out creatures. Dionysus, we noted, is "the Many," all-inclusive and ever-changing. Life's totality is summer *and* winter, floridity and devastation. The Great Mother is both seasons in her benevolent and malevolent halves. If the beautiful boy is pink and white, she is the red and purple of her labial maw. The beautiful boy represents a hopeless attempt to separate imagination from death and decay. He is form seceding from form-making, *natura naturata* dreaming itself free of *natura naturans*. As an epiphany, eye-created, he binds up the many into a transient vision of the one, like art itself.

Besides the *Kritios Boy*, the preeminent examples of this persona are the bronze *Benevento Boy* of the Louvre, the Antinous sculptures commissioned by the emperor Hadrian, Donatello's *David*, and Thomas Mann's Tadzio in *Death in Venice*. The Apollonian is a mode of silence, suppressing rhythm to focus the eye. The beautiful boy, sexually self-complete, is sealed in silence, behind a wall of aristocratic disdain. The adolescent dreaminess of the Antinous sculptures is not true inwardness but a melancholy premonition of death. Antinous drowned, like Icarus. The beautiful boy dreams but neither thinks nor feels. His eyes fix on nothing. His face is a pale oval upon which nothing is written. A real person could not remain at this stage without decadence and mummification. The

beautiful boy is cruel in his indifference, remoteness, and serene self-containment. We rarely see these things in a girl, but when we do, as in the magnificent portrait photographs of the young Virginia Woolf, we sense catatonia and autism. Narcissistic beauty in a postadolescent (like Hitchcock's Marnie) may mean malice and ruthlessness, a psychopathic amorality. There is danger in beauty.

The beautiful boy has flowing or richly textured hyacinthine hair, the only luxuriance in this chastity. Long male hair, sometimes wrapped round the head, was an aristocratic fashion in Athens. Antinous' thick hair is crisply layered, as in Van Dyck's silky princes or Seventies rock stars. In its artful negligence and allure, the hair traps the beholder's eye. It is a nimbus, a pre-Christian halo, scintillating with fiery flakes of stars. The beautiful boy, glittering with charisma, is matter transformed, penetrated by Apollonian light. Greek visionary materialism makes hard crystal of our gross fleshiness. The beautiful boy is without motive force or deed; hence he is not a hero. Because of his emotional detachment, he is not a heroine. He occupies an ideal space between male and female, effect and affect. Like the Olympians, he is an *objet d'art,* which also affects without acting or being acted upon. The beautiful boy is the product of chance or destiny, a sport thrown up by the universe. He is, I suggested, a secular saint. Light makes beautiful boys incandescent. Divinity swoops down to ennoble them, like the eagle falling upon Ganymede, who is kidnapped to Olympus, unlike the pack of female lovers like Leda whom Zeus casually abandons as types of the generative mother.

In the *Phaedrus,* Plato sets forth Greek homosexuality's ritualization of the eye. Socrates says the man who gazes upon "a god-like countenance or physical form," a copy of "true beauty," is overcome by a shudder of awe, "an unusual fever and perspiration": "Beholding it, he reverences it as he would a god; and if he were not afraid of being accounted stark mad, he would offer sacrifice to the beloved as to a holy image of divinity." Beauty is the first step of a ladder leading to God. Writing in the fourth century about memories of the fifth, Plato is already postclassical. He is suspicious of art, which he banishes from his ideal republic. Visionary materialism has failed. In the *Phaedrus*, however, we still see the aesthetic distance vibrating between Greek personae. Plato has Sappho's fever, but it is cooled by the dominating and dominated western eye. In Greece, beauty was sacred and ugliness or deformity hateful. When Odysseus bludgeons Thersites, a lame, hunchback commoner, Homer's heroes laugh. Christ's ministry to the lepers was unthinkable in Greek terms. In the Greek cult of beauty, there was mystical elevation and hierarchical submission, but significantly without moral obligation.

The Greek principle of domination by the beautiful person as work of art is implicit in western culture, rising to view at charged historical moments. I see it in Dante and Beatrice and in Petrarch and Laura. There must be distance, of space or time. The eye elects a narcissistic personality as galvanizing object and formalizes the relation in art. The artist imposes a hieratic sexual character on the beloved, making himself the receptor (or more feminine receptacle) of the beloved's mana. The structure is sadomasochistic. Western sexual personae are hostile with dramatic tension. Naturalistically, Beatrice's expansion into a gigantic heavenly body is grandiose and even absurd, but she achieves her preeminence through the poet's sexually hierarchizing western imagination. The aesthetic distance between personae is like a vacuum between poles, discharging electric tension by a bolt of lightning. Little is known of the real Beatrice and Laura. But I think they resembled the beautiful boy of homosexual tradition: they were dreamy, remote, autistic, lost in a world of androgynous self-completion. Beatrice, after all, was barely eight when Dante fell in love with her in her crimson dress. Laura's impenetrability inspired the "fire and ice" metaphor of Petrarch's sonnets, which revolutionized European poetry. "Fire and ice" is western alchemy. It is the chills and fever of Sappho's and Plato's uncanny love experience. Agonized ambivalence of body and mind was Sappho's contribution to poetry, imitated by Catullus and transmitted to us through folk ballads and pop torch songs. Western love, Denis de Rougemont shows, is unhappy or death-ridden. In Dante and Petrarch, self-frustrating love is not neurotic but ritualistic and conceptualizing. The west makes art and thought out of the cold manipulation of our hard sexual personae.

Domination by the beautiful personality is central to Romanticism, specifically in its dark Coleridgean line passing through Poe and Baudelaire to Wilde. The Pre-Raphaelite Dante Gabriel Rossetti, imitating his namesake, invented his own Beatrice, the sickly Elizabeth Siddal, who obsessively appears throughout his work. That Siddal, like Beatrice and Laura, was a female version of the beautiful boy is suggested by the speed with which her face turned into the face of beautiful young men in the paintings of Rossetti's disciple, Edward Burne-Jones. The beautiful boy's narcissistic remoteness and latent autism became somnambulism in Rossetti's pensive Muse. Antinous, Beatrice, Laura, and Elizabeth Siddal passed with ease into art because in their cool, untouchable impersonality they already had the abstract removal of an objet d'art. Transcendence of sexual identity is the key.

The bungling brooder, John Hinckley, infatuated with the boyish Jodie Foster, replicates Dante's submission to distant Beatrice. Dante's love was just as preposterous, but he made poetry out of it. The untalented literalist, failing to recognize the aggression already inherent in the western eye, picks up a gun instead of a pen. The sexual ambiguity of Jodie Foster's onscreen persona supports my point about Beatrice. The absence of moral obligation in this sexual religiosity explains the amorality of aestheticism. Oscar Wilde believed the beautiful person has absolute rights to commit any act. Beauty replaces morality as the divine order. As Cocteau said, following Wilde, "The privileges of beauty are enormous."

The beautiful boy, the object of all eyes, looks downward or away or keeps his eyes in soft focus because he does not recognize the reality of other persons or things. By making the glamorous Alcibiades burst drunk into the *Symposium,* ending the intellectual debate, Plato is commenting in retrospect on the political damage done to Athens by its fascination with beauty. Spoiled, captivating Alcibiades was to betray his city and end in exile and disgrace. When the beautiful boy leaves the realm of contemplation for the realm of action, the result is chaos and crime. Wilde's Alcibiades, Dorian Gray, makes a science of corruption. Refusing to accept the early death that preserved the beauty of Adonis and Antinous, Dorian compacts with a fellow art object, his portrait, projecting human mutability onto it. The ephebic Dorian is serene and heartless, the beautiful boy as destroyer. In *Death in Venice,* Mann's homage to Wilde, the beautiful boy does not even have to act to destroy.

His blinding Apollonian light is a radiation disintegrating the moral world.

The beautiful boy is the representational paradigm of high classic Athens. He is pure Apollonian objectification, a public sex object. His lucid contour and hardness originate in Egypt's monumental architectonics and in Homer's gleaming Olympian sky-cult. The Apollonian beautiful boy dramatizes the special horror of dissolved form to Pheidian Athens, with its passionate vision of the sunlit human figure. Unity of image and unity of personality were the Athenian norm, satirized by Euripides in his chthonian dismemberments, symbol of fragmentation and multiplicity. The androgynous beautiful boy has an androgynous sponsor, the male-born Uranian Aphrodite whom Plato identifies with homosexual love. While the Archaic kouros is vigorously masculine, the early and high classic beautiful boy perfectly harmonizes masculine and feminine. With the Hellenistic tilt toward women, prefigured by Euripides, the beautiful boy slides toward the feminine, a symptom of decadence.

Praxiteles registers this shift in his ephebic *Hermes* (ca. 350 B.C.), which misaligns the elegance of classic contrapposto. Hermes awkwardly leans away from the engaged leg rather than toward it, curving his hips in a peculiar swish. His arm, supporting infant Dionysus, rests heavily on a stump. Farnell says of the Praxitelean "languor," "Even the gods are becoming fatigued." Kenneth Clark finds in high classic Greek art a perfect "physical balance of strength and grace." In the Hellenistic beautiful boy, grace drains strength. Rhys Carpenter sees Praxiteles' *Knidian Aphrodite* as a sexual degeneration of

Polycleitus' canonical fifth-century *Doryphoros,* a "languid devi-talization of the male victor-athlete into an equivalent feminine canon." Hauser says of the *Hermes* and Lysippus' *Apoxyomenos,* "They give the impression of being dancers rather than athletes." Jane Harrison denounces Praxiteles' Hermes on the grounds that as *Kourotrophos* ("boy-rearer") he "usurps the function of the mother": "The man doing woman's work has all the inherent futility and something of the ugly dissonance of the man masquerading in woman's clothes." Again, Harrison recognizes sexual duality but finds it repugnant. Clark points out that wherever contrapposto appears in world art, it shows Greek influence, even in India, to which it was carried by Alexander. Originally a male motif, it entered female iconography to become "a vivid symbol of desire." What seems overlooked is that contrapposto was erotic from the start, in the dignified exhibitionism of the early classic kouros. Hellenistic ephebes use a more extreme hip-shot pose, ripe with sexual solicitation. It is the street stance of harlot and drag queen, ancient or modern. Male contrapposto with hand on hip, as in Donatello's *David,* is provocative and epicene.

Portraits of Dionysus illustrate the sensual feminization of male personae in Greek art. The Archaic transvestite Dionysus fuses a bearded adult man with a sexually mature woman. In the fifth century, he loses his beard and becomes indistinguishable from the ephebic Apollo of the Parthenon frieze. The Hellenistic Dionysus is a voluptuously appealing beautiful boy. A third-century head at Thasos could be mistaken for a woman, a movie queen, with thick shoulder-length hair and expectant parted lips. Scholars have gen-erally been repelled by these beautiful objects, with their overt homoeroticism. Even Marie Delcourt, in her excellent study, *Hermaphrodite,* attacks the "effeminacy" of the Hellenistic Dionysus, which "pandered" to Greek homosexual desire. But it was the Hellenistic Dionysus and Apollo who were the androgynous models for the exquisite Antinous sculptures.

The long, decentralized Hellenistic era was like our own time, lively, anxious, and sensationalistic. Hellenistic art teems with sex and violence. High classic Greek art honors ideal youth, while Hellenistic art is full of babies, brutes, and drunks. Athenian eroticism is pornographic in kitchen and tavern pottery but sublime and restrained in major sculpture. Hellenistic sculpture, on the other hand, likes large-scale wrestling and rapine—massacre, pugilism, and priapism. Hellenistic sex is in such free flow that the gender of shattered statues can be doubtful. Misidentifications have been common.

Dover speaks of the change in homosexual taste in Athens from the fifth century, which glorified athletic physiques, to the fourth, when softer, passive minions came into vogue. It is in the fourth century that the hermaphrodite first appears in classical art. The plush creature with female breasts manages to expose its male genitals, either by a slipping cloak or a tunic boldly raised in ritual exhibitionism. The *Sleeping Hermaphrodite* influenced later art, like eighteenth-century reclining female nudes. From one side, the drowsy figure displays ambiguously smooth buttocks and the half-swell of a breast; from the other, female breast and male genitals pop out clear as day. I found the Villa Borghese copy prudently pushed against the wall to discourage inspection! The decorative popularity of hermaphrodites is paradoxical, for everywhere in

antiquity the birth of a real hermaphrodite was greeted with horror. This condition, hypospadias, may be examined *ad stuporem* in
the hundreds of photographs of Hugh Hampton Young's pioneer-
ing text, *Genital Abnormalities, Hermaphroditism, and Related
Adrenal Diseases* (1937). Since a hermaphrodite birth was a bad
omen presaging war, disaster, or pestilence, the infant was usually
destroyed or left to die by exposure. As late as Paracelsus, her-
maphroditic children were thought "monstrous signs of secret sins
in the parents." The annalist Diodorus Siculus, in the Roman era,
records a case where an Arabian girl's tumor burst open to reveal
male genitals. She then changed her name, donned men's clothes,
and joined the cavalry.

The source of the Hermaphrodite legend is unknown. It may
be a vestige of the sexual duality of early fertility deities of Asia Minor.
Later stories improvised upon the name to claim he/she was the child
of Hermes and Aphrodite. Ovid started a mythographic muddle with
his version in the *Metamorphoses*, possibly based on a lost Alexandrian
romance. The amorous nymph Salmacis traps the beautiful boy
Hermaphroditus in her forest pool, entwining him with her arms and
legs, until the gods grant her prayer and unite them into one being, like
Plato's primeval androgynes. The tale may have begun as a folk legend
about a cursed pool sapping the virility of men who bathed in it.

Greek androgyny evolved from chthonian to Apollonian
and back: vitalistic energy to godlike charisma to loss of manhood.
I do not agree with the disparagement of the later androgyne by
Jane Harrison and Marie Delcourt. Effeminate men have suffered
a bad press the world over. I accept decadence as a complex historical mode. In late phases, maleness is always in retreat. Women

have ironically enjoyed a greater symbolic, if not practical freedom. Thus it is that male and not female homosexuality has usually been harshly punished by law. A debater in Lucian declares, "Far better that a woman, in the madness of her lust, should usurp the nature of man, than that man's noble nature should be so degraded as to play the woman." Similarly today, lesbian interludes are a staple of heterosexual pornography. Ever since man emerged from the dominance of nature, masculinity has been the most fragile and problematic of psychic states.

Hymn to Beauty

D O Y O U come from
on high or out of the abyss,
O Beauty? Godless yet divine, your gaze
indifferently showers favor and shame,
and therefore some have likened you to wine.

Your eyes reflect the sunset and the dawn;
you scatter perfumes like a windy night;
your kisses are a drug, your mouth the urn
dispensing fear to heroes, fervor to boys.

CHARLES BAUDELAIRE'S *stunning recognition of beauty in unusual places foreshadowed much in modern writing. Baudelaire published only a single volume of poetry,* Les Fleurs du Mal *(1857).*

Whether spawned by hell or sprung from
        the stars,
Fate like a spaniel follows at your heel;
you sow haphazard fortune and despair,
ruling all things, responsible for none.

You walk on corpses, Beauty, undismayed,
and Horror coruscates among your gems;
Murder, one of your dearest trinkets, throbs
on your shameless belly: make it dance!

Dazzled, the dayfly flutters round your wick,
crackles, flares, and cries: I bless this torch!
The pining lover for his lady swoons
like a dying man adoring his own tomb.

Who cares if you come from paradise or hell,
appalling Beauty, artless and monstrous
        scourge,
if only your eyes, your smile or your foot reveal
the Infinite I love and have never known?

Come from Satan, come from God—who cares,
Angel or Siren, rhythm, fragrance, light,
provided you transform—O my one queen!
this hideous universe, this heavy hour?

Two Tales of Beauty

·ᴗ

FABIO HAS A forty-four-inch chest, just about the only male model in Manhattan who does. The rest can all share clothes. Suit size forty to forty-two. Height six feet to six-two. Waist thirty to thirty-two. The size is uniform, same as female models. The only difference is there are a lot more six-foot-tall men with forty-inch chests than there are five-ten women who are a size six. But again, it's about selling clothes and photographing well. The camera adds pounds, doesn't take them away, so the taller and trimmer the better.

There are some distinguished older gentlemen models, but youth is beauty. Almost any male model can easily be styled to look like a beautiful fraternity boy.

A male model lives one flight above me, in the penthouse apartment. His ads are always in the newspapers and magazines. I

KEN SIMAN'S *"Two Tales of Beauty" is found in his very personal, very recent collection of interviews, gossip and general beauteous thoughts,* The Beauty Trip *(1995).*

want to talk to him about beauty, but he has a girlfriend and I'm afraid if I brought up the subject in the elevator or laundry room, he'll think I'm making a pass. So I look him up in the Wilhelmina Men catalog (Josh, 6'1", 40L), and write to him, care of his agent.

"I'd like to help you out, man," he says, "but I don't have anything to say about beauty. If it was real estate or music you wanted to talk about . . ."

I call Dorothy. She told me once that a lot of male models who pose in *Playboy* fashion spreads come to her office. Does she know any?

Not really.

"How about the guys you work with, do they ever talk about male beauty?"

"All the guys here are straight, and all they'll admit to wanting is a flat stomach and a full head of hair."

So I figure Sy Sperling is a straight man who would be comfortable talking—if not about male beauty, at least about all the beautiful male hair he has for sale.

Sy is the businessman who was unself-conscious enough to make a TV commercial that showed viewers he's a chrome dome who happens to wear a rug, I mean, a hair-replacement system. "I'm not only president of the Hair Club for Men," he said, "I'm also a client." It was the most successful before/after ad since that skinny guy bought a Charles Atlas muscle kit and stopped getting sand kicked in his face.

Sy tells Dorothy and me he never worried about getting beaten up on account of being so tough that he was in a Bronx gang called the Golden Guineas, even though he was Jewish. "I was considered the toughest guy in the school, the toughest guy in the neighborhood, probably the toughest guy in the region—the entire North Bronx region."

This was in the 1950s, before gangs started using guns, but Sy would pull out a knife if he had to. But now that Sy has so much money that he's appeared on *Lifestyles of the Rich and Famous*, he'd back away from a fight. If Sy whupped someone who got a look at his famous head, he'd be sued big time.

Sy's a strict vegetarian now, and there's no meat or dairy allowed at this restaurant. If you want cream in your coffee, it's BYO. Dorothy and I order the vegetarian duck and share.

Sy is wearing his hair-replacement system. Dorothy says it looks real to her and that Sy is taller, more confident and handsome than he appears on TV.

I look at Sy's system and wonder about my own hair. I've always hoped that since I was so plagued by acne, fate would kindly spare me baldness. But I worry because my father has lost most of his hair. Then again, my uncle—my mother's brother—collects social security and still has a full head of hair. It's as black as Ronald Reagan's was when he was in office.

If I do go bald, I'm sure I'd consider purchasing Sy's product. It does fit well on Sy, but I'm afraid I would always be self-conscious if I was wearing it, probably feeling the same way I did when I wore foundation (Clinique, porcelain beige). Whenever people looked at me, I wasn't sure if they were admiring my outfit or thinking that my makeup wasn't blended properly. Likewise, if I had on someone else's hair, I'd be afraid that it would either fall off or I'd run into the person who used to own it.

"Sy, where does the hair you use come from?"

"India," he says.

"Dead people?"

"Ken, gross," says Dorothy.

"No," says Sy. It's from people who evidently have long hair and a notion to sell it, like the lady in the O. Henry story, "Gift of the Magi." Sy says the hair is anonymous, so clients can't communicate or become pen pals with the people whose hair they are wearing.

Does Sy go to India and check all the hair out himself? No, but if you look in the Yellow Pages under hair supplies, you'll find wholesalers who sell human hair by the pound. Since Sy practically buys by the ton and has a lot of leverage in the business, he gets the choicest stuff.

But everybody in India has black hair, and guys in Sy's commercials are blond, brunette, even some carrot tops.

"The hair is dyed," says Sy.

Sy's father was a bald-headed Bronx plumber. He had "the Bozo look," says Sy. "He allowed the side of his hair to grow and that accentuated the baldness." He was bothered by it enough to rub his scalp with wintergreen oil. It smelled up the house worse than limburger cheese, but Sy's dad swore it was making his hair sprout. Sy was a good son and would say, "Yeah, Dad, right, it's true. That's a true statement."

The baldness didn't bother Sy's mother, though. She was more concerned about his making a living. "She was very practical, like most Jewish mothers."

Sy was very looks conscious as a teenager. Like his dad, he had a hair-loss problem early in life. He had a high forehead, plus thinning hair to boot (you could see his scalp when he used Brylcreem). That's why the young people called him Chrome Dome.

"Sometimes I'd look in the mirror and say to myself, 'You know, I have pretty good features,' but for some reason when I flirted with women, I was very unsuccessful and I never really knew why."

Sy would get turned down at social events when he asked women to dance. The neighborhood girls wouldn't go out with him. "They loved me like a *brothuh*," says Sy. "Everybody loved me like a *brothuh*."

Sy knew it wasn't all about looks. It was class, too. He had moved from "the Bronx ghettos" to a more middle-class neighborhood. The girl he fancied, Sharon Finkelstein, wanted to go out with guys who were going to be doctors or lawyers. Sy didn't know about the hair-fusion method then, he didn't have a five-year career plan, so he went to the air force after high school.

He boxed a lot and beat up several pilots in the ring. Sy says he defeated the eighth-ranked heavyweight of the world in a three-round match. "I couldn't have beaten Ali," he says. "But I probably could have beaten Patterson, Quarry . . ." Still, Sy saw what happened to a lot of boxers and didn't want to become an idiot with a caved-in head. Boxing was out as a career option. He started selling pools and carpets and purchased a rug to make himself more appealing. The product turned into a hair ball when Sy wore it in the shower, and it took almost two hours to untangle.

In 1968, Sy created one of his first hair-replacement systems and put it on his father's head. It didn't fit, and the old man accused his son of giving him a secondhand hairpiece. Not much later, his father passed away.

"When women say hair loss doesn't bother them, what they mean is they're not going to divorce a guy they're married to if he's losing his hair," says Sy. "But when a guy with a full head of hair approaches a woman in a bar, she's more likely to talk to him than to a guy who's balding."

It's really simple when you think about it, says Sy, like a formula: "If a guy is twenty-five and doesn't have hair on top, why would a twenty-three-year-old woman talk to him if he looks forty, when she can talk to someone who looks her own age?"

Sy is fifty-two. Not too long ago, he separated from his wife, Amy, who invented the Hair Club strand-by-strand system that Sy's now wearing. They're still friends, but Sy hit the singles bars until he met his new girlfriend:

"Now, if I didn't have hair, I'd probably be talking to women forty to fifty. But I [wore hair] and I met my girlfriend, who's thirty-six years old and very attractive, very charming, and we have a great relationship. I'm sure if I didn't look youthful to her she wouldn't have talked to me the first night we met."

"But, Sy," Dorothy says, "you're a celebrity. Of course women want to meet you."

"I don't want women to be attracted to me because I'm a wealthy entrepreneur," says Sy. "I'm not a bald, fat celebrity. I'm somebody who is well groomed. If Don Rickles went to a club, they might want his autograph, but I don't know how well he'd do socially. Besides, I didn't become famous because I broke the four-minute mile or I won the Nobel prize. I'm famous because I made a commercial. I paid for my own celebrity. So what's the big deal?"

"It's still celebrity," I say. "What gives you more confidence—fame or hair?"

"I want to have sex appeal, I want to be able to relate to a woman thirty-five years old. I want to market myself so that I can appeal to a woman who is two decades younger. I want to have as much appeal as possible in the same way [I want my ads] to appeal to as many people as possible."

Whenever they get the chance, men go for youth and beauty.

"At least he's being honest about it," Dorothy whispers to me.

But when does it end? If you're an older man—but rich or famous—you will probably always be able to attract youth and beauty until you keel over.

"Do you think that maybe you'd have stayed with your wife if you'd stayed bald?" I want to say: "Did your new hair and fame distract you from the real thing?" but I don't because how do I know how real his marriage was?

Sy says if he'd never gotten hair, then he'd be more unhappy with himself and "very insecure with my wife. I would have made her miserable. I would have been getting on her case, you know. 'Why are you looking at that guy?'"

"What do you think of hair in a can?" I ask. "You know, the stuff you spray on your bald spot?"

Sy says it's nothing compared to what Hair Club can do.

"My commercial changed the way people think. At one time wearing any kind of artificial hair was considered to be an embarrassment. I removed the shroud of secrecy. Here I am, bald, here I am with hair, there's nothing wrong with it." Sy didn't remove his hair during dinner to make the point.

"We were the first to offer a nonsurgical semipermanent type of hair replacement. You never hear the word toupee anymore, it's an anachronism."

Sy hates bad hair jobs. They stand out like a sore thumb and give his business a bad name. "I'd pay Howard Cosell not to wear a piece," says Sy.

A lot of style-conscious Manhattan liberals had a problem voting for Mayor Giuliani because he was a Republican and they didn't like his haircut. What was the deal? Was it a toupee or a comb-over?

Sy says he gave money to Giuliani's campaign the first time he ran for mayor, but not the second.

"If I write his campaign a check again, I want to get something in return, and that would be fun for him to become a client and give us a testimonial. So if somebody says to him, 'Hey, Rudy, your hair looks terrific,' he would say, 'Hair Club is my stylist.' I don't want to promote a guy who is promoting the bald or covered look. I'm very pragmatic as a businessman. I don't want people thinking this guy is a client. One hand washes the other. I want him to be a client of ours because he looks like he's a bad client of ours now."

I ask Sy about beautiful guys, the ones in Bruce Weber photos and Calvin Klein ads with perfect faces and pecs.

"Over ninety percent of the male public does not have an interest in that," says Sy.

Sy will admit to hair envy, going to the gym to keep his body fit, even to getting the bags under his eyes removed. He wants to look good, but isn't tortured by not being an ideal. And he's not interested in discussing the ideal, either. That's for the other ten percent of the "male public"—mostly gay homosexuals like me—to agonize over.

"A lot of people who know me think of me as an anomaly," says Sy. "What do you think of me? Sometimes you question where you fit in the universe."

"You're very on the table," says Dorothy, and I nod.

Beauty-with-the-Seven-Dresses

.‿

ONCE THERE WAS a father of two boys. Sensing his last hour approach, he called in his older son and said, "Son, I'm about to die. There's no more hope for me. Tell me which you prefer, my solemn blessing or a sum of money?"

Without beating around the bush, the son replied, "Give me the money, for with just the blessing I'd go hungry."

Then the father called his younger son and put the same question to him.

"Money matters little to me," said the younger boy. "I prefer your solemn blessing."

The father died and they carried him to the cemetery. The little boy, who'd received only the solemn blessing, wept heartily, while the big boy, who'd inherited all the property, was thinking of the best way to use it. He ended up opening a café and taking

ITALO CALVINO *is the author of such classics as* Mr. Palomar *and* Invisible Cities. *"Beauty-with-the-Seven-Dresses" is from* Italian Folktales.

his place behind the counter, while the little brother, whose name was Francesco, went out into the world to seek his fortune.

One evening after walking quite a distance, he saw a little light far ahead of him and said, "If the Lord so wills, I must get to that place." He thus came to a house and knocked. Accompanied by seven ladies, Beauty-with-the-Seven-Dresses came down and offered him food and shelter. In the morning Beauty got into conversation with the young man, and was so taken with his good looks and manners, that she ended up saying she wanted him for her husband. She was a very beautiful and gracious maiden, and a few days later they got married.

One day while they were looking out the window at the garden, Beauty said to her husband, "Ciccillo, do you see that fine seven-part frock there?" (She spoke of it that way, since it included seven dresses, one inside the other.) "Do you see that seven-part frock hanging on the tree?"

"I certainly do!" he answered. "Why do you ask me?"

"I'm going to tell you. If a bird should light on the frock and you caught it, you wouldn't see me any more. If you shot the bird, the frock would fly away, and I would go through fire and water. Should worse come to worst, dress in a red outfit, which has already been laid out in this room, and leave home in search of me. I'll see to it that you find me again."

It happened one day that while the husband was out hunting and shooting birds, a bird lit right on the seven-part frock. So wrapped up in the hunt was Ciccillo that, without thinking, he fired at the bird. The seven-part frock immediately soared into the air and vanished from sight. Ciccillo then remembered his wife's warning. Frantic, he ran back to the palace at once, fearing the worst. When Beauty saw him, she asked, "What's the matter?" but he dared not tell her. Then she looked up at the tree and found the seven-part frock gone. At that she began pulling out her hair and saying, "I've been betrayed! Betrayed! Now they'll come and take me away. Remember, if that happens, husband, to dress in red and don't abandon me."

Let's leave them and follow the seven-part frock which had taken flight at the shot. On and on it flew until it reached a palace, went through the window, and came to rest before the table of a king who was in the process of writing. The king scrutinized the seven-part frock and wondered whose it was. He asked all around, but no one knew a thing about it. Then an old woman, aware of the king's inquiries about the owner of the seven-part frock, went to the palace, announcing, "Majesty and lords, I can find the owner of this dress."

"What will it take to do so?" asked the king.

"Here's what I need. Fix me a bottle of drugged rosolio and a pound of sweets that have also been drugged. Leave everything else to me. Then I'll need a carriage with a good driver; I'll ride in it with a dagger concealed in my bosom."

The king provided her with all those things, and the old woman rode off in style.

When they had gone a certain distance, she said to the coachman, "Wait for me here and be sure to come when I call you." It was raining, but the old woman walked straight up to the palace of Beauty-with-the-Seven-Dresses. She knocked at the front door, and the husband came down with the seven ladies to let her in. The old woman asked for shelter for the night because it was raining, and he gladly welcomed her and invited her to table with them. At the table the old woman pulled out the rosolio and sweets, which were all drugged, and said, "These are not fit for important people like you, but do eat them for my sake. My daughter has just married, and I brought along this little bit so that you can celebrate the occasion too."

Once the sweets were eaten, the couple and all the other guests dropped to the floor like pears. The old woman then pulled out the dagger and thrust it all the way through the husband. Then she called the coachman, who was waiting outside, and the two of them together picked up Beauty, one by the head, the other by the feet, and carried her into the carriage as she slept. Once they had her inside, they galloped off to the king.

The king was anxiously awaiting them, and when the old woman arrived, he had Beauty-with-the-Seven-Dresses put in a room by herself until she should awaken. In the morning he went to her and found her awake and weeping over her misfortune. He tried to comfort her a bit, then all of a sudden asked, "When shall we get married?" At that proposition, Beauty began screaming at the top of her voice. Since there was no way to quiet her, the king took to his heels. A month later, he returned and repeated his proposal. Beauty replied, "When you find a man dressed entirely in red." The king drew a sigh of relief, and telegraphed at once throughout the world. But Ciccillo was dead, stabbed by that old woman, and the man dressed in red was not to be found.

One day the big brother who had opened up a café went broke; reduced to poverty, he decided to change countries and try his luck elsewhere. He happened to take the same road as his brother Ciccillo, and when the seven ladies answered the door, they thought he was the dead man, so much did the two resemble one another.

"You've risen from the dead?" they asked.

"What!" he replied, amazed.

"Or maybe you had a brother who looked like you?"

"Yes, I did," he said. "But why do you ask me?"

"Come with us and you will see," answered the ladies, drawing him into a room where there was a dead man. This dead man was his brother, and the minute he saw him he began weeping and wailing. "Oh, my brother! My brother!" The ladies comforted him, telling him how Ciccillo had been treacherously slain, and they invited him to remain there with them.

While this youth was standing on the doorstep one morning, he saw two lizards, a little one and a big one. The big one killed the little one, then went and pulled up a herb, with which it rubbed the dead little lizard until it revived. Seeing that, the young man thought, Who knows but what my brother might revive if rubbed with that same herb. It certainly won't hurt to try. He pulled the herb, rubbed his brother's entire body with it, and he too came back to life. He asked about his wife at once and, remembering her warning, he dressed in red and left home to look the world over for her.

Now that very day Beauty was to marry the king: they'd not been able to find the man in red, whom she had finally given up for dead. He came into the city where the marriage was to be celebrated, and the inhabitants, at the sight of a man dressed in red after so much fruitless searching on their part, stopped him and carried him to the king. The king hastened to tell Beauty that the man in red had been found, thus fulfilling her one condition and clearing the way for the wedding. Beauty replied that she first had to talk to the man in red, alone and behind closed doors, so he was brought into her room, where they spent the night relating their misfortunes and making plans for the future. Beauty had all the keys of the palace, and once the king was fast asleep, they got up, loaded two donkeys with sacks of money, and fled.

After traveling all day long it grew dark again and they saw a stable. They made their bed as best they could on the hay under a loft. In the loft above, a drunkard snored and tossed in his sleep. Tossing and turning, he fell from the loft and ended up between the husband and wife, sinking down into the hay without even waking up or ceasing to snore. In the morning Beauty was the first one awake, and called her husband, "Ciccillo, get up, it's late. Let's get on our donkeys with the money and be off." Her husband was still fast asleep, though, and didn't hear her. But the drunkard, at the mention of money, answered right off the bat, "By all means, let's be on our way!" It was still dark, and the two of them groped their way to the donkeys laden with money and left. When it was day, Beauty realized her companion was not her husband and began to protest. His only response was to reach out and knock her to the ground, leaving her there weeping as he made off with the two donkeys. She had no idea how to find her husband again, for she had already gone a good way with the drunkard. She went back until she came to a haystack and saw a farm boy. She begged and pleaded with him until he gave her his clothes, and thus dressed as a man, she was able to continue her journey in less peril.

Not a trace of her husband was to be found. In order to support herself, she therefore decided to work for a miller, who happened to be miller to the king's notary. She kept the miller's accounts and wrote such a beautiful hand that the notary, who had never seen such fine writing, asked the miller who kept his accounts. Learning that a farm boy did, the notary took Beauty into his service, and she kept the notary's accounts, which were presented to the king. The king too was impressed with the beautiful writing and just had to have the talented farm boy to work for him.

In the meantime, the other king who wanted to marry Beauty-with-the-Seven-Dresses had died. He had taken his own life, butting his head against the wall upon finding his bride missing the morning of the wedding. Who should inherit his kingdom but the king who kept the farm boy in his service! This king called the farm boy and ordered him to go to the dead king's city and announce throughout the realm that he would govern them on behalf of their new king. The farm boy replied that if he was to govern, he needed absolute authority over every citizen, which the king granted him.

On his arrival at the dead king's, he had the news published in all the towns, inviting everybody marked by any unusual event to come before the new governor, who would give them each a purse of money.

The news spread, and the first person to show up to tell her story was the old woman who had stabbed the husband and kidnapped his wife. "You old wretch!" exclaimed the governor. "You have the nerve to come and tell me that?"

He ordered her seized and thrown into a caldron of boiling water.

The old woman was followed by the drunkard, who told his story. "You thief!" exclaimed the governor. "You robbed a woman and have the nerve to admit it?" He had him dragged to the gallows and hanged as a dangerous thief. After those two were taken care of, here came the husband to tell his story.

They recognized one another and fell into each other's arms. Then the governor went and changed clothes, reappearing in the seven-part frock and every bit as lovely as a rosebud. They had a fine dinner and were reunited with the big brother and the seven ladies. Ciccillo was named king, and thus ended his misfortunes.

The Arts of Beauty; or Secrets of a Ladies' Toilet

FEMALE BEAUTY.

"Look upon this face,

Examine every feature and proportion,

And you with me must grant this rare piece finish'd.

Nature, despairing e'er to make the like,

Brake suddenly the mould in which 'twas fashion'd;

Yet, to increase your pity, and call on

Your justice with severity, this fair outside

Was but the cover of a fairer mind."

MASSINGER'S *Parliament of Love.*

MADAME LOLA MONTEZ *divulged her secrets of beauty and attraction in an 1858 tell-all,* The Arts of Beauty; or Secrets of a Ladies' Toilet.

It is a most difficult task to fix upon any general and satisfactory standard of female beauty, since forms and qualities the most opposite and contradictory are looked upon by different nations, and by different individuals, as the perfection of beauty. Some will have it that a beautiful woman must be *fair*, while others conceive nothing but brunettes to be handsome. A Chinese belle must be fat, have small eyes, short nose, high cheeks, and feet which are not longer than a man's finger. In the Labrador Islands no woman is beautiful who has not black teeth and white hair. In Greenland and some other northern countries, the women paint their faces blue, and some yellow. Some nations squeeze the heads of children between boards to make them *square*, while others prefer the shape of a *sugar-loaf* as the highest type of beauty for that important top-piece to the "human form divine." So that there is nothing truer than the old proverb, that "there is no accounting for tastes." This difference of opinion with respect to beauty in various countries is, however, principally confined to *color* and *form*, and may, undoubtedly, be traced to national habits and customs. Nor is it fair, perhaps, to oppose the tastes of uncivilized people to the opinions of civilized nations. But then it must not be overlooked that the standard of beauty in civilized countries is by no means agreed upon. Neither the *buona roba* of the Italians, nor the *linda* of the Spaniards, nor the *embonpoint* of the French, can fully reach the mystical standard of *beauty* to the eye of American taste. And if I were to say that it consists of an indescribable combination of all these, still you would go beyond even that, before you would be content with the definition. Perhaps the best definition of beauty ever given, was by a French poet, who called it a certain *je ne sais quoi,* or *I don't know what!*

The following classical synopsis of female beauty, which has been attributed to Felibien, is the best I remember to have seen:

"The head should be well rounded and look rather inclining to small than large.

"The forehead white, smooth, and open (not with the hair growing down too deep upon it), neither flat nor prominent, but, like the head, well rounded, and rather small in proportion than large.

"The hair either black, bright brown, or auburn, not thin, but full and waving, and if it falls in moderate curls, the better— the black is particularly useful in setting off the whiteness of the neck and skin.

"The eyes black, chestnut, or blue; clear, bright, and lively, and rather large in proportion than small.

"The eyebrows well divided, full, semicircular, and broader in the middle than at the ends, of a neat turn, but not formal.

"The cheeks should not be wide, should have a degree of plumpness, with the red and white finely blended together, and should look firm and soft.

"The ear should be rather small, well folded, and have an agreeable tinge of red.

"The nose should be placed so as to divide the face into equal parts; should be of a moderate size, straight, and well squared, though sometimes a little rising in the middle, which is just perceivable, may give a very graceful look to it.

"The mouth should be small, and the lips not of equal thickness; they should be well turned, small, rather than gross, soft even to the eye, and with a living red in them; a truly pretty mouth is like a rosebud that is beginning to blow. The teeth should be middle-sized, white, well ranged and even.

"The chin of a moderate size, white, soft, and agreeably rounded.

"The neck should be white, straight, and of a soft, easy, flexible make; rather long than short, less above, and increasing gently towards the shoulders; the whiteness and delicacy of its skin should be continued, or rather go on improving to the bosom; the skin in general should be white, properly tinged with red, and a look of thriving health in it.

"The shoulders should be white, gently spread, and with a much softer appearance of strength than in those of men.

"The arm should be white, round, firm and soft, and more particularly so from the elbow to the hands.

"The hand should unite insensibly with the arm; it should be long and delicate, and even the joints and nervous parts of it should be without either any hardness or dryness.

"The fingers should be fine, long, round and soft; small and lessening to the tips, and the nails rather long, round at the ends, and pellucid.

"The bosom should be white and charming, neither too large nor too small; the breasts equal in roundness and firmness, rising gently, and very distinctly separated.

"The sides should be rather long and the hips wider than the shoulders, and go down rounding and lessening gradually to the knee.

"The knee should be even and well rounded.

"The legs straight but varied by proper rounding of the more fleshy parts of them, and finely turned, white, and small at the ankle."

It is very fortunate, however, for the human race that *all* men do not have exactly a correct taste in the matter of female beauty, for if they had, a fatal degree of strife would be likely to ensue as to who should possess the few types of perfect beauty. The old man who rejoiced that all did not see alike, as, if they did, all would be after his wife, was not far out of the way.

A Handsome Form

Many women who can lay no claims to a beautiful face have carried captive the hearts of plenty of men by the beauty of their form. Indeed it may be questioned if a perfect form does not possess a power of captivation beyond any charms that the most beautiful face possesses. You will often hear men say of such and such a girl, "to be sure she has not a beautiful face, but then she has a most exquisite form"; and this they speak with such a peculiar earnestness that it is quite evident they mean what they say.

Those gloomy and ascetic beings who contemn the human body as only a cumbersome lump of clay, as a piece of corruption, and as the charnel-house of the soul, insult their maker, by despising the most ingenious and beautiful piece of mechanism of his physical creation. God has displayed so much care and love upon our bodies that He not only created them for usefulness, but He adorned them with loveliness. If it was not beneath our maker's glory to frame them in beauty, it certainly cannot be beneath us to respect and preserve the charms which we have received from His loving hand. To slight these gifts is to despise the giver. He that has made the temple of our souls beautiful, certainly would not have us neglect the means of preserving that beauty. Every woman owes it not only to herself, but to society, to be as beautiful and charming as she possibly can. The popular cant about the *beauty of the mind* as something which is inconsistent with, and in opposition to the *beauty of the body*, is a superstition which cannot be for a moment entertained by any sound and rational mind. To despise the *temple* is to insult its *occupant*. The divine intelligence which has planted the roses of beauty in the human cheeks, and lighted its fires in the eyes, has also intrusted us with a mission to multiply and increase these charms, as well as to develop and educate our intellects.

Let every woman feel, then, that so far from doing wrong, she is in the pleasant ways of duty when she is studying how to develop and preserve the natural beauty of her body.

"There's nothing ill can dwell in such a temple:
If the ill spirit have so fair a house,
Good things will strive to dwell with it."

SHAKESPEARE.

How to Acquire a Bright and Smooth Skin

The most perfect form will avail a woman little, unless it possess also that *brightness* which is the finishing touch and final polish of a beautiful lady. What avails a plump and well-rounded neck or shoulder if it is dim and dingy withal? What charm can be found in the finest modelled arm if its skin is coarse and rusty? A *grater,* even though moulded in the shape of the most charming female arm, would possess small attractions to a man of taste and refinement.

I have to tell you, ladies—and the same must be said to the gentlemen, too—that the great secret of acquiring a bright and beautiful skin lies in three simple things, as I have said in my lecture on Beautiful Women—temperance, exercise, and cleanliness. A young lady, were she as fair as Hebe, as charming as Venus herself, would soon destroy it all by too high living and late hours. "Take the ordinary fare of a fashionable woman, and you have a style of living which is sufficient to destroy the greatest beauty. It is not the *quantity* so much as the *quality* of the dishes that produces the mischief. Take, for instance, only strong coffee and hot bread and butter, and you have a diet which is most destructive to beauty. The heated grease, long indulged in, is sure to derange the stomach, and by creating or increasing bilious disorders, gradually overspreads the fair skin with a wan or yellow hue. After this meal comes the long fast from nine in the morning till five or six in the afternoon, when dinner is served, and the half-famished beauty sits down to sate a keen appetite with peppered soups, fish, roast, boiled, broiled, and fried meat; game, tarts, sweet-meats, ices, fruits, etc., etc., etc. How must the constitution suffer in trying to digest this *mélange!* How does the heated complexion bear witness to the combustion within! Let the fashionable lady keep up this habit, and add the other one of late hours, and her own looking-glass will tell her that 'we all do fade as the leaf.' The firm texture of the rounded form gives way to a flabby softness, or yields to a scraggy leanness, or shapeless fate. The once fair skin assumes a pallid rigidity or bloated redness, which the deluded victim would still regard as the roses of health and beauty. And when she at last becomes aware of her condition, to repair the ravages she flies to paddings, to give shape where there is none; to stays, to compress into form the swelling chaos of flesh; and to paints, to rectify the dingy complexion. But vain are all these attempts. No; if dissipation, late hours, and immoderation have once wrecked the fair vessel of female charms, it is not in the power of Esculapius himself to right the shattered bark, and make it ride the sea in gallant trim again."

Cleanliness is a subject of indispensable consideration in the pursuit of a beautiful skin. The frequent use of the tepid bath is the best cosmetic I can recommend to my readers in this connection. By such ablutions, the accidental corporeal impurities are thrown off, cutaneous obstructions removed; and while the surface of the body is preserved in its original brightness, many threatening disorders are prevented. It is by this means that the women of the East render their skins as soft and fair as those of the tenderest babes. I wish to impress upon every beautiful woman, and especially upon the one who leads a city life, that she cannot long preserve the brightness of her charms without a daily resort to this purifying agent. She should make the bath as indispensable an article in her house as her looking-glass.

Beauty of Elasticity

The most perfect form, and the most brilliant skin will avail a woman little, unless she possess, also, that physical *agility*, or elasticity, which is the *soul* of a beautiful form in woman. A half-alive and sluggish body, however perfectly formed, is, to say the most, but half beautiful. When you behold a woman who is like a wood-nymph, with a form elastic in all its parts, and a foot as light as that of the goddess, whose flying step "scarcely brushed the unbending corn," whose conscious limbs and agile grace moved in harmony with the light of her sparkling eyes, you may be sure that she carries all hearts before her. There are women whose exquisite forms seem as flexible, wavy and undulating as the graceful lilies of the field. The stuff and prim city belle, incased in hoops and buckram, may well envy that agile, bouncing country romp, who, with nature's roses in her cheeks, skips it like a fawn, and sends out a laugh as natural and merry as the notes of song-birds in June. And she may be sure that her husband or lover never looks upon such a specimen of nature's own beauty, but that he quietly wishes in his heart that his wife, or sweetheart, were like her. Let the city belle learn a lesson from this. She can have the same charms on the same conditions that the country lass has obtained them. But, by high living, late hours, and all the other dissipations of fashionable city life—*never!* That country lass goes to bed with the robin, and is up with the lark. Her life is after nature's fashion, and she is rewarded with nature's most sprightly gifts. Whereas this city belle goes to bed at indefinite midnight hours, and crawls languidly out at mid-day, with a jaded body and a feverish mind, to mope through the tedious rounds of daily dullness, until night again rallies her faint and exhausted spirits. Her life is by gaslight.

Most that I have said in the chapter on the means of obtaining a bright and handsome form, applies equally to the subject of this chapter. But, there are some artificial tricks which I have known beautiful ladies to resort to for the purpose of giving elasticity and sprightliness to the animal frame. The ladies of France and Italy, especially those who are professionally, or as amateurs, engaged in exercises which require great activity of the limbs, as dancing, or playing on instruments, sometimes rub themselves, on retiring to bed, with the following preparation:

Fat of the stag, or deer	8 oz.
Florence oil (or olive oil)	6 oz.
Virgin wax	3 oz.
Musk	1 grain.
White brandy	$\frac{1}{2}$ pint.
Rose water	4 oz.

Put the fat, oil, and wax into a well glazed earthen vessel, and let them simmer over a slow fire until they are assimilated; then pour in the other ingredients, and let the whole gradually cool, when it will be fit for use. There is no doubt but that this mixture, frequently and thoroughly rubbed upon the body on going to bed, will impart a remarkable degree of elasticity to the muscles. In the morning, after this preparation has been used, the body should be thoroughly wiped with a sponge, dampened with cold water.

A Beautiful Face

If it be true "that the face is the index of the mind," the recipe for a beautiful face must be something that reaches the soul. What can be done for a human face, that has a sluggish, sullen, arrogant, angry mind looking out of every feature? An habitually ill-natured, discontented mind ploughs the face with inevitable marks of its own vice. However well shaped, or however bright its complexion, no such face can ever become really beautiful. If a woman's soul is without cultivation, without taste, without refinement, without the sweetness of a happy mind, not all the mysteries of art can ever make her face beautiful. And, on the other hand, it is impossible to dim the brightness of an elegant and polished intellect. The radiance of a charming mind strikes through all deformity of features, and still asserts its sway over the world of the affections. It has been my privilege to see the most celebrated beauties that shine in all the gilded courts of fashion throughout the world, from St. James's to St. Petersburgh, from Paris to Hindostan, and yet I have found no art which can atone for an unpolished mind, and an unlovely heart. That chastened and delightful activity of soul, that spiritual energy which gives animation, grace, and living light to the animal frame, is, after all, the real source of beauty in a woman. It is *that* which gives eloquence to the language of her eyes, which sends the sweetest vermilion mantling to the cheek, and lights up the whole *personnel* as if her very body thought. That, ladies, is the ensign of beauty, and the herald of charms, which are sure to fill the beholder with answering emotion, and irrepressible delight. I never see a creature of such lively and lovely animation, but I fall in love with her myself, and only wish that I were a man, that I might marry her.

I cannot resist the temptation to close this chapter with a beautiful quotation from an old Greek poet, which proves that common sense on this subject of beauty is not by any means of recent date in the world.

> "Why tinge the cheek of youth? the snowy neck,
> Why load with jewels? why anoint the hair?
> Oh, lady, scorn these arts; but richly deck
> Thy soul with virtues: thus for love prepare.
> Lo, with what vermil tints the apple blooms!
> Say, doth the rose the painter's hand require?
> Away, then, with cosmetics and perfumes!
> The charms of nature most excite desire."

How to Obtain a Beautiful Complexion

Though it is true that a beautiful mind is the first thing requisite for a beautiful face, yet how much more charming will the whole become through the aid of a fine complexion? It is not easy to overrate the importance of *complexion*. The features of a Juno with a dull skin would never fascinate. The forehead, the nose, the lips, may all be faultless in size and shape; but still, they can hardly look beautiful without the aid of a bright complexion. Even the finest eyes lose more than half their power, if they are surrounded by an inexpressive complexion. It is in the *coloring* or *complexion* that the artist shows his great skill in giving expression to the face. Overlooking entirely the matter of *vanity*, it is a woman's *duty* to use all the means in her power to beautify and preserve her complexion. It is fitting that the "index of the soul" should be kept as clean and bright and beautiful as possible.

All that I have said in chapters IV. and V., apply also to the subject of the present chapter. A stomach frequently crowded with greasy food, or with artificial stimulants of any kind, will in a short time spoil the brightest complexion. All *excesses* tend to do the same thing. Frequent ablution with pure cold water, followed by gentle and very frequent rubbing with a dry napkin, is one of the best cosmetics ever employed.

It is amusing to reflect upon the tricks which vain beauties will resort to in order to obtain this paramount aid to female charms. Nor is it any wonder that woman should exhaust all her resources in this pursuit, for her face is such a public thing, that there is no hiding the least deformity in it. She can, to some extent, hide an ugly neck, or shoulder, or hand, or foot—but there is no hiding-place for an ugly face.

I knew many fashionable ladies in Paris who used to bind their faces, every night on going to bed, with thin slices of raw beef, which is said to keep the skin from wrinkles, while it gives a youthful freshness and brilliancy to the complexion. I have no doubt of its efficacy. The celebrated Madam Vestris used to sleep every night with her face plastered up with a kind of paste to ward off the threatening wrinkles, and keep her charming complexion from fading. I will give the recipe for making the Vestris' Paste for the benefit of any of my readers whose looking-glass warns them that the dimness and wrinkles of age are extinguishing the roses of youth:

The whites of four eggs boiled in rose water, half an ounce of alum, half an ounce of oil of sweet almonds; beat the whole together till it assumes the consistence of a paste.

The above, spread upon a silk or muslin mask, and worn at night, will not only keep back the wrinkles and preserve the complexion fair, but it is a great remedy where the skin becomes too loosely attached to the muscles, as it gives firmness to the parts. When I was last in Paris (1857) I was shown a recent invention of ready-made masks for the face, composed of fine thick white silk, lined, or plastered, with some kind of fard, or paste, which is designed to beautify and preserve the complexion. I do not know the component parts of this preparation; but I doubt if it is any better than the recipe which was given to me by Madam Vestris, and which I have given above. This trick is so entirely French that there is little danger of its getting into *general* practice in this country. In Bohemia I have seen the ladies flock to arsenic springs and drink the waters, which gave their skins a transparent whiteness; but there is a terrible penalty attached to this folly; for when once they habituate themselves to the practice, they are obliged to keep it up the rest of their days, or death would speedily follow. The beauties of the court of George I were in the habit of taking minute doses of quicksilver to obtain a white and fair complexion; and I have read in Pepys's Diary of some ridiculous scenes which occurred at dancing parties from this practice. Young girls of the present day sometimes eat such things as chalk, slate, and tea-grounds to give themselves a white complexion. I have no doubt that this is a good way to get a *pale* complexion; for it destroys the health, and surely drives out of the face the natural roses of beauty, and, instead of a bright complexion, produces a wan and sickly one. Every young girl ought early to be impressed that whatever destroys health spoils her beauty.

The most remarkable wash for the face which I have ever known, and which is said to have been known to the beauties of the court of Charles II, is made of a simple tincture of *benzoin* precipitated by water. All you have to do in preparing it is to *take a small piece of the gum benzoin and boil it in spirits of wine till it becomes a rich tincture. Fifteen drops of this, poured into a glass of water, will produce a mixture which will look like milk, and emits a most agreeable perfume.*

This delightful wash seems to have the effect of calling the purple stream of the blood to the external fibres of the face, and gives the cheeks a beautiful rosy color. If left on the face to dry, it will render the skin clear and brilliant. It is also an excellent remedy for spots, freckles, pimples, and eruptions, if they have not been of long standing.

Habits which Destroy the Complexion

There are many disorders of the skin which are induced by culpable ignorance, and which owe their origin entirely to the circumstances connected with *fashion* or *habit*. The frequent and sudden changes in this country from heat to cold, by abruptly exciting or repressing the secretions of the skin, roughen its texture, injure its hue, and often deform it with unseemly eruptions. And many of the fashions of dressing the head, are still more inimical to the complexion, than the climate. The habit the ladies have of going into the open air without a bonnet, and often without a veil, is a ruinous one for the skin. Indeed, the fashion of the ladies' bonnets, which only cover a few inches of the back of the head, is a great tax upon the beauty of the complexion. In this climate, especially, the head and face need protection from the atmosphere. Not only a woman's *beauty*, but her *health* requires that she should never step into the open air, particularly in autumnal evenings, without a sufficient covering of her head. And, if she regards the beauty of her complexion, she must never go out into the hot sun without her veil.

The custom, common among ladies, of drying the perspiration from their faces by powdering, or of cooling them when they are hot, from exposure to the sun or dancing, by washing with cold water, is most destructive to the complexion, and not infrequently spreads a humor over the face which renders it hideous for ever. A little common sense ought to teach a woman that, when she is overheated, she ought to allow herself to cool gradually; and, by all means, to avoid going into the air, or allowing a draught through an open door, or window, to blow upon her while she is thus heated. If she will not attend to these rules, she will be fortunate, saying nothing about her beauty, if her *life* does not pay the penalty of her thoughtlessness.

Ladies ought also to know that excessive heat is as bad as excessive cold for the complexion, and often causes distempers of the skin, which are difficult of cure. Look at the rough and dingy face of the desert-wandering gipsy, and you behold the effects of exposure to alternate heats and colds.

To remedy the rigidity of the muscles of the face, and to cure any roughness which may be induced by daily exposure, the following wash may be applied with almost certain relief:

Mix two parts of white brandy with one part of rose water, and wash the face with it night and morning.

The brandy keeps up a gentle action of the skin, which is so essential to its healthy appearance, also thoroughly cleanses the surface, while the rose water counteracts the drying nature of the brandy, and leaves the skin in a natural, soft, and flexible state.

At a trifling expense, a lady may provide herself with a delightful wash for the face, which is a thousand times better than the expensive *lotions* which she purchases at the apothecaries. Besides, she has the advantage of knowing what she is using, which is far from being the case where she buys the prepared patent lotions. These preparations are generally put up by ignorant quacks and pretenders; and I have known the most loathsome, beauty-destroying, indolent ulcers to be produced by the use of them.

The following is a recipe for making another wash for the face, which is a favorite with the ladies of France.

Take equal parts of the seeds of the melon pumpkin, gourd and cucumber, pounded till they are reduced to powder; add to it sufficient fresh cream to dilute the flour, and then add milk enough to reduce the whole to a thin paste. Add a grain of musk, and a few drops of the oil of lemon. Anoint the face with this, leave it on twenty or thirty minutes, or overnight if convenient, and wash off with warm water. It gives a remarkable purity and brightness to the complexion.

A fashionable beauty at St. Petersburgh gave me the following recipe for a wash, which imparts a remarkable lustre to the face, and is the greatest favorite of a Russian lady's toilet.

Infuse a handful of well sifted wheat bran for four hours in white wine vinegar; add to it five yolks of eggs and two grains of musk, and distill the whole. Bottle it, keep carefully corked, fifteen days, when it will be fit for use. Apply it overnight, and wash in the morning with tepid water.

PIMPERNEL WATER is a sovereign wash with the ladies all over the continent of Europe, for whitening the complexion. All they do to prepare it is simply to steep that wholesome plant in pure rain water. It is such a favorite that it is regarded as almost indispensable to a lady's toilet, who is particularly attentive to the brightness of her complexion.

Paints and Powders

If Satan has ever had any direct agency in inducing woman to spoil or deform her own beauty, it must have been in tempting her to use *paints* and *enamelling.* Nothing so effectually writes *memento mori!* on the cheek of beauty as this ridiculous and culpable practice. Ladies ought to know that it is a sure spoiler of the skin, and good taste ought to teach them that it is a frightful distorter and deformer of the natural beauty of the "human face divine." The greatest charm of beauty is in the *expression* of a lovely face; in those divine flashes of joy, and good-nature, and love, which beam in the human countenance. But what expression can there be in "a face bedaubed with white paint and enamelled? No flush of pleasure, no thrill of hope, no light of love can shine through the incrusted mould." Her face is as expressionless as that of a painted mummy. And let no woman imagine that the men do not readily detect this poisonous mask upon the skin. Many a time have I seen a gentleman shrink from saluting a brilliant lady, as though it was a death's head he were compelled to kiss. The secret was, that her face and lips were bedaubed with paints. All white paints are not only destructive to the skin, but they are ruinous to the health. I have known paralytic affections and premature death to be traced to their use. But alas! I am afraid that there never was a time when many of the gay and fashionable of my sex, did not make themselves both contemptible and ridiculous by this disgusting trick. The ancient ladies seem to have outdone even modern belles in this painting business. The terrible old Juvenal draws the following picture of one of the flirts of his day:

> But tell me yet; this thing, thus daubed and oiled,
> Poulticed, plastered, baked by turns, and boiled,
> Thus with pomatums, ointments, lacquered o'er,
> Is it a *face*, Usidius, or a *sore?*

But it is proper to remark, that what has been said against white paints and enamels does not apply with equal force to the use of *rouge*. Rouging still leaves the neck and arms, and more than three-quarters of the face to their natural complexion, and the language of the heart, expressed by the general complexion, is not obstructed. A little vegetable *rouge* tinging the cheek of a beautiful woman, who, from ill health or an anxious mind, loses her roses, may be excusable; and so transparent is the texture of such *rouge* (if unadulterated with lead) that when the blood does mount to the face, it speaks through the slight covering, and enhances the fading bloom. But even this allowable artificial aid must be used with the most delicate taste, and discretion. The tint on the cheek, should always be fainter than what nature's pallet would have painted. A violently rouged woman is a disgusting sight. The excessive red on the face gives a coarseness to every feature, and a general fierceness to the countenance, which transforms the elegant lady of fashion into a vulgar harridan. But, in no case, can even *rouge* be used by ladies who have passed the age of life when roses are natural to the cheek. A *rouged* old woman is a horrible sight—a distortion of nature's harmony!

Excessive use of *powder* is also a vulgar trick. None but the very finest powder should ever be used, and the lady should be especially careful that sufficient is not left upon the face to be noticeable to the eye of a gentleman. She must be very particular that particles of it are not left visible about the base of the nose, and in the hollow of the chin. Ladies sometimes catch up their powder, and rub it on in a hurry, without even stopping to look in the glass, and go into company with their faces looking as though they just came out of a meal-bag. It is a ridiculous sight, and ladies may be sure it is disgusting to gentlemen.

A Beautiful Bosom

I am aware that this is a subject which must be handled with great delicacy; but my book would be incomplete without some notice of this "greatest claim of lovely woman." And, besides, it is undoubtedly true, that a proper discussion of this subject will seem *peculiar* only to the most vulgar minded of both sexes. If it be true, as the old poet sung, that

"Heaven rests on those two heaving hills of snow,"

why should not a woman be suitably instructed in the right management of such extraordinary charms?

The first thing to be impressed upon the mind of a lady is, that very low-necked dresses are in exceeding bad taste, and are quite sure to leave upon the mind of a gentleman an equivocal idea, to say the least. A word to the wise on this subject is sufficient. If a young lady has no father, or brother, or husband to direct her taste in this matter, she will do well to sit down and commit the above statement to memory. It is a charm which a woman, who understands herself, will leave not to the public eye of man, but to his imagination. She knows that *modesty* is the divine spell that binds the heart of man to her forever. But my observation has taught me that few women are well informed as to the physical management of this part of their bodies. The bosom, which nature has formed with exquisite symmetry in itself, and admirable adaptation to the parts of the figure to which it is united, is often transformed into a shape, and transplanted to a place, which deprive it of its original beauty and harmony with the rest of the person. This deforming metamorphosis is effected by means of stiff stays, or corsets, which force the part out of its natural position, and destroy the natural tension and firmness in which so much of its beauty consists. A young lady should be instructed that she is not to allow even her own hand to press it too roughly. But, above all things, to avoid, especially when young, the constant pressure of such hard substances as whalebone and steel; for, besides the destruction to beauty, they are liable to produce all the terrible consequences of abscesses and cancers. Even the padding which ladies use to give a full appearance, where there is a deficient bosom, is sure, in a little time, to entirely destroy all the natural beauty of the parts. As soon as it becomes apparent that the bosom lacks the rounded fullness due to the rest of her form, instead of trying to repair the deficiency with artificial padding, it should be clothed as loosely as possible, so as to avoid the least artificial pressure. Not only its growth is stopped, but its complexion is spoiled by these tricks. Let the growth of this beautiful part be left as unconfined as the young cedar, or as the lily of the field. And for that reason the bodice should be flexible to the motion of the body and the undulations of the shape. The artificial india-rubber bosoms are not only ridiculous contrivances, but they are absolutely ruinous to the beauty of the part.

The following preparation, very softly rubbed upon the bosom for five or ten minutes, two or three times a day has been uscd with success to promote its growth.

Tincture of myrrh	$1/_2$ oz.
Pimpernel water	4 oz.
Elder-flower water	4 oz.
Musk	1 gr.
Rectified spirits of wine	6 oz.

I have known ladies to take a preparation of iodine internally to remedy a too large development of the bosom. But this must be a dangerous experiment for the general health. The following external application has been recommended for this purpose.

Strong essence of mint	1 oz.
Iodine of zinc	2 gr.
Aromatic vinegar	2 gr.
Essence of cedrat	10 drops.

If, from sickness, or any other cause, the bosom has lost its beauty by becoming soft, the following wash, applied as gently as possible morning and night, will have a most beneficial effect.

Alum water	$^{1}/_{2}$ oz.
Strong camomile water	1 oz.
White brandy	2 oz.

If the whole body is not afflicted with a general decay and flabbiness, the use of this wash for a month or two will be quite sure to produce the happiest effects.

The Living Beauty

·ᴗ

I BADE, BECAUSE THE wick and oil
are spent
And frozen are the channels of the blood,
My discontented heart to draw content
From beauty that is cast out of a mould
In bronze, or that in dazzling marble appears,
Appears, but when we have gone is gone again,
Being more indifferent to our solitude
Than 'twere an apparition. O heart, we are old;
The living beauty is for younger men:
We cannot pay its tribute of wild tears.

W. B. YEATS *is considered one of the greatest writers of the twentieth century. The Irish poet's work was largely dedicated to the ideas of art, beauty, and the occult. "The Living Beauty" is from his* Collected Poems.

Memoirs of an Ex-Prom Queen

.⌣

L

EAVE IT TO the philosophers to have a weighty German name for the question of whether or not to procreate. *Zeugungsproblem.* An aspect of axiology, a branch of ethics. Hear the learned professors contemplate the consequences of birth for the race of Man, the metaphysical implications of existence, and not one word about the effects of procreation on a woman's body.

Schopenhauer, the profoundest of pessimists, meets the gloomy Byron on a holiday stroll through Venice. The two giants greet each other, remark the shimmer of the air, the futility of life, while their inamoratas, each leaning on her lover's arm and shifting her weight from foot to foot, looks the other over, smiles sweetly, twirls her parasol, straightens her skirts. Ah, sighs Lord Byron, how painful this life. Aye, nods

---

ALIX KATES SHULMAN'S *autobiography,* Memoirs of an Ex-Prom Queen, *appeared in 1972.*

Schopenhauer, we must put a stop to it. They part, the one to suicide, the other to misogyny.

But see what the tiniest baby will do to the woman. Stretching her belly and waist into the ghastliest shapes before it even emerges from the womb, ruining her breasts, turning her pink nipples brown. Producing spots at the hairline, dark hairs down her midline, bleeding gums, stretch marks, varicosities, blues, alterations of the hormones and perhaps the DNA—and that's only the beginning. In time comes the ugly crease in the brow between the eyes hewn by incessant anxiety and sporadic rage, the rasp in the voice, the knot in the gut, the regret. Fear alters the features, and in time the sweetest child will make a shrew of her.

Schopenhauer, the misogynist, resolves his *Zeugungsproblem* by remaining a bachelor and sometime celibate. He rises punctually each morning to write his books, blames his mother, takes his meals in his favorite restaurant, in a temper shoves an old woman down a flight of stairs, and discourses at length on the futility of life and the deception in women.

It was partly because of the way Willy noted the girls on the street that summer, partly because of the new fashions, that I finally decided to cut my hair. The sixties had started while I was having my babies, and I felt I had to do something about it. The threat of abandonment or another woman had crept into the nursery, and I was going out of my mind.

I did not act on impulse. I spent a long time thinking it over, studying the ads and my old photos, before I finally made an appointment with a hairdresser and hired a sitter. And even then, I would never have had the nerve to go through with it if Willy, who had declared himself against the haircut, hadn't left town for a week to supervise a computer installation in Waterbury, Connecticut. He said.

At first I tried to reach Andrew, the man who had regularly cut my hair when I was at Columbia before I had married and let it grow long. He would have known exactly the look I wanted. But I was told on the phone he had long since left to open a shop in Queens, and I accepted an appointment with a Mr. John instead.

Standing on an Eighth Street crosstown bus edging through traffic, I was fairly optimistic about the results. My reflection in the bus window was not unattractive. It skipped the details and gave no hint of texture. Depending on how I chose to focus, I could see at a single spot on the windowpane my nose or a building across the street.

I had never been one to dwell on my failings. Rather, since the miraculous removal of my braces back in 1945, I, raised on Emerson, had always believed that whatever faults surfaced, there was always some cure, some program or remedy to apply, to reverse the symptoms. A diet, a haircut, sun, sleep, exercise, a change of scene, a new lover, a husband, determination, suicide if all else failed. Through the years I had found my own standards more exacting than others'; and examining my reflection as we stopped to take on passengers, I was reasonably confident of the expedition's outcome.

The moment I sat down before the beauty parlor mirror, however, surrounded by regular customers and Muzak, I knew I was making a mistake. Reflections in a dirty window are one thing; in a fluorescent-lit mirror another. There was a crease beside my mouth it was useless to deny, and other shocking imperfections. Not in my skin only. My very bones had shifted: narrower cheeks, more prominent cheekbones. The hairline was new, and there were several small, as yet inconspicuous moles destined to enlarge. I had evidently undergone some reversal of luck.

The operator covered me—hands, purse, and all—in a green smock, then looked me over in the mirror. "A Cap Cut, I think," he suggested.

"Okay," I said, "but short enough that I won't have to set it."

"Aren't you down for a shampoo and set?" He checked his book.

I did not believe in hair setting. It was a fraud, like a wig or a padded bra. They all corrupted the user, robbing her of dignity. The women in the mirror surrounding me, staring at their green-smocked reflections, their hair wrapped in towels, set in rollers, teased, straightened, frizzed, dyed; eyebrows red from plucking, lips foaming with peroxide, hands soaking in softener— they had all been robbed, like the mannequins in Rome and the secretaries in offices.

"No. Just a cut."

"Well, I'll wet you down then. You could use a styling. With that much hair I'm going to have to charge you for a styling anyway."

I suddenly recalled the sorry fate of Veronica Lake and her famous "peekaboo bang." When the peekaboo bangs of thousands of women working in factories during World War II began getting caught in the machinery and fouling the War Effort, the Department of War asked Miss Lake to set an example by changing her hairdo for the Duration. A patriot, she complied. It ruined her. Directly she changed her hair, she fell into obscurity and then oblivion.

Mr. John sprinkled water on my hair and my fluff flattened, leaving only my naked face.

Under the circumstances, I thought, a haircut might prove a disaster.

He reached for his scissors. I gripped the arms of the chair underneath my smock. I tried not to wince as Mr. John picked up my long front lock and made his initial snip; watched horrified as pieces of me fell to the floor. Remnants of my past, to be swept away by a porter's broom, too late to get back.

"Remember," I cautioned, "very short. But soft. Not severe."

Though I aimed to convey only reasonable concern, something in my manner must have betrayed anxiety, for Mr. John, holding scissors poised midair, gently reprimanded my reflection with:

"Why don't you wait till I finish before you judge?"

A new operator, I thought, inexperienced. Too late to change, and Will expected home tomorrow. I held my head absolutely still as he proceeded to cut, my features frozen as though caked in mudpack.

Mr. John hummed with the Muzak, then paused to examine his work.

"Shorter at the ears," I instructed. "I'd like a more tousled look." No going back.

Mr. John ignored me, pursuing some ideal of his own.

"I may have a picture here of the look I want," I admitted at last. And as casually as I could, I brought out from under the green smock my old graduation photo that had been reprinted years before in the Cleveland *Post* with the Former-Prom-Queen caption. With pride and shame I tried to present the picture as though, despite its yellowed crumbling edges, I had clipped it from some ad in last week's *News*.

"More like that."

Mr. John glanced at it quickly without recognition and shrugged.

"Of course, I'll cut it any way you say, but frankly, your ears are not the daintiest."

There was a blinding flash as for an instant the mirror lit up with revelations.

My ears, never before worth noticing, were suddenly to be regarded! Like my skin and my hair, heretofore unobjectionable, suddenly my ears, too, were factors in the total picture. How the considerations proliferated!

The clothes you're wearing are the clothes you wore,

The smile you are smiling you were smiling then,

But I don't remember where, or whhhh-en,

sang Mr. John to the Muzak, snipping away. Of course I was glad to have escaped detection in that old clipping, but I was vexed to discover that we no longer bore any recognizable resemblance to each other. Perhaps, as Mr. John suggested, it was time to be restyled. All the magazines proclaimed times had changed. The sixties were news. What had been in was out; what out, in. Taking the clipping out of my drawer the night before, I had even then sensed an anachronism, like my paltry total of twenty-six lovers on the coded list beside it, now regularly surpassed by every industrious contender, like the four-minute mile.

I made no protest as Mr. John severed my remaining locks, wrapped the stumps in tissues and rolled them on rollers, then stuffed my ears with cotton and shoved me under a dryer.

"Want me to bring you some magazines?" he mouthed, as a barrage of hot molecules battered my ears, drowning out the opening strains of Muzak "Stardust."

Oh, why had I neglected to bring a book? The truth was, years had passed since I had read a book. I had looked things up and read reviews on Sundays, had even browsed in bookstores on Eighth Street with Willy after the movies. But in my daily life of clutter and climax my attentions had been so splintered, my concerns so manifold, that the concentration required to read a book through had evidently atrophied in me, and except for survival manuals like Dr. Guttmacher's and Dr. Spock's, never intended for reflection anyway, books were but titles to me, like lovers' names, documents of my biography. Even the tiny volumes of the Little Leather Library, now collectors' items, were stored safely away with the baby clothes to be handed down to a daughter. The most I managed was now and then a poem from a quarterly, to commit to memory and replay for solace.

"I said, would you like some magazines?" repeated Mr. John, raising the headpiece for a moment so I could hear him.

"Yes, thanks."

He returned with a handful of slick paper. And within moments, there I was under a dryer leafing through magazines, without even a book to distinguish me, as though I too had come to be patched and repaired, styled, shampooed, and set. Rather than simply trimmed.

Does she . . . or doesn't she? Hair color so natural only her hairdresser knows for sure.

Starting at puberty in *Seventeen* magazines all my life I had noticed ads for skin care and hair rinses, but I had never understood them. Not that I had been smug—I had simply not believed in cosmetics, not known what all that talk of pores and textures was about.

Radiant color that never rubs off on pillows, towels, collars, or him.

Suddenly under the influence of the extremely hot air, the pages of *McCall's* and *Glamour* yielded intelligences I had frankly never suspected. At last, in my thirty-first year, I began to understand those ads for the first time in my life.

Can a cream really make dramatic improvements in aging skin? Is such an achievement possible? Today, Science tells us, the probability exists as never before.

Perhaps such things, like sex and motherhood, can be understood only when it is too late. Are not the products promoted in the magazines intended to halt precisely those developments that cannot be halted? Afflictions like acne have nothing in common with this other condition, despite surface appearances; one, time alone will cure; the other, time will only worsen.

Gives you back that flat tummy of your teens.

Gone forever that flaky caky feeling, washed away with Beauty Bar.

Suddenly under the dryer I saw that those very remedies I had come to count on—haircuts, diets, sun, lovers—would produce in time such terrible symptoms of their own that more cures, more tricks, more devices would be necessary to control them. Bleach your hair and it will turn out coarser; shave your legs and it will grow in thicker; have a mole removed and two more will pop out. My own once-radiant skin had begun to show imperfections which to camouflage would be to aggravate. It would dry out in the sun, hang loose if I dieted, puff up if I slept; and even if I did nothing at all, the pores would enlarge, hairs sprout, dimples crease, pimples scar. The whole process was out of control. Once the grey got a start in my hair, it could only spread. And a lover—the ultimate cure—a lover was absolutely out of the question for the simple reason that I could not bear for him to see my thirty-year-old thighs quiver!

It was all coming startlingly clear. The hot air waves bombarding my head and burning my ears were no doubt transmitting cosmic messages. In the *Ladies' Home Journal* at last I began to see the necessary connections between causes and effects that had eluded me in all my study of philosophy. Perhaps every stimulus, as Dr. Watson testified, had its response and every act, as Spinoza maintained, its consequences given from the beginning of time, but the responses and consequences were not those I had grown to expect. Who would have predicted that the crooked smile I had artfully cultivated for its power to charm would leave an entirely different mark beside my mouth? The particular fate I had spent a lifetime fleeing across two continents and decades had been here waiting for me all the while I was looking back over my shoulder. Neither course I had followed had saved me from it. To find myself at thirty locked under a dryer eagerly studying ads in magazines while I worry about the sitter and my husband is away on a business trip; now, after my schemes and triumphs, my visions and dares, to be, without income or skill, dependent on a man and a fading skin—it can only be the fulfillment of a curse!

Q u e e n   E s t h e r

I T IS A LITTLE singular that the words GOD or
PROVIDENCE are not mentioned in the whole book of Esther. The
writer seems studiously to have avoided any reference to them, as
if he did not wish to recognize the interposition of Heaven in any
of the events that transpired; while his *narrative* is evidently
designed to teach nothing else. The hand of Providence is everywhere seen managing the whole scheme.

Ahasuerus, king over a hundred and twenty-seven
provinces, and prosperous to the extent of his vast ambition,
made a grand exhibition of his wealth to his subjects, which
lasted six months. At the end of this time, he gave a feast to continue a week. The court of the garden of his palace was paved
with the choicest marbles, black, red, blue, and white. From this
costly floor, pillars of polished marble arose, supporting a gor-

REV. J. T. HEADLEY'S *"Queen Esther" is from his 1853 tract,* The Power of
Beauty.

geous canopy; while all around were the richest hangings, upheld by cords and rings of silver. Beneath this magnificent drapery, were spread couches, covered only with gold and silver cloths. In the midst the table was laid—groaning under a weight of gold—every goblet being of solid gold, and each differing from the other in its form and elaborate workmanship. The queen had a similar feast in her apartments for the women, and all was mirth and festivity. At the end of the week, however, when the dissipation had reached its height, the king being merry and uxorious from his long and deep libations, sent for his wife to come and show herself to his guests, that he might praise her beauty. Knowing the state her husband was in, and also the shocks her delicacy would receive in the interview, she refused to go. The king was just drunk enough to be dignified, and hence regarded this refusal as a mortal offense. He asked the wise men about him, what should be done in such an extraordinary case. Much wiser than if they had been sober, they one after another expressed proper horror at the monstrous act, and stroking their long beards and looking grave and sage, told him that it was a matter that concerned not only him, but husbands the world over; for if such a thing should be passed by in silence, all authority over their wives would end—in short, it would be a sort of moral earthquake. Poor Vashti had not the least idea she was creating such a revolution in human affairs: however, she was unqueened at once, and the catastrophe of husbands being ruled by their wives, postponed if not averted.

When the king, however, came out of his dissipation, he began to pine for his beautiful wife. His favorites no sooner perceived this, than they set on foot a plan to wean him entirely from her. They knew her restoration would be the signal of their disgrace and banishment—so all the beautiful virgins of that vast realm were brought before him, from whom, after a trial which does as much honor to the morals, as to the wisdom of those sages, he was to select one as a wife. Among these was Hadassah, a Hebrew maiden whose parents were dead, and who had been reared by her cousin Mordecai, one of the prisoners carried away, when the king of Babylon took and sacked Jerusalem.

The character of Esther is here exhibited at the outset; for when she went into the presence of the king for his inspection, instead of asking for gifts as allowed by him, and as the others did, she took only what the chamberlain gave her.

Of exquisite form and faultless features, her rare beauty at once captivated the king, and he made her his wife. Following the advice of her cousin, she had never told him her lineage, and the enthralled monarch forgot his former queen.

Mordecai always reminds one of Hamlet. Of a noble heart, grand intellect, and unwavering integrity, there was nevertheless an air of severity about him—a haughty, unbending spirit; which with his high sense of honor, and scorn of meanness, would prompt him to lead an isolated life. I have sometimes thought that even he had not been able to resist the fascinations of his young and beautiful cousin, and that the effort to conceal his feelings had given a greater severity to his manner than he naturally possessed. Too noble, however, to sacrifice such a beautiful being by uniting her fate with his own, when a throne was offered her; or perceiving that the lovely and gentle being he had seen ripen into faultless womanhood, could never return his love—indeed could cherish no feeling but that of a fond daughter, he crushed by his strong will his fruitless passion. In no other way can I account for the life he led, lingering forever around the palace gates, where now and then he might get a glimpse of her who had been the light of his soul, the one bright bird which had cheered his exile's home. That home he wished no longer to see, and day after day he took his old station at the gates of Shushan, and looked upon the magnificent walls that divided him from all that had made life desirable. It seems, also, as if some latent fear that Haman, the favorite of the king—younger than his master and of vast ambition—might attempt to exert too great an influence over his cousin, must have prompted him to treat the latter with disrespect, and refuse him that homage which was his due. No reason is given for the hostility he manifested, and which he must have known would end in his own destruction. Whenever Haman with his retinue came from the palace, all paid him the reverence due to the king's favorite, but Mordecai, who sat like a statue, not even turning his head to notice him. He acted like one tired of life, and at length succeeded in arousing the deadly hostility of the haughty minister. The latter, however, scorning to be revenged on *one* man, and he a person of low birth, persuaded the king to decree the slaughter of all the Jews in his realm. The news fell like a thunderbolt on Mordecai. Sullen, proud, and indifferent to his own fate, he had defied his enemy to do his worst; but such a savage vengeance had never entered his mind. It was too late, however, to regret his behavior. Right or wrong, he had been the cause of the bloody sentence, and he roused himself to avert the awful catastrophe. With rent garments, and sackcloth on his head, he travelled the city with a loud and bitter cry, and his voice rang even over the walls of the palace, in tones that startled its slumbering inmates. It was told to Esther, and she ordered garments to be given him; but he refused to receive them, and sent back a copy of the king's decree, respecting the massacre of the Jews, and bade her go in, and supplicate him to remit the sentence. She replied that it was certain death to enter the king's presence unbidden, unless he chose to hold out his sceptre; and that for a whole month he had not requested to see her. Her stern cousin, however, unmoved by the danger to herself, and thinking only of his people, replied haughtily that she might do as she chose—if she preferred to save herself, delivery would come to the Jews from some other quarter, but she should die.

From this moment the character of Esther unfolds itself. It was only a passing weakness that prompted her to put in a word for her own life, and she at once arose to the dignity of a martyr. The blood of the proud and heroic Mordecai flowed in her veins, and she said, "Go, tell my cousin to assemble all the Jews in Shushan, and fast three days and three nights, neither eating nor drinking; I and my maidens will do the same, and on the third day I will go before the king, and *if I perish, I perish.*" Noble and brave heart! death—a violent death is terrible, but thou art equal to it!

There, in that magnificent apartment, filled with perfume—and where the softened light, stealing through the gorgeous windows by day, and shed from golden lamps by night on marble columns and gold-covered couches, makes a scene of enchantment—behold Esther, with her royal apparel thrown aside, kneeling on the tessellated floor. There she has been two days and nights, neither eating nor drinking, while hunger, and thirst, and mental agony, have made fearful inroads on her beauty. Her cheeks are sunken and haggard, her large and lustrous eyes dim with weeping, and her lips parched and dry, yet ever moving in inward prayer. Mental and physical suffering have crushed her young heart within her, and now the hour of her destiny is approaching. Ah! who can tell the desperate effort it required to prepare for that terrible interview? Never before did it become her to look so fascinating as then; and removing with tremulous anxiety the traces of her suffering, she decked herself in the most becoming apparel she could select. Her long black tresses were never before so carefully braided over her polished forehead, and never before did she put forth such an effort to enhance every charm, and make her beauty irresistible to the king. At length fully arrayed, and looking more like a goddess dropped from the clouds, than a being of clay, she stole tremblingly towards the king's chamber. Stopping a moment at the threshold to swallow down the choking sensation that almost suffocated her, and to gather her failing strength, she passed slowly into the room, while her maidens stood breathless without, listening, and waiting with the intensest anxiety the issue. Hearing a slight rustling, the king, with a sudden frown, looked up to see who was so sick of life as to dare come unbidden in his presence, and lo! Esther stood speechless before him. Her long fastings and watchings had taken the color from her cheeks, but had given a greater transparency in its place, and as she stood, half shrinking, with the shadow of profound melancholy on her pallid, but indescribably beautiful countenance—her pencilled brow slightly contracted in the intensity of her excitement—her long lashes dripping in tears, and her lips trembling with agitation; she was—though silent—in herself an appeal that a heart of stone could not resist. The monarch gazed long and silently on her, as she stood waiting her doom. Shall she die? No; the golden sceptre slowly rises and points to her. The beautiful intruder is welcome, and sinks like a snow-wreath at his feet. Never before did the monarch gaze on such transcendent loveliness; and spellbound and conquered by it, he said in a gentle voice: "What wilt thou, queen Esther? What is thy request?—it shall be granted thee, even to the *half of my kingdom!*"

Woman-like, she did not wish to risk the influence she had thus suddenly gained, by asking the destruction of his favorite, and the reversion of his unalterable decree, and so she prayed only that he and Haman might banquet with her the next day. She had thrown her fetters over him, and was determined to fascinate him still more deeply before she ventured on so bold a movement. At the banquet he again asked her what she desired, for he well knew it was no ordinary matter that had induced her to peril her life by entering, unbidden, his presence.

She invited him to a second feast, and at that to a third. But the night previous to the last, the king could not sleep, and after tossing awhile on his troubled couch, he called for the record of the court, and there found that Mordecai had a short time before informed him, through the queen, of an attempt to assassinate him, and no reward been bestowed. The next day, therefore, he made Haman perform the humiliating office of leading his enemy in triumph through the streets, proclaiming before him, "This is the man whom the king delighteth to honor." As he passed by the gallows he had the day before erected for that very man, a shudder crept through his frame, and the first omen of coming evil cast its shadow on his spirit.

The way was now clear to Esther, and so the next day, at the banquet, as the king repeated his former offer, she, reclining on the couch, her chiselled form and ravishing beauty inflaming the ardent monarch with love and desire, said, in pleading accents, "I ask, O king, for *my life*, and that of my people. If we had all been sold as bondmen and bondwomen, I had held my tongue, great as the evil would have been to thee." The king started, as if stung by an adder, and with a brow dark as wrath, and a voice that sent Haman to his feet, exclaimed: "*Thy life!* my queen? *Who* is he? *where* is he that dare even think such a thought in his heart? He who strikes at thy life, radiant creature, plants his presumptuous blow in his monarch's bosom." "*That man,*" said the lovely pleader, "*is the wicked Haman.*" Darting one look of vengeance on the petrified favorite, he strode forth into the garden to control his boiling passions. Haman saw at once that his only hope now was, in moving the sympathies of the queen in his behalf; and approaching her, he began to plead most piteously for his life. In his agony he fell on the couch where she lay, and while in this position, the king returned. "What!" he exclaimed, "will he violate the queen here in my own palace!" Nothing more was said: no order was given. The look and voice of terrible wrath in which this was said were sufficient. The attendants simply spread a cloth over Haman's face, and not a word was spoken. Those who came in, when they saw the covered countenance, knew the import. It was the sentence of death. The vaulting favorite himself dare not remove it—he must *die,* and the quicker the agony is over, the better. In a few hours he was swinging on the gallows he had erected for Mordecai.

After this, the queen's power was supreme—everything she asked was granted. To please her, he let his palace flow in the blood of five hundred of his subjects, whom the Jews slew in self-defence. For her he hung Haman's ten sons on the gallows where the father had suffered before them. For her he made Mordecai prime minister, and lavished boundless favors on the hitherto oppressed Hebrews. And right worthy was she of all he did for her. Lovely in character as she was in person, her sudden elevation did not make her vain, nor her power haughty. The same gentle, pure, and noble creature when queen, as when living in the lowly habitation of her cousin—generous, disinterested, and ready to die for others, she is one of the loveliest characters furnished in the annals of history.

Snow White

∙⤳

SHE IS A tall dark beauty containing a great many beauty spots: one above the breast, one above the belly, one above the knee, one above the ankle, one above the buttock, one on the back of the neck. All of these are on the left side, more or less in a row, as you go up and down:

o

o

o

o

o

o

The hair is black as ebony, the skin white as snow.

DONALD BARTHELME *happily mixed the absurd, comic, and violent in his writings; perhaps no more than in the 1983* Snow White. *This excerpt opens the book.*

Autobiography of a Face

M Y FRIEND STEPHEN and I used to do pony
parties together. The festivities took place on the well-tended
lawns of the vast suburban communities that had sprung up
around Diamond D Stables in the rural acres of Rockland
County. Mrs. Daniels, the owner of Diamond D, took advantage
of the opportunity and readily dispatched a couple of ponies for
birthday parties. In the early years Mrs. Daniels used to attend
the parties with us, something Stephen and I dreaded. She fancied herself a sort of Mrs. Roy Rogers and dressed in embar-
rassing accordance: fringed shirts, oversized belt buckles,
ramshackle hats. I'd stand there holding a pony, cringing
inwardly with mortification as if she were my own mother. But
as we got older and Stephen got his driver's license, and as

LUCY GREALY *penned a memoir for* Harper's *magazine. The article, which*
won a National Magazine award, was the basis for her first book,
Autobiography of a Face *(1984).*

Diamond D itself slowly sank into a somewhat surreal, muddy, and orphaned state of anarchy, we worked the parties by ourselves, which I relished.

We were invariably late for the birthday party, a result of loading the ponies at the last minute, combined with our truly remarkable propensity for getting lost. I never really minded, though. I enjoyed the drive through those precisely planned streets as the summer air swirled through the cab of the pickup, rustling the crepe-paper ribbons temporarily draped over the rear-view mirror. When we finally found our destination, we'd clip the ribbons into the ponies' manes and tails in a rather sad attempt to imbue a festive air. The neighborhoods were varied, from close, tree-laden streets crammed with ranch-style houses to more spacious boulevards dotted with outsized Tudors. Still, all the communities seemed to share a certain carbon-copy quality: house after house looked exactly like the one next to it, save for the occasional cement deer or sculpted shrub. A dog would always appear and chase the trailer for a set number of lawns— some mysterious canine demarcation of territory—before suddenly dropping away, to be replaced by another dog running and barking behind us a few lawns later.

I liked those dogs, liked their sense of purpose and enjoyment and responsibility. I especially liked being lost, tooling through strange neighborhoods with Stephen. As we drove by the houses, I gazed into the windows, imagining what the families inside were like. My ideas were loosely based on what I had learned from TV and films. I pictured a father in a reclining chair next to a lamp, its shade trimmed with small white tassels.

Somewhere nearby a wife in a coordinated outfit chatted on the phone with friends while their children set the dinner table. As they ate their home-cooked food, passing assorted white serving dishes, they'd casually ask each other about the day. Perhaps someone would mention the unusual sight of a horse trailer going past the house that day. Certain that these families were nothing like my own, a certainty wrought with a sense of vague superiority and even vaguer longing, I took pride and pleasure in knowing that I was the person in that strangely surreal trailer with the kicking ponies and angry muffler, that I had driven by their house that day, that I had brushed against their lives, and past them, like that.

Once we reached the party, there was a great rush of excitement. The children, realizing that the ponies had arrived, would come running from the back yard in their silly hats; their now forgotten balloons, bobbing colorfully behind them, would fly off in search of some tree or telephone wire. The ponies, reacting to the excitement of new sounds and smells, would promptly take a crap in the driveway, to a chorus of disgusted groans.

My pleasure at the sight of the children didn't last long, however. I knew what was coming. As soon as they got over the thrill of being near the ponies, they'd notice me. Half my jaw was missing, which gave my face a strange triangular shape, accentuated by the fact that I was unable to keep my mouth completely closed. When I first started doing pony parties, my hair was still short and wispy, still growing in from the chemo. But as it grew I made things worse by continuously bowing my head and hiding behind the curtain of hair, furtively peering out at the world like some nervous actor. Unlike the actor, though, I didn't secretly relish my audience, and if it were possible I would have stood behind that curtain forever, my head bent in an eternal act of deference. I was, however, dependent upon my audience. Their approval or disapproval defined everything for me, and I believed with every cell in my body that approval wasn't written into my particular script. I was fourteen years old.

"I *hate* this, why am I doing this?" I'd ask myself each time, but I had no choice if I wanted to keep my job at the stable. Everyone who worked at Diamond D had to do pony parties—no exceptions. Years later a friend remarked how odd it was that an adult would even think to send a disfigured child to work at a kid's party, but at the time it was never an issue. If my presence in these back yards was something of an anomaly, it wasn't just because of my face. In fact, my physical oddness seemed somehow to fit in with the general oddness and failings of Diamond D.

The stable was a small place near the bottom of a gently sloping hill. Each spring the melting snow left behind ankle-deep mud that wouldn't dry up completely until midsummer. Mrs. Daniels possessed a number of peculiar traits that made life at Diamond D unpredictable. When she wasn't trying to save our souls, or treating Stephen's rumored homosexuality by unexpectedly exposing her breasts to him, she was taking us on shoplifting sprees, dropping criminal hints like some Artful Dodger.

No one at Diamond D knew how to properly care for horses. Most of the animals were kept outside in three small, grassless corrals. The barn was on the verge of collapse; our every entry was accompanied by the fluttering sounds of startled rats.

The "staff" consisted of a bunch of junior high and high school kids willing to work in exchange for riding privileges. And the main source of income, apart from pony parties, was hacking—renting out the horses for ten dollars an hour to anyone willing to pay. Mrs. Daniels bought the horses at an auction whose main customer was the meat dealer for a dog-food company; Diamond D, more often than not, was merely a way station. The general air of neglect surrounding the stable was the result more of ignorance than of apathy. It's not as if we didn't care about the horses—we simply didn't know any better. And for most of us, especially me, Diamond D was a haven. Though I had to suffer through the pony parties, I was more willing to do so to spend time alone with the horses. I considered animals bearers of higher truth, and I wanted to align myself with their knowledge. I thought animals were the only beings capable of understanding me.

I had finished chemotherapy only a few months before I started looking in the Yellow Pages for stables where I might work. Just fourteen and still unclear about the exact details of my surgery, I made my way down the listings. It was the July Fourth weekend, and Mrs. Daniels, typically overbooked, said I had called at exactly the right moment. Overjoyed, I went into the kitchen to tell my mother I had a job at a stable. She looked at me dubiously.

"Did you tell them about yourself?"

I hesitated, and lied. "Yes, of course I did."

"Are you sure they know you were sick? Will you be up for this?"

"Of *course* I am," I replied in my most petulant adolescent tone.

In actuality it hadn't even occurred to me to mention cancer, or my face, to Mrs. Daniels. I was still blissfully unaware, somehow believing that the only reason people stared at me was because my hair was still growing in. So my mother obligingly drove all sixty-odd pounds of me down to Diamond D, where my pale and misshapen face seemed to surprise all of us. They let me water a few horses, imagining I wouldn't last more than a day. I stayed for four years.

That first day I walked a small pinto in circle after circle, practically drunk with the aroma of the horses. But with each circle, each new child lifted into the tiny saddle, I became more and more uncomfortable, and with each circuit my head dropped just a little bit further in shame. With time I became adept at handling the horses, and even more adept at avoiding the direct stares of the children.

When our trailer pulled into the driveway for a pony party, I would briefly remember my own excitement at being around ponies for the first time. But I also knew that these children lived apart from me. Through them I learned the language of paranoia: every whisper I heard was a comment about the way I looked, every laugh a joke at my expense.

Partly I was honing my self-consciousness into a torture device, sharp and efficient enough to last me the rest of my life. Partly I was right: they *were* staring at me, laughing at me. The cruelty of children is immense, almost startling in its precision. The kids at the parties were fairly young and, surrounded by adults, they rarely made cruel remarks outright. But their open, uncensored stares were more painful than the deliberate taunts of my peers at school, where insecurities drove everything and everyone like some looming, evil presence in a haunted machine. But in those back yards, where the grass was mown so short and sharp it would have hurt to walk on it, there was only the fact of me, my face, my ugliness.

This singularity of meaning—I *was* my face, I *was* ugliness—though sometimes unbearable, also offered a possible point of escape. It became the launching pad from which to lift off, the one immediately recognizable place to point to when asked what was wrong with my life. Everything led to it, everything receded from it—my face as personal vanishing point. The pain these children brought with their stares engulfed every other pain in my life. Yet occasionally, just as that vast ocean threatened to swallow me whole, some greater force would lift me out and enable me to walk among them easily and carelessly, as alien as the pony that trotted beside me, his tail held high in excitement, his nostrils wide in anticipation of a brief encounter with a world beyond his comprehension.

The parents would trail behind the kids, iced drinks clinking, making their own, more practical comments about the fresh horse manure in their driveway. If Stephen and I liked their looks (all our judgments were instantaneous), we'd shovel it up; if not, we'd tell them cleanup wasn't included in the fee. Stephen came from a large, all-American family, but for me these grownups provided a secret fascination. The mothers had frosted lipstick and long bright fingernails; the fathers sported gold watches and smelled of too much aftershave.

This was the late seventies, and a number of corporate headquarters had sprung up across the border in New Jersey.

Complete with duck ponds and fountains, these "industrial parks" looked more like fancy hotels than office buildings. The newly planted suburban lawns I found myself parading ponies on were a direct result of their proliferation.

My feelings of being an outsider were strengthened by the reminder of what my own family didn't have: money. We *should* have had money: this was true in practical terms, for my father was a successful journalist, and it was also true within my family mythology, which conjured up images of Fallen Aristocracy. We were displaced foreigners, Europeans newly arrived in an alien landscape. If we had had the money we felt entitled to, we would never have spent it on anything as mundane as a house in Spring Valley or as silly and trivial as a pony party.

Unfortunately, the mythologically endowed money didn't materialize. Despite my father's good job with a major television network, we were barraged by collection agencies, and our house was falling apart around us. Either unwilling or unable, I'm not sure which, to spend money on plumbers and electricians and general handymen, my father kept our house barely together by a complex system of odd bits of wire, duct tape, and putty, which he applied rather haphazardly and good-naturedly on weekend afternoons. He sang when he worked. Bits of opera, slapped together jauntily with the current top forty and ancient ditties from his childhood, were periodically interrupted as he patiently explained his work to the dog, who always listened attentively.

Anything my father fixed usually did not stay fixed for more than a few months. Flushing our toilets when it rained required coaxing with a Zenlike ritual of jiggles to avoid spilling the entire contents of the septic tank onto the basement floor. One walked by the oven door with a sense of near reverence, lest it fall open with an operatic crash. Pantheism ruled.

Similarly, when dealing with my mother, one always had to act in a delicate and prescribed way, though the exact rules of protocol seemed to shift frequently and without advance notice. One day, running out of milk was a problem easily dealt with, but on the next it was a symbol of her children's selfishness, our father's failure, and her tragic, wasted life. Lack of money, it was driven into us, was the root of all our unhappiness. So as Stephen and I drove through those "bourgeois" suburbs (my radical older brothers had taught me to identify them as such), I genuinely believed that if our family were as well-off as those families, the extra carton of milk would not have been an issue, and my mother would have been more than delighted to buy gallon after gallon until the house fairly spilled over with fresh milk.

Though our whole family shared the burden of my mother's anger, in my heart I suspected that part of it was my fault and my fault alone. Cancer is an obscenely expensive illness; I saw the bills, I heard their fights. There was no doubt that I was personally responsible for a great deal of my family's money problems: ergo, I was responsible for my mother's unhappy life. During my parents' many fights over money, I would sit in the kitchen in silence, unable to move even after my brothers and sisters had fled to their bedrooms. I sat listening as some kind of penance.

The parents who presided over the pony parties never fought, or at least not about anything significant, of this I felt sure. Resentment made me scorn them, their gauche houses, their spoiled children. These feelings might have been purely political, like those of my left-wing brothers (whose philosophies I understood very little of), if it weren't for the painfully personal detail of my face.

"What's wrong with her face?"

The mothers bent down to hear this question and, still bent over, they'd look over at me, their glances refracting away as quickly and predictably as light through a prism. I couldn't always hear their response, but I knew from experience that vague pleas for politeness would hardly satisfy a child's curiosity.

While the eyes of these perfectly formed children swiftly and deftly bored into the deepest part of me, the glances from their parents provided me with an exotic sense of power as I watched them inexpertly pretend not to notice me. After I passed the swing sets and looped around to pick up the next child waiting near the picnic table littered with cake plates, juice bottles, and party favors, I'd pause confrontationally, like some Dickensian ghost, imagining that my presence served as an uneasy reminder of what might be. What had happened to me was any parent's nightmare, and I allowed myself to believe that I was dangerous to them. The parents obliged me in this: they brushed past me, around me, sometimes even smiled at me. But not once in the three or so years that I worked pony parties did anyone ask me directly what had happened.

They were uncomfortable because of my face. I ignored the deep hurt by allowing the side of me that was desperate for any kind of definition to staunchly act out, if not exactly relish, this macabre status.

Zoom lenses, fancy flash systems, perfect focus—these cameras probably were worth more than the ponies instigating the pictures. A physical sense of dread came over me as soon as I spotted the thickly padded case, heard the sound of the zipper, noted the ridiculous, almost surgical protection provided by the fitted foam compartment. I'd automatically hold the pony's halter, careful to keep his head tight and high in case he suddenly decided to pull down for a bite of lawn. I'd expertly turn my own head away, pretending I was only just then aware of something more important off to the side. I'd tilt away at exactly the same angle each time, my hair falling in a perfect sheet of camouflage between me and the camera.

I stood there perfectly still, just as I had sat for countless medical photographs: full face, turn to the left, the right, now a three-quarter shot to the left. I took a certain pride in knowing the routine so well. I've even seen some of these medical photographs in publications. Curiously, those sterile, bright photos are easy for me to look at. For one thing, I know that only doctors look at them, and perhaps I'm even slightly proud that I'm such an interesting case, worthy of documentation. Or maybe I do not really think it is me sitting there, *Case 3, figure 6-A*.

Once, when my doctor left me waiting too long in his examining room, I leafed though my file, which I knew was strictly off-limits. I was thrilled to find a whole section of slides housed in a clear plastic folder. Removing one, I lifted it up to the fluorescent light, stared for a moment, then carefully, calmly replaced it. It was a photograph taken of me on the operating table. Most of the skin of the right side of my face had been pulled over and back, exposing something with the general shape of a face and neck but with the color and consistency of raw steak. A clamp gleamed off to the side, holding something unidentifiable in place. I wasn't particularly bothered; I've always had a fascination with gore, and had it been someone else I'd have stared endlessly. But I simply put the slide in its slot and made a mental note not to look at slides from my file again, ever.

With the same numbed yet cavalier stance, I waited for a father to click the shutter. At least these were photographs I'd never have to see, though to this day I fantasize about meeting someone who eventually shows me their photo album and there, inexplicably, in the middle of a page, is me holding a pony. I have seen one pony party photo of me. In it I'm holding on to a small dark bay pony whose name I don't remember. I look frail and thin and certainly peculiar, but I don't look anywhere near as repulsive as I then believed I did. There's a gaggle of children around me, waiting for their turn on the pony. My stomach was always in knots then, surrounded by so many children, but I can tell by my expression that I'm convincing myself I don't care as I point to the back of the line. The children look older than most of the kids at the backyard parties: some of them are even older than nine, the age I was when I got sick. I'm probably thinking about this, too, as I order them into line.

I can still hear the rubbery, metallic thump of hooves on the trailer's ramp as we loaded the ponies back into the hot and smelly box for the ride back to Diamond D. Fifteen years later, when I see that photo, I am filled with questions I rarely allow myself, such as, how do we go about turning into the people we are meant to be? What relation do the human beings in that picture have to the people they are now? How is it that all of us were caught together in that brief moment of time, me standing there pretending I wasn't hurt by a single thing in this world while they lined up for their turn on the pony, some of them excited and some of them scared, but all of them neatly, at my insistence, one in front of the other, like all the days ahead.

·

The general plot of life is sometimes shaped by the different ways genuine intelligence combines with equally genuine ignorance. I put all my effort into looking at the world as openly, unbiasedly, and honestly as possible, but I could not recognize my own self as a part of this world. I took great pains to infuse a sense of grace and meaning into everything I saw, but I could not apply those values to myself. Personally, I felt meaningless, or, more precisely, I felt I meant nothing to no one.

Even though I now possessed many rich friendships, had people who valued me, not having a lover meant I was ultimately unlovable. I didn't realize what a major step forward it was for me to begin to own my desires. But rather than finding affirmation in knowing my friends loved me, I turned it against myself: if so many people thought I was such a lovable person, the fact that I still wasn't able to get a lover proved I was too ugly. Whatever sense of inner worth I developed was eroded by the knowledge that I could only compensate for, but never overcome, the obstacle of my face.

I was consumed with self-pity, but try as I might I couldn't shake it. Because I had grown up denying myself any feeling that even hinted at self-pity, I now had to find a way to reshape it. Just as I had been comforted by the Christian pamphlets that came in the mail, I now read the Bible, though I could not find it within myself to believe. In the Old and New Testaments I recognized a certain movement of time, a cycle of mourning that began with expulsion and moved toward reconciliation. It was the dynamic of my own life, reaffirmed in a different language. I read various philosophers and imagined my soul, separate and clear of my heart and mind. At times I was so lonely I was amazed I didn't just expire right there on the spot, as if loneliness that strong were a divine thunderbolt that could strike me down at any moment, whether I was in bed, at a crowded dinner table, or at an empty roadside stop.

Not surprisingly, I saw sex as my salvation. If only I could get someone to have sex with me, it would mean that I was attractive, that someone could love me. I never doubted my own ability to love, only that the love would never be returned. The longing for someone and the fear that there would never be anyone intermingled to the point where I couldn't tell the difference. My longing itself, my neediness, transformed itself into a firm belief that my love would never be reciprocated. The major reason I was still a virgin when I graduated from college was obviously the lack of genuine opportunities combined with my crippling lack of self-esteem, but I persisted in seeing it as proof that I had lost out on the world of love only because of my looks.

All of this would change when I went to graduate school. Having long given up on the idea of going to medical school, I applied to MFA programs in poetry. If sex wasn't going to be my salvation, writing and poetry would be. But within two days of arriving at the University of Iowa, I met the man who would become my first lover. There was no doubt I was an easy mark. On the surface Jude was everything I imagined I wanted: an older, handsome writer who drove an antique sports car and had an unusual name and a quirky personality. He had lived a difficult, interesting life. On the whole he was, as he loved to hear me describe him, terribly dashing.

The relationship was a disaster. I never for a moment thought I was in love with Jude or that he was in love with me, but it was a highly charged sexual relationship. At last I had found a man who was attracted to me, and I allowed his attraction to define me. At his prompting, I began dressing more like "a woman," even though I still could not bring myself to use the personal pronoun and the word *woman* in the same sentence. At first I felt like an imposter, but as time wore on even I had to admit I had a sexy body. I went from looking like a boy to wearing miniskirts, garter belts, and high heels. Once I started dressing provocatively I couldn't stop. It was just as much a costume as dressing androgynously had been, and even though these new dresses hid none of my curves, I believed they hid my fear of being ugly. I thought I could use my body to distract people from my face. It made me feel worthy: I even got dressed up to go to the supermarket.

All of my parading around couldn't hide the fact that the bone graft was slowly going the way of the other grafts. I didn't really notice it until the day after Jude broke up with me. Looking in the mirror, I saw the telltale signs and felt a huge dread come over me. It had all been a lie. I had fooled Jude into thinking I was something other that what I was, and now reality was slowly, relentlessly manifesting itself again. This is when I began dressing in earnest slinkiness. I began spending two hours a day at the gym, imposing a killer regime on myself. My body was one thing I had control over. If I had put a tenth of the energy I spent obsessing over my face and my body into my work, I could have written *War and Peace* ten times over.

Bent on proving I was desirable, I started collecting lovers, having a series of short-term relationships that always ended, I was certain, because I wasn't beautiful enough. I became convinced that anyone who wanted to have a real relationship with me was automatically someone I didn't want. It was the classic Groucho Marx paradox: I didn't want to belong to any club that would have me as a member.

Dr. Baker and I decided to try another soft-tissue free flap. So much of the original irradiated tissue had been replaced with nonirradiated tissue that he felt there was a good chance this graft would stick. But a few months before the operation, I discovered that Medicaid would not pay my hospital bills. The accumulated reasons ranged from my not living in the state where the operation was to be performed to my being a full-time student with a teaching fellowship. I had to put off the operation until the following summer.

Dr. Baker suggested I go to the University of Iowa hospital for a consultation with the head of plastic surgery, who was an old friend of his. Perhaps there was a way for him to do the operation. Because Iowa's Medicaid system was on a first-come, first-serve funding basis, I could not apply for funding before the operation: I had to have it, submit the bills, and wait to see if there was enough left in the budget to pay for it. I wasn't very optimistic when I went for my appointment.

The surgeon was from the old school. Of course my free flaps had shrunk, he told me; they always did. He suggested sticking with the pedestal method that Dr. Conley had outlined for me so many years ago. He was very enthusiastic, explaining in far greater detail than Conley had about all the different incisions he'd make. He described how I could stay in the hospital for the six weeks when my hand was sewn to my stomach and then to my face; while my hand was sewn to my face he would rig up a special cast to hold everything in place. He even introduced me to a patient of his who was having a pedestal to rebuild his nose. This patient's nose had been shot off with a gun, and he was sporting a very complicated and uncomfortable-looking cast that was forcibly holding his wrist to his face. Connecting his wrist to the area of his nose was a pale tube of skin with a red row of sutures down the side. I felt totally repulsed, and ashamed of my repulsion.

After this patient had left, and not wanting to be rude, I calmly told the surgeon that I probably couldn't go through with the operations after all because of the money involved. "Oh, don't let that worry you. You wait right here." He disappeared for a long fifteen minutes, leaving me alone in the office. I decided this was as good a time as any to see if I could have an out-of-body experience. Having read only in passing about out-of-body experiences, and these mostly in supermarket tabloids, I thought you were supposed to follow an actual physical route, so I closed my eyes and tried imagining what the air duct over my head would look like if I were inside it.

Eventually the surgeon returned with a hospital financial officer, who outlined a payment plan for the three major operations and the minor follow-up, as well as the extended inpatient stays. When he had finished his calculations, he assured me that with payments of only a hundred dollars a month I could pay off the original bill and all the accumulated interest by the time I was forty-two. He was very affable, and I shook his hand, telling him I'd think about it.

I stayed calm until I reached the street, when I broke into a run and didn't stop until I got home, four miles away. There I started to hyperventilate. I was even more upset that my body should betray me now, just when I most needed it. There was no way I was going to put myself through those operations, let alone have the pleasure of paying them off just when I should be rightfully starting my midlife crisis along with everybody else.

There I was with my short skirts and sharp mind and list of lovers, trying so hard to convince myself that maybe all I really needed to do was learn how to treat myself better. I was on the verge of learning this, yet I was still so suspicious, so certain that only another's love could prove my worth absolutely. Forget all that now, though, because here was the ugly truth. I felt I had been shown a mirror of what my life really was, what I really was, and I did not want to look. I was someone whom doctors talked to about sewing her hand to her face. I was trying to believe there really wasn't all that much wrong with me, but here were my worst suspicions, confirmed.

Lying in my usual abject heap on the living-room carpet, a pose I often adopted in dire times, I mouthed the words "I'm tired. I don't want to do this anymore." For once I didn't adopt either a noble or a catastrophic interpretation of events. I'd been so hell-bent on accepting everything that happened, on trying to inject some grand scheme of meaning, that the thought of simply rejecting everything felt akin to heresy. It was reality, after all: I did have cancer once, I did have a disfigured face now, there was no denying these two things. I felt pulled in two different directions. I had tasted what it was like to feel loved, to feel whole, and I had liked that taste. But fear kept insisting that I needed someone else's longing to believe in that love. No matter how philosophical my ideals, I boiled every equation down to these simple terms: was I lovable or was I ugly?

As radical a decision as it was to simply *not* try to reach a conclusion, I knew that one way or another I would have an operation. This, I felt, was beyond my control. After a great deal of finagling, I managed to find funding for the next free flap from a charity through the New York University Center for Reconstructive Surgery. Dr. Baker did the operation that summer, and it was the usual story of hope and disappointment. I looked horrendous for a few months, then I looked better, and just as I was getting used to the new face, the graft started disappearing. I thought about trying another bone graft, but when I discovered that there was a limit to the number of times I could apply for funds, I decided to give it up. This was me, this was my face, like it or lump it.

I opted for a geographic cure, deciding to go live in Europe once school was finished. I took on extra jobs, worked around the clock, and in a few months saved two thousand dollars and bought a ticket to Berlin. An old college friend was living there, which seemed as good a reason as any to pick that destination.

West Berlin, the Wall still intact at the time, fueled every romantic notion I had about living the bohemian life. I lived in a flat heated by giant prewar porcelain stoves, with no proper bathroom. Each morning I bathed in the kitchen sink. I applied for jobs teaching English at various schools and went to Kreuzberg, a poor, rundown area near the Wall, for very cheap German lessons, along with a room full of Turkish immigrants. While waiting to hear about jobs, I spent my days sitting in cafés, trying to write the ultimate poem about beauty and truth while simultaneously plotting to get rich from writing the great transatlantic trashy novel.

Living in a country where I didn't speak the language suited me just fine. Everything was an adventure, including buying milk at the corner store. I developed the art of getting lost. Intending to ride one U-Bahn line, I'd often end up in a completely different part of town, with only my own wits and the help of strangers to get me back home. It was a safe kind of chaos, and at some point I understood that I was cultivating my "aloneness" in this strange place as a method for putting off loneliness.

I maintained a romantic picture of myself as an expat artist in Berlin for as long as possible, until all my job possibilities fell through. Running low on funds, I decided to go to London and live with my sister Susie. I figured I'd find work more readily in a country where I spoke the language.

Usually cities offered me the refuge of anonymity, but everything felt different in London. Though I'd toned down my fashion sense quite a bit since Iowa, I still enjoyed wearing clothes that showed off my figure. Groups of men, mostly young and drunk, would spot me from a distance and follow me, catcalling. It was like junior high school all over again. As soon as they got near enough to see my face clearly, they'd start teasing me, calling me ugly, thinking it hysterically funny to challenge one another to ask me out on a date. I always stayed calm, kept right on walking, keeping my composure, but it was exhausting. I knew it had to do with their being drunk, that they would have targeted anyone in their path, that I just happened to be in the wrong place at the wrong time, but none of this helped.

One evening, after I'd come home visibly upset from some teasing, my sister mentioned a surgeon named Oliver Fenton. While I was in Iowa, just after my last failed free flap, she'd read about a new method for plastic surgery he was working on, known as a tissue expander. She had written to him and asked whether this new procedure might be of any benefit to me. He called her back himself and told her he thought it might work. When she had called me from London, I was very doubtful.

People were always telling me about the "wonderful things they can do today." It was difficult explaining to them—

even apologizing for the fact—that plastic surgery wasn't like the movies. There was never a dramatic moment when the bandages came off, nor a single procedure that would make it all right. As soon as my sister told me about this new doctor, I forgot all about him. Now she mentioned him again, how nice he'd sounded on the phone, how it couldn't hurt to at least go see him. He lived in Aberdeen, Scotland, seven hours by train from London. I couldn't afford the train ticket, and in all likelihood I would have skipped it if Susie hadn't generously offered to buy the ticket as a present.

Fenton explained the whole procedure to me. First he would insert a tissue expander, to be followed by a vascularized bone graft. Because the bone graft would have its own blood supply, the chances of it being reabsorbed were minimal. The procedure would take at least six months to finish; I knew enough about plastic surgery by then to know this probably meant a year. Telling him I'd think about it, I boarded the train back to London. In the dining car I encountered yet another pack of drunken men more than willing to judge my looks for me.

I was frightened that none of Fenton's proposed operations would work, that I would only be letting myself in again for that familiar disappointment. But, again but, how could I pass up the possibility that it might work, that at long last I might finally fix my face, fix my life, my soul? And thanks to my Irish passport and socialized medicine, the operations would be free. Remembering the drunken but nonetheless cruel comments of those men on the train, I called up the doctor and told him yes.

. . .

An empty balloon was inserted under the skin on the
right side of my face and then slowly blown up by daily injections
of a few milliliters of saline solution into a special port beside my
ear. The objective was to slowly stretch out the skin, much the
way a pregnancy stretches the belly, so that there would be
enough of my own skin to pull down and cover the bone graft.
The whole process took about three months, and I spent the
entire time in the hospital. All in all, I had a great time.

The others on the ward took it upon themselves to teach
me about Scotland. The dialect was almost impenetrable at first,
but I wasn't half bad at understanding it by the time I left. Certain
patients became my good friends, and after they were released,
they took me for day trips to the beautiful countryside surrounding the city. The landscape brought up long-distant memories of
Ireland. One of the doctors, a German woman named Eva, com-
miserated with me on our shared foreignness and invited me
home with her sometimes after work to enjoy a good meal, which
made me feel special, not like just another patient.

I was happy to be in the hospital, relieved not to have to
go out into the world looking this way. My face transformed on a
daily basis into something rather monstrous. It was beginning to
look as if a big balloon had been put in my face. I knew my
appearance was strange, but there were other people on the ward
with tissue expanders, people worse off than myself, and I never
felt the need to explain or apologize or feel ashamed of my
appearance. Since physically I was capable of taking care of
myself, and medically there was no need for me to be an inpa-

tient, it did not escape my attention that I was being treated like a sick person simply because I did not look like other people.

The big day finally came, and in what turned out to be an almost thirteen-hour operation, due to some minor unforeseen difficulties, the tissue expander was removed and the graft from my hip put in. I was severely disoriented when I woke up, a feeling exacerbated by the morphine they were giving me. The morphine didn't actually lessen the pain; rather, it diminished my scope of awareness. As I kept waking and sinking back under, I was overtaken by a brutal paranoia, convinced that because I had chosen to do this to myself, I deserved everything I got. Such long operations are rare, and I don't think the staff was aware of this side effect. I was a complete wreck, and no one knew how to reassure me. It wasn't until Susie came up from London a couple of days later to visit me that the paranoia began to wear off. I don't think I'd ever been so happy to see someone in all my life.

Because of the bone taken from my hip, I was very lame for a long time. I tried not to think about the results. There were more revision operations to come, and I patiently waited for each of them. After a few, my face was beginning to look acceptable to me; the new graft was solid and didn't seem to be in jeopardy. But then something unexpected happened: the original bone on the left side of my jaw, which had also been heavily irradiated, was starting to shrink, probably spurred by the stress of such a large operation. The doctor proposed putting a tissue expander in on the left side, followed by yet another free flap.

I could not imagine going through it *again*, and just as I'd done all my life, I searched and searched for a way to make it okay, make it bearable, for a way to *do* it. I lay awake all night on the train back to London. I realized then that I had no obligation to improve my situation, that I could simply let it happen. By the time the train pulled into King's Cross Station I felt able to bear it yet again, not entirely sure what other choice I had.

I moved to Scotland, partly to be near the hospital and partly because I wanted more independence. Eligible for social security benefits, I was able to get my own, albeit very cold, flat overlooking a bridge under which whores congregated at night.

When I arrived at the hospital to set up a date to have the tissue expander inserted, I was informed that I would spend only three or four days there after the initial procedure. Almost in a whisper, I asked if I would be staying in the hospital for the three months of expansion time. No—instead I was to come in every day to the outpatient ward. Horrified by this prospect, I left there speechless. I would have to live and move about in the outside world for three months with a giant balloon stuck in my face. In the few days before I went into the hospital I spent a great deal of time drinking alone, both in bars and at home. I even picked up man, a sweet and handsome man, probably every bit as lonely as I was. Lying next to him after it was over, I remember thinking I was fooling him, that he didn't have any idea who, or what, he was really with.

I went into the hospital, had the operation, and went home at the end of the week. The only things that gave me any comfort during the months I lived with my face gradually ballooning out were my writing and my reading. I wrote for hours and hours each day and lost myself reading everything from Kafka to Jackie Collins. I'd usually walk to the hospital, even though it was several miles, because I didn't want to get on the bus and feel trapped that way. Luckily it was also cold, so I could wrap my whole head in a scarf. As the tissue expander grew and grew, this became harder to do. I stopped going out except to the hospital and to the little store around the corner from me to buy food. I knew the people who worked there, and I kept wondering when they were going to ask what was wrong. I assumed they thought I had some massive tumor and were afraid to ask.

Finally I couldn't stand the polite silence any longer. I blurted out my whole life story to the man behind the counter. I was holding a glass bottle of milk, letting the whole saga stream out of me, when the bells tied to the door jangled. The man who walked in was completely covered with tattoos. I stopped in mid-sentence and stared at him. He stopped in midstride and stared at me. There was a puma reaching across his cheek toward his nose, which had some kind of tree on it, the trunk of it running along the bridge, then flowering up on his forehead. He hadn't even one inch of naturally colored skin: his ears, neck and hands were covered with lush jungle scenes and half-naked women with seashells covering their breasts.

I don't know why, but I felt immensely sorry for him. We finally broke our mutual stares, I paid for my milk, he bought a pack of cigarettes, and we walked out together, turning different ways at the corner. In the same way that imagining living in Cambodia had helped me as a child, I walked the streets of my dark little Scottish city by the sea and knew without doubt that I was living in a story Kafka would have been proud to write.

The one good thing about a tissue expander is that you look so bad with it in that no matter what you look like when it's finally removed, it has to be better. I had the graft and some revision operations, and by that summer, yes, even I had to admit I looked better. But I didn't look like me. Something was wrong: was *this* the face I had waited for through eighteen years and almost thirty operations? I couldn't make what I saw in the mirror correspond to the person I thought I was. It wasn't only that I continued to feel ugly; I simply could not conceive of the image as belonging to me. I had known this feeling before, but that had been when my face was "unfinished," when I still had a large gap where my jaw should have been. I'd been through twelve operations in the three years I'd been living in Scotland: Fenton was running out of things to do to me. There were still some minor operations, but for the most part it was over. Was this it? How could this be? Even as people confirmed that this was now my face, even as people congratulated me, I felt I was being mistaken for someone else. The person in the mirror was an imposter—why couldn't anyone else see this?

The only solution I could think of was to stop looking. It wasn't easy. I'd never suspected just how omnipresent our own images are. I became an expert on the reflected image, its numerous tricks and wiles, how it can spring up at you at any moment from a glass tabletop, a well-polished door handle, a darkened window, a pair of sunglasses, a restaurant's otherwise magnificent brass-plated coffee machine sitting innocently by the cash register. I perfected the technique of brushing my teeth without a mirror, grew my hair in such a way that it would require only a quick, simple brush, and wore clothes that were easily put on, with no complex layers or lines that might require even a minor visual adjustment. I did this for almost a year.

The journey back to my face was a long one. Between operations, thanks to some unexpected money inherited from my grandmother, I traveled around Europe. I kept writing. I returned to Berlin and sat in the same cafés as before, but now without my image, without the framework of *when my face gets fixed, then I'll start living.* I felt there was something empty about me. I didn't tell anyone, not my sister, not my closest friends, that I had stopped looking in mirrors. I found that I could stare straight through a mirror, allowing none of the reflection to get back to me.

Unlike some stroke victims, who are physically unable to name the person in the mirror as themselves, my trick of the eye was the result of my lifelong refusal to learn *how* to name the person in the mirror. My face had been changing for so long that I had never had time to become acquainted with it, to develop anything other than an ephemeral relationship with it. It was easy for me to ascribe to physical beauty certain qualities that I thought I simply had to wait for. It was easier to think that I was still not beautiful enough or lovable enough than to admit that perhaps these qualities did not really belong to this thing I thought was called beauty after all.

Without another operation to hang all my hopes on, I was completely on my own. And now something inside me started to miss me. A part of me, one that had always been there, organically *knew* I was whole. It was as if this part had known it was necessary to wait so long, to wait until the impatient din around it had quieted down, until the other internal voices had grown exhausted and hoarse before it could begin to speak, before I would begin to listen.

·

One evening near the end of my long separation from the mirror, I was sitting in a café talking to a man I found quite attractive when I suddenly wondered what I looked like to him. What was he actually *seeing* in me? I asked myself this old question, and startlingly, for the first time in my life, I had no ready answer. I had not looked in a mirror for so long that I had no idea what I objectively looked like. I studied the man as he spoke; for all those years I'd handed my ugliness over to people and seen only the different ways it was reflected back to me. As reluctant as I was to admit it now, the only indication in my companion's behavior was positive.

And then I experienced a moment of freedom I'd been practicing for behind my Halloween mask all those years ago. As a child I had expected my liberation to come from getting a new face to put on, but now I saw it came from shedding something, shedding my image.

I used to think truth was eternal, that once I *knew*, once I *saw*, it would be with me forever, a constant by which everything else could be measured. I know now that this isn't so, that most truths are inherently unretainable, that we have to work hard all our lives to remember the most basic things. Society is no help. It tells us again and again that we can most be ourselves by acting and looking like someone else, only to leave our original faces behind to turn into ghosts that will inevitably resent and haunt us. As I sat there in the café, it suddenly occurred to me that it is no mistake when sometimes in films and literature the dead know they are dead only after being offered that most irrefutable proof: they can no longer see themselves in the mirror.

Feeling the warmth of the cup against my palm, I felt this small observation as a great revelation. I wanted to tell the man I was with about it, but he was involved in his own thoughts and I did not want to interrupt him, so instead I looked with curiosity at the window behind him, its night-silvered glass reflecting the entire café, to see if I could, now, recognize myself.

Bringing Up a Beauty

N EXT TO BEING beautiful herself, almost the nicest thing that can happen to a woman is to have a beautiful daughter. All the bother of mothering a girl child up to her teens is repaid when you begin to hear people whispering about her, "Isn't she lovely?"

How much can you do to bring up your girl to be a beauty? A surprising lot. It is not an accident that there are so many lovely debutantes among society families every year. It is simply proof of what wise, devoted attention can do to make a girl grow good-looking as she grows up.

You can't begin too young. Almost from the moment you have a daughter, all soft and hugable, keep remembering that you can mold that softness into grace or ugliness.

Take her ears, for example. Begin in her very cradle to

DOROTHY COCKS'S *"Bringing Up a Beauty" appeared in the July 1933 edition of* Ladies' Home Journal.

make them lie flat to her head. She will never forgive you if you let her grow up with them standing out! Tape her baby ears down, if necessary, with adhesive straps. Make her wear smooth-fitted caps that hold her ears close. Be watchful all during her childhood that she doesn't jam on a béret or a tam o' shanter with her ears pushed forward and out. That's one thing you can do toward bringing up a beauty.

And you can help her to grow up with nice finger nails. Don't let her bite them. Many nails never outgrow the ugly shape, the bruised matrix, that result from habitual nail biting in childhood. If admonishing does not break the habit, then paint your daughter's nails with something so bitter that she will be painfully reminded to keep her fingers away from her mouth. Your druggist will put up a harmless but horrid-tasting mixture for this purpose.

And don't let your child bite or tear or pick the cuticle around her nails. This habit makes the cuticles grow thick and horny, ugly for years afterward. It may injure the soft nail root under the edge of the cuticle, and give rise to dents, ridges or spots in the nails that she will deeply regret when she grows up to the age of manicuring. Tie up in mittens or cotton gloves the hands of a little girl who has this habit.

You can do a great deal to give your child a pretty mouth. Don't let her suck a pacifier or her finger! Besides all the reasons of health against this device, there are the reasons of beauty. Its use may make a child's lips take on an ugly form that is permanent. It distorts the shape of the jaw bones. It may give rise to buck teeth. You'll hate them when she grows up, much worse than you hate her fretting now.

Keep her hair clean. That is easy in her bald baby days. Be just as conscientious about it when her hair is longer, and tangled and grimy from play. Shampoo at least once a week. Brush your little girl's hair faithfully every day; brushing contributes enormously to beautiful hair growth. It exercises and stimulates the scalp; cleans the hair of dust; distributes the natural oil down the length of the hair, to keep it glossy and pliable.

One of the greatest gifts of beauty you can give your daughter is a graceful walk, a pair of healthy, normally shaped, strong-arched and untiring feet. See that your daughter has shoes properly fitted, shoes built for health as well as looks. As soon as she graduates from booties, begin taking her for footwear to a good shop that specializes in children's shoes and has salespeople trained and experienced in fitting children's feet. Don't nag her to "toe out," for we know now that placing the feet parallel and straight ahead is a natural, easy walk. But if she noticeably "toes in," or if she experiences difficulty in finding comfortable shoes, ask your doctor or nearest large hospital to suggest a pediatrist who will prescribe exercises and specially made shoes to correct faulty posture or instill proper walking habits.

Beauty and the Beast

·↲

ONCE UPON A time, there lived a very rich merchant who had six children, three boys and three girls. And as he was a wise man he spared his children nothing for their education, and provided them with several tutors. The elder daughters were very beautiful; but the youngest was more beautiful still. As a child she was always called "Little Beauty"; and her sisters were very jealous because this name stuck to her. Not only was the youngest more beautiful, but also kinder and more modest. Her sisters were both very proud merely because they were rich; they put on airs, behaving like ladies of fashion, fawning after people of high society, and spurning to know girls of their own class. They spent their time promenading about, going to balls and plays, and looked down on their young sister who spent most of her time

---

The fairy tale "Beauty and the Beast" was first recorded by Straparola in 1550. A more common version was written in France by **MADAME LEPRINCE DE BEAUMONT,** *circa 1750.*

reading at home. As the whole town knew that these two girls were very rich, several important merchants asked for their hand in marriage; but they refused such offers because they were looking for a Duke, or at least a Count. Whereas Beauty (for as I said, that was what the youngest was called) would thank those who wished to marry her, but always refused; saying that she wanted to look after her father for a few more years.

Then suddenly the merchant lost all his wealth and nothing remained of his estate but a little country house a good way from the town. Weeping he told his children that there was nothing left but to go and live there, adding that if they all worked like peasants they might manage to survive. To which the two eldest daughters replied that they did not wish to leave the town, and that anyhow, fortune or no fortune, they both had several suitors who were only too anxious to marry them; but in this, of course, they were mistaken; for their wealth had been their only attraction. As they had always been so proud, people said: "They don't deserve to be pitied. It's just as well that they've been taken down a peg. Perhaps the sheep which they now have to tend will appreciate their fine airs!" But on the other hand, everybody pitied Beauty's misfortune, saying how sorry they were that this should happen to such a good girl who had always been so charitable and kind to the poor.

And though Beauty was as penniless as the others, even so, several gentlemen still continued to court her; but she discouraged their attentions saying she could not possibly leave her father now he was so worried and that she intended to go and look after him in the country. At first she, too, had been very upset at losing her fortune. But she soon realized that weeping would not redeem it, and resolved to try and be happy without money.

When they were settled in their little country house, the merchant and his three sons spent all their time working the fields. Beauty used to get up at four o'clock in the morning, clean the home and prepare the family dinner. At first she found it very hard, for she was not used to working like a servant; but after a time she became stronger and the work even made her healthier. Of an evening, when her work was finished, she would read, play the harpsichord, or sing at the spinning wheel. But her sisters were bored to death; they rose at ten in the morning, strolled about all day, and passed their time bemoaning the loss of their beautiful clothes and gay companions. And they used to try and undermine Beauty's contentment by saying "It's only because you're so stupid that you are content to live as a peasant." But the merchant did not agree with them. For he knew that Beauty was far more intelligent than her sisters and he admired the patience of his youngest daughter, who not only did the chores of the house but tolerated her sisters' taunts and insults.

The merchant and his family had been living like this for a year, when one day he received a letter informing him that one of his boats, which he had believed lost, had reached port loaded with merchandise. This news went straight to the heads of the two oldest daughters, who immediately saw themselves being able to leave the little house where they were so bored. As their father started off for the harbor, they anticipated their new fortune by asking him to bring back dresses, fur tippets and baubles of every kind. But Beauty didn't ask for anything, for she could see that the merchant would have no money left once he had carried out her sisters' commissions.

"But don't you want anything?" her father asked her.

She hesitated and then said: "I beg of you to bring me a rose—for none grow here."

She didn't really want a rose and had only asked for one rather than ask for nothing, for she felt that if she had done that, her sisters would have turned on her for being indifferent and for making an example of them. The good man rode off; but when he arrived he found that all his goods had been distrained by his creditors; and after all his efforts had failed, he set off as poor as when he had arrived. When he had still thirty miles to go to reach his house, he began to rejoice at the thought of seeing his children again; then he came to a great wood in which he lost his way. It was snowing heavily and the blizzard was so strong that twice he was almost blown from his horse. As night began to fall, he thought he would either perish from exposure or be eaten by the wolves he could hear baying around him. Suddenly, through the trees, he saw a bright light shining in the distance. He turned and led his horse towards it, and discovered that the light came from a great castle. The merchant uttered a prayer for his delivery and hurried towards it; but to his surprise he found no one in the courtyard. But his horse found a great open stable full of hay and straw, and as the poor animal was nearly dead with exhaustion, its head was soon buried in the fodder. The merchant tied it up in the stable and then entered the castle, where he could find nobody; then he came to a great hall where a log fire burned in the hearth, and a table stood loaded with food, but laid only for one. As the poor man was soaked to the skin, he went to dry himself by the fire, thinking that the master of the house would surely forgive him the liberty he was taking, and would, no doubt, soon appear. He waited for a considerable time, but when eleven o'clock struck and he had still seen nobody, and being unable to resist the pangs of hunger any longer, he took a chicken from the table, which he ate in two mouthfuls, trembling as he did so. He also drank several glasses of wine, and then, becoming bolder, left the hall and explored several great rooms, which he found magnificently furnished. Finally he came to a room which contained a wonderful bed, and, as it was past midnight and he was so tired, he took the liberty of closing the door and lying down there.

It was ten o'clock in the morning before he awoke, and to his surprise, he found a clean coat in the place of his old one. "Assuredly," he said to himself, "this castle must belong to some good fairy who has had pity on me." Looking out of the window, he found that all the snow had disappeared, revealing beds of flowers to enchant his sight. He returned to the great hall where he had supped on the previous night, to find a little table laid with a cup of hot chocolate. "Thank you, Madame Fairy," he said aloud, "for being so kind to think of my breakfast." When the good man had drunk his chocolate, he went out to see to his horse; and passing beneath a bower of roses he suddenly remembered Beauty's request. He stopped to pluck one, for there were so many. At that moment he heard a terrible roar, and looking up saw a hideous beast, so horrible that the merchant nearly fainted at the sight. "How ungrateful you are," said the Beast, in a terrible voice. "I saved your life by taking you

into my castle, and in return for my hospitality, I find you stealing my roses, which I love better than anything in the whole
world; you must therefore die to expiate this crime and I shall
give you only a quarter of an hour to make your peace with
God." The poor merchant threw himself on his knees, wringing
his hands: "My lord," he pleaded, "I did not think I would
offend so gravely by plucking a rose for my daughter who had
asked me to bring her one."

"I am not a lord," replied the monster, "I am a Beast. I do
not like compliments. I prefer people who say what they think,
and you do not move me with your flattery. But since you tell me
you have some daughters I will forgive you on condition that one
of them comes here willingly to die in your place. Do not argue
with me; go immediately but before you do, swear that you will
return in three months if one of your daughters does not come
meanwhile to die in your place."

The good man had no intention of sacrificing one of his precious children to this ugly monster, but thinking that this would at
least give him the pleasure of embracing them once more, he swore
that he would return; upon which the Beast told him he could leave
when he wished. "But," he added, "I do not wish you to return empty
handed. Go back to the room where you slept; there you will find a
great empty chest. You may fill it with anything you see, and I will
have it carried to your house." At this, the Beast withdrew, leaving
the poor man saying to himself, "If I am to die I shall at least now
have the consolation of leaving my children provided for."

He returned to the chamber where he had slept and filled
the great chest with a huge quantity of gold and closed it down.

Then he saddled his horse in the stable, and rode from the castle feeling as sad as he had been happy when he found it the previous evening. His horse now found its way through the forest paths, and within a few hours, the good man reached his home again. His children gathered round him excitedly; but instead of responding to their kisses, the merchant began to weep as he looked down on them. Holding out the rose which he had brought for Beauty, he gave it to her and said: "Here you are, Beauty, take this rose. It has cost your father very dear." Whereupon he told his family of his mysterious adventure. After this recital, his two elder daughters turned on Beauty and heaped all the blame upon her. "See," they cried, "what this little missy's pride has brought us to! Why couldn't she ask for sensible things as we did! But oh no, Miss Beauty must always be different. And now that she has been the means of condemning our father to death, she doesn't even weep."

"What good would that do?" Beauty replied, "and besides, why should I weep for my father's death since he need not perish; for the monster is willing to accept one of his daughters in his place and I intend to deliver myself to his fury, and am thankful for the opportunity; since, in dying to save him, I shall prove I love him." But her brothers would have none of this.

"You shall not go," they cried, "we will go, and find this monster and if we cannot kill him we will perish in the attempt."

"It is useless to try," said the merchant, "for this Beast's power is so great you have no chance of destroying him. I am deeply touched by Beauty's willingness to go, but I will not permit it. I am already old and have only a short time to live; at the worst I shall be losing only a few years of my life, which I shall not regret as it is for your sakes, my dear children."

"You shall not go back to the castle without me," said Beauty. "And you cannot prevent me from following you. I am not attached to life although I am young; and I would rather be devoured by this monster than die of the grief your death would cause me."

In spite of her father's refusal, Beauty insisted that she would go to the mysterious castle, and her sisters were delighted at her decision; because her virtue always aggravated them, and made them furious with jealousy. The merchant was so occupied with his grief at the thought of losing his daughter that he forgot all about the chest he had filled with gold; but when he went to bed that night, he was astonished to find it there in the room. He decided not to tell his children of his new wealth, because he knew that his two elder daughters would immediately wish to return to the town, and he had resolved to die in the country; but he confided in Beauty, who told him that several gentlemen had called at the house during his absence, two of whom had been to pay suit to her sisters. She begged her father to endower them; for she was so good, she loved them with all her heart in spite of the evil they had done her. These two wicked girls then rubbed their eyes with onions so that they could feign tears when Beauty set out with her father; but her brothers wept as genuinely as the merchant. Beauty, alone, did not weep, because she did not wish to add her grief to theirs.

The horse took the same road back to the castle, and by evening they saw it ahead of them, illuminated as it was the first time. Again the horse went of its own accord to the stable, and the good man entered the great hall with his daughter where they found a table, magnificently dressed and laid with two places. The merchant hadn't the heart to eat; but Beauty, pretending to be at ease, sat down at the table and served her father; then she said to herself, "I suppose the Beast gives me such good food because he wants to fatten me up before eating me."

When they had supped, they heard a great roar and the merchant, knowing it was the Beast, wept and began to say farewell to his daughter. When Beauty saw the Beast's hideous face she could not stop herself from trembling; but she tried to control her fear, and when the monster asked her if she had come willingly, she replied that it was so.

"That is good of you," said the Beast, "and I am much obliged." Then, turning to her father, he said: "You must leave tomorrow morning and never try to return." Then he wished Beauty good night and immediately withdrew.

"Oh my daughter," cried the merchant, embracing Beauty, "I am already half dead with fear. I beg of you to go and leave me here."

"No, Father," said Beauty, with all firmness, "you must leave tomorrow morning, and perhaps heaven will have pity on me."

They went to bed, thinking that they would not sleep at all, but hardly had their heads touched the pillows, than they sank into a deep slumber. During her dream, Beauty saw a lady who said to her: "I am pleased with your virtue, Beauty; your sacrifice in giving up your life to save your father's will not go without reward." When she awoke, Beauty told her father of this dream, and though she was consoled by it, he uttered a groan of remorse, as he came to separate himself from his beloved daughter.

When he had gone, Beauty sat down in the great hall, and began to weep too; but as she had a great deal of courage, she gave herself up to God, resolving not to grieve during the little time she had left to live. For she was now resigned to the fact that the Beast would devour her that evening. Whilst waiting she decided to go for a walk, and explore this beautiful castle. Even in her distress she could not help admiring its grandeur; then, to her surprise, she saw a door, on which was written, *Beauty's Apartment*. She immediately opened it and was dazzled by its elegance. But what pleased her most was a huge bookcase, a harpsichord, and her favorite volumes of music. "I can see no one wants me to be bored," she said to herself, and then wondered why such pains had been taken to make her comfortable if she had only that day to life. This thought revived her courage. She opened the bookcase and saw a book in which, in letters of gold, were written these words: *Desire, command; here, you are the Queen; you are the mistress.* "Alas," she whispered to herself, "the only thing I wish is to see my father and to know how he is at the moment." And as she said this, she glanced into a great mirror, and to her amazement, saw her home in it, with the father just arriving there, looking extremely sad. She watched and saw her sisters run to meet him; and in spite of all the grimaces they made to appear distressed, the joy they felt at the loss of their sister was plainly written on their faces. After a moment, the mirror cleared. Beauty began to think that the Beast was not so cruel after all, and perhaps she might not have anything to fear. At midday she found the table laid, and whilst she ate the meal, she listened to an exquisite concert, although she could not see any players. But in the evening, as she was about to sit at the table she again heard the Beast's roar, and in spite of herself, she shivered with terror.

"Beauty," said the monster, "will you be gracious enough to let me watch you sup?"

"You are the master here," she cried, trembling.

"No," replied the Beast, "I am your servant. If I weary you, you have only to tell me to go away, and I shall do so at once. I suppose you find me very ugly, don't you?"

"That is true," said Beauty, "for I do not know how to lie; but I think that you are very kind."

"You are right," said the Beast; "but not only am I extremely ugly, I am also simple. And I know very well I am only a Beast."

"You can't be so simple," Beauty replied, "if you say you are, for fools never recognize their stupidity."

"Then eat, Beauty," said the monster, "and try not to be sad in your house; for everything here is yours, and I shall grieve if you are not happy."

"You are very hospitable," said Beauty. "I must confess that your kindness pleases me; and when I come to think of it, you no longer seem so ugly."

"Yes, Beauty, I have a good heart, but for all that, I am a Beast."

"Many men are more bestial than you," Beauty replied. "And I like you with your head better than those who, beneath a man's face, hide a false, evil and inhuman heart."

"If I were not so stupid," he replied, "I would compliment you, but as I am, all I can say is, thank you."

Beauty enjoyed her supper, for she no longer feared the monster so much; but she nearly died with terror when he suddenly said to her: "Beauty, will you be my wife?" For a long time she made no answer, for she was afraid that her refusal might arouse his wrath. But finally she summoned up the courage to whisper "No, Beast."

And the poor monster's sigh echoed round the castle; but Beauty had no need to fear, for the Beast turned to her sadly and bade her farewell, then slowly walked out of the room, turning back at the door to look pathetically at her. Once Beauty was alone, she was overwhelmed with sympathy for this poor Beast. "What a pity," she said to herself, "that he is so ugly, for he is very kind!"

Beauty passed three peaceful months in the castle. Every evening the Beast came to watch her eat her supper, and though he would talk good enough sense, he never displayed what the world would call wit. And each day, Beauty discovered fresh signs of the monster's kindness; from seeing him every day, she had grown accustomed to his ugliness and she no longer feared his visits; and, indeed, she began to look forward to them: constantly looking at her watch to see when it would be nine o'clock for the Beast never failed to appear at that time. The only thing that caused Beauty any distress was that before the monster disappeared every evening, he always asked her if she would be his wife; and when she refused, he looked as though in pain with grief. One day she said to him: "You cause me much distress. I would like to marry you, Beast, but I have too much respect for you to make you believe that that could happen. But I shall always be your friend; you must try to content yourself with that."

"Yes, I must," replied the Beast, "for in truth, I know I am most horrible to look at, though I love you so very much; nevertheless, I shall be happy so long as you remain here. Promise me that you will never leave me."

Beauty blushed at these words; for in the mirror in her room, she had seen that her father was ill and pining away at losing her; and consequently, at that moment she was wishing to leave the castle and return to him. "I could," she said, eventually, "promise never to leave you altogether; but I am so homesick to see my father that I shall die if you refuse me that pleasure."

"I would rather die myself," said the Beast "than cause you any unhappiness; I shall send you home to your father, where you will stay and it will then be your poor Beast who will pine away at your loss."

Then Beauty began to weep, and weeping, said "I like you too much to make you suffer so, and I promise to return in a week. You have let me see in your mirror that my sisters are now married, and that my brothers have gone away with the army; so my father is all alone. Do allow me to remain with him for just one week."

"Tomorrow morning you will be there" said the Beast, "but remember your promise. You have only to lay your ring on the table when you go to bed, and you will return. Farewell, Beauty."

With these words he sighed, as he often did, and Beauty went to bed very sad, at having saddened him. When she woke up in the morning, she found herself in her father's house, and, ringing a bell which was beside her bed, a maid entered, who cried out in surprise at seeing her. At this the good merchant ran up to her room and was overwhelmed with joy at the sight of his daughter, and for more than a quarter of an hour they embraced each other. Then Beauty realized that she had no clothes; but the maid told her that she had just found a huge chest in the next room full of dresses embroidered with gold and studded with diamonds. Beauty thanked her good Beast for his forethought, and taking the most modest dress for herself, she told the maid she wished to give the others to her sisters; whereupon the chest immediately disappeared.

Her father warned her that this was a sign that the Beast wished her to keep the dresses for herself, and no sooner had he said this, than they appeared again. Whilst Beauty dressed herself, she sent a message to her sisters who, with their husbands, came hurrying to the house. The eldest had married a man who was as beautiful as Adonis, but as he was so much in love with his own face, busy admiring it from morning till night, he had no time to admire his wife. The second had married a man who had considerable wit, with which he used to tease and annoy everyone, beginning with his wife. Beauty's sisters were nearly consumed with jealousy when they saw her dressed like a princess and more radiant than the day. And though she welcomed them with such tenderness, they could not stifle their spite, which became more venomous as she told them of the happiness she had found. Then these two jealous sisters took themselves into the garden to give full vent to their bitterness. "Why should that little hussy be happier than we, when we are so much more lovable than she?" said one.

"Sister," said the other, "an idea has occurred to me. Let us try and keep her here beyond the week. If we can do that, her stupid Beast will become so angry with her for breaking her promise, he will probably devour her."

"That's a good idea," replied the other. "To do that, we had best make a great fuss of her."

With this scheme in mind they immediately went upstairs again and feigned so much affection towards their sister, that Beauty wept at the pleasure they gave her. And when the week was nearly over, these crafty sisters tore their hair, pretending to be so distraught at her going that she promised to stay for one more week.

Nevertheless, Beauty reproached herself for the unhappiness she was causing her poor Beast whom she now loved with all her heart, and whom she longed to see again. On the tenth night at her father's home, she dreamt that she was back in the castle garden, and that she saw the Beast lying prostrate on the grass about to die, and reproaching her for her ingratitude. Beauty woke and wept.

"How wicked I am," she said to herself, "to make a Beast suffer so when he has been so kind to me. It is not his fault that he is so ugly or so simple. He is kind, which, of itself, is worth all the rest. Why did I refuse to marry him? I should be happier with him than my sisters are with their husbands, for it is neither beauty nor wit in a husband which makes his wife content; it is their goodness of character, their kindness and their care; and the Beast has just these three qualities. Though I am not in love with him, yet I respect him and feel love towards him. I must not make him unhappy. If I do, I shall reproach myself all my life."

With this, she got up and placed the ring on the table and got back to bed, and very soon was asleep. When she woke in the morning it was with joy that she found herself back in the Beast's castle. She dressed herself magnificently to please him, and then waited impatiently through the day for nine o'clock; but when the clock struck that hour, the Beast failed to appear. The thought then occurred to her that perhaps she had already caused his death. Frantically, she ran through the castle, loudly calling his name. After searching everywhere, she suddenly remembered her dream, and ran down the garden to the moat where she had seen him lying. There she found the poor Beast lying unconscious on his back. And believing him to be dead, she threw herself on his body, no longer feeling any revulsion at his appearance. And as she lay there she felt his heart still beating, so taking some water from the moat, she revived him by sprinkling it on his forehead. Then the Beast opened his eyes, "You forgot your promise," he said, "and my remorse at losing you made me no longer want to live; but I shall now die content since you have given me the plea-sure of seeing you once again."

"Oh my dear Beast, you must not die," cried Beauty, "but live to marry me; for I now give you my hand and swear that I will be yours alone. I thought that it was only friendship that I felt for you, but the grief I felt when I thought you were dead made me see that I cannot live without you."

No sooner had Beauty said these words than the whole castle lit up; with fireworks and music. But Beauty paid little attention to them, she turned her eyes back to her Beast, for whose health she still trembled, and to her amazement, the Beast had disappeared and she saw a Prince more beautiful than Love himself, lying at her feet. The Prince began to thank her for breaking the spell under which he had laid for so many years. And though he deserved all her attentions, she could not help herself from interrupting him to ask where her poor Beast was.

"You see him at your feet," replied the Prince, "a wicked fairy had cast a spell on me that I had to remain disguised as a simple beast until a beautiful girl consented to marry me. No one in the world but you had virtue enough to see what goodness there was in me, and though I offer you my crown I cannot repay the debt I owe you."

Beauty, delightfully surprised, gave her hand to lift this beautiful Prince from the ground. Together they went inside the castle, and to her joy, she found her father and all her family there in the great hall, where they had been transported by the beautiful fairy who had first appeared to Beauty in her dream. "Beauty," said the fairy, "come and receive the reward for the choice you have made; you have preferred virtue to beauty and wit, and you now deserve to find all these qualities in the one you love. You will become a great queen; may your throne not destroy your virtue."

"But as for you," said the fairy, turning to Beauty's elder sisters, "I know your little hearts and all the malice they contain. You will become two statues, yet keep your reason within the stone that shall embalm you. You will stand for ever at the gate of your sister's castle and I impose no other punishment on you but this: that you must watch and witness her happiness. But you can break the spell the moment you recognize your own faults and I'm very much afraid you will always remain as statues. For though you may correct your pride, your bad temper, greediness and sloth, only a miracle can take envy from your heart."

At that moment the fairy waved her wand and all the others in the hall were transported to the Prince's kingdom where his subjects welcomed him with joy, where he married Beauty, where they lived a very long time, in perfect happiness because their love was founded on virtue.

Beauty and the Beast

·⸝

ONCE UPON A TIME, in a land none other than that vague country we call Fairyland, there lived a merchant who had been ruined by losing his ships at sea as they were returning home, laden with merchandise. He had three daughters and a son. The latter, called Ludovic, was a charming scamp; he was always getting into trouble with his friend, Avenant. Two of the daughters, Félicie and Adélaïde, were very wicked, and had made a slave out of the third daughter, Beauty, and had treated her as the Cinderella of the family.

Amongst all their bickerings and troubles, Beauty serves at table and polishes the floor. Avenant loves her. He asks her to marry him, but she refuses. She thinks she ought to remain unmarried and live with her father, a good man if a little weak. He has just received some good news. One of his

---

JEAN COCTEAU *filmed the classic fairy tale "Beauty and the Beast" in 1946. This is the introduction to his screenplay,* "La Belle et la Bête."

ships, which he believed lost, has reached harbour after all. People of fashion who had previously ignored him, again make their calls. Again Félicie and Adélaïde clamor for dresses and jewels. Ludovic borrows money from a usurer. As her father rides away to the harbour, Beauty asks him to bring her back a rose, "for none grow here."

That's where the story begins. The sisters laugh at her request which she made rather than ask for nothing. When the merchant reaches the quay he finds to his dismay that his creditors have got there first, and seized the ship and all his goods, leaving him nothing, not even enough to pay for a single night's lodging at one of the inns. There is nothing he can do but ride back through the thick forest, though night has already fallen. It is obvious as he rides into the mist that the poor man will lose his way. He hunts for the path by leading his horse by its bridle, and he sees a light which the branches part to reveal. He steps forward and finds himself on a bridlepath. Then the branches close behind him. Before him is an immense empty castle, bristling with riddles: candles which light themselves and statues which seem to be alive. He comes to a terrifying table, loaded with wine and fruit; but, worn out, he sits down only to sleep. The death cry of some wild animal in the distance wakes him. He flies for his life. He loses his way again, and then, finding himself in an arbor of roses, he remembers Beauty's strange request, which is now the only one he will be able to fulfil. He picks one. Immediately the echoes of his cries: "Hello! Is there anyone there" are answered by a terrible voice roaring: "Who's there!"

He turns and stands before the Beast, who looks like a great nobleman, except that his hands and face are those of a beast of prey. Whereupon the Beast pronounces the mysterious theme of the story: "You have stolen my roses, therefore you must die. Unless one of your daughters will die in your place."

It is very probable that this rose is one of the jaws of a trap set through all eternity which will now ensnare Beauty.

The father is given a horse called Magnificent to ride home on. All he has to do is whisper in its ear: "Go where I wish, Magnificent—go, go, go!" And no doubt this horse is the other lip of the trap.

The sisters are furious. Beauty offers to go to the Beast, Father refuses. Avenant is angry and, in the middle of a violent scene, the old man collapses, and Beauty seizes the opportunity to escape through the night. Mounting Magnificent, she whispers the magic password, and gallops towards her martyrdom.

But once in the Beast's castle, Beauty finds a different fate from the one she expected. The trap has worked well. The Beast surrounds her with luxury and kindness, for though he looks ferocious, he has a kind heart. He suffers because of his ugliness and his ugliness moves one to pity.

Gradually Beauty will also be moved by it, but her father is ill. A magic mirror shows him to her. She falls ill. The Beast, finally, opens his trap. Beauty is given eight days in which to go home to her father, under a promise that she will return to the castle. The Beast has several magic objects which are the secrets of his power. To show his trust in Beauty he gives them to her; his glove which will take her where she wishes, the golden key which opens the Pavilion of Diana where his treasure is piled, and which no one must touch till his death.

"I know your heart," he says to Beauty, "and this key will be the pledge of your return."

Once home, Beauty's jewels excite the jealousy of her sisters. They try flattery on her, and then, to dupe her, feign tears to move her to pity and so prevent her from returning to the castle, for they want to turn her into a servant again. By this trick Beauty is made to break her promise, and then no longer dares to return. Félicie and Adélaïde steal her golden key. Magnificent arrives. He is the only magic object that the Beast did not give away. That and the mirror which he bears. Without doubt these have been sent as a last appeal from her forsaken love. It is not Beauty, however, who rides Magnificent to the castle, but Ludovic and Avenant, whom the sisters have persuaded to kill the Beast and steal his treasure. They give them the golden key.

Looking into the magic mirror, Beauty sees the Beast weeping. She is all alone. She puts on the glove. She is at the castle. Where is the Beast? She calls him, she runs about looking for him, and finds him beside the lake dying.

Meanwhile Ludovic and Avenant have reached the pavilion of Diana. Fearing some trap, they dare not use the key. So they climb onto the roof of the pavilion and through the skylight they see the treasure, a statue of Diana and snow circulating as it used to do in those glass balls which one had as a child. Ludovic is afraid. Avenant breaks the panes of glass. He is a doubting Thomas: "It is only glass," he cries. Ludovic [sic] will let himself down holding his friend's hands; he will jump down into the pavilion and will make his way as best he can afterwards. At the lake Beauty is lamenting. She begs the Beast to listen to her. The Beast murmurs: "Too late." Beauty is almost at the point of saying: "I love you."

Back at the pavilion, Avenant is letting himself down through the broken glass. Just then the statue of Diana moves, raises her bow, aims. The arrow strikes him in the back. Ludovic, terrified, sees Avenant's face contorted with agony as it turns into the Beast's. He falls. At that very moment the Beast must have been transformed under Beauty's eyes as they filled with love. It was only this loving look from a young girl which could break the curse. Beauty jumps back, for now a Prince Charming stands before her, bowing and explaining the marvel.

This Prince Charming looks extraordinarily like Avenant, and the likeness worries Beauty. She seems to miss the kind Beast a little, and to be a little afraid of this unexpected Avenant. But the end of a fairy story is the end of a fairy story. Beauty is docile. And it is with the Prince with three faces that she flies to a kingdom where, as he says: "You will be a great queen, you will find your father, and your sisters will carry your train."

The Late Show

•‿

A RE WE OLDER FEMALES utter nitwits to care so much (*still*) about beauty? Certainly we are, but the world rewards beauty so lavishly it's hard not to take it seriously even at this late date. Men—if you want to use *them* as a yardstick—still value beauty in a woman—and we are talking here about the outside stuff as in Diane Sawyer, Kim Basinger and Cindy Crawford, not inner as in Mother Teresa—more than any other asset, no matter *what* they say, and they say a lot of silly stuff like what they care about most is intelligence, pleasing personality and "she should be fun to be with." Don Johnson said in a *Cosmo* interview, "The most important ingredient for a woman is a good sense of humor. If she can make me laugh, the rest is workable." We should give him perhaps Phyllis Diller? Sylvia Miles? Reizl

HELEN GURLEY BROWN *is the founder and longtime editor of* Cosmopolitan *magazine. Her stories and wisdom on beauty are collected in the 1986 book,* The Late Show.

Bozyk as the divine matchmaking hag in *Crossing Delancey*? What they mean is that after the requisite *beautiful* is taken care of (Don has married beauteous Melanie Griffith *twice*), they can *then* start to appreciate other things.

Of course, after marriage they do start caring more about whether we can get the septic tank unclogged than whether our eyes are clear emerald pools of light, but going in, beauty zonks. I never knew a beautiful woman who couldn't find a man if she wanted one until she got to be about sixty; after that the going gets tougher. Brains, humor, charm—even goodness, in a pinch— are what some of us use to make *up* for not being gorgeous. Sometimes I, not a great beauty, make myself *sick* being so perky and sweet all the time with doormen, elevator men, gas-station attendants, flight attendants, bus drivers, receptionists, mani- curists, hairdressers, masseuses, salesgirls, doctors' and dentists' nurses, hostesses, hostess's children, hostess's husband, hostess's mother, hostess's aunt visiting from Witchcraft, Wisconsin, the busboy who puts down the rolls and butter, the one who picks up the dishes . . . you name it and I am nice to it! If I were gor- geouser, I know I would be less adorable!

If you want to let us *all* off the hook for our preoccupation with beauty, I will just reprise the primordial reason I mentioned in Chapter Three about why men respond to youth and beauty as they do. Men have to get their genes into the gene pool, i.e., reproduce. To do that their penis has to get all perked up. It does that *best* when its owner encounters young and beautiful. And our sex *wants* the other one to get its genes into our pool (give us a baby) so that the race will continue, so we go around trying to be gorgeous and, if we can't make it all the way, we do the best we *can*. Striving to be beautiful to have babies may seem a little far-fetched *now* (it's twenty years too late) but that's how the whole birdbrained thing got started and maybe what continues to fuel the scramble on a subliminal level. In addition to baby-production needs, beauty has always been such a *negotiable* asset; whether man *or* woman, if you're a smasher you get offered worship, dinner in Paris via the Concorde, roles in movies, *big* diamonds, blue chips—things like that!

Men like to be beautiful, too, of course, though their looks don't deliver quite as well as ours except in the gay world. A man married for his beauty who doesn't also *do* something in life will tend to be denigrated. (Did anyone ever really admire Joan Collins's Peter Holm other than for his looks and his chutzpah?) Still, a darling CEO I know sighs wistfully when he talks about the blond, sculptured look of the actor who played Sebastian in the TV miniseries *Brideshead Revisited*. "It wouldn't hurt to look like that," he says. I'll bet nearly every man you know knows another man about whom he thinks, "It wouldn't hurt to look like that," though looks-envy in men is rarely revealed. (Thank *God!* We've got enough to cheer them up about!) Occasionally it slips out. The first words out of the mouth of a man I know who'd just read a major story about himself in *The Wall Street Journal*—flattering, almost idolatrous—were "Do I really look like that?," referring to a *not* flattering line drawing that accompanied the article.

I'm going to say this just once again, having said it so often I've really become a bore: Not being beautiful doesn't make any difference to one's friends, loved ones or employers most of the time. The friends figure our being plain makes *them* look better. Parents love you anyway even if you're a turnip . . . bone of my bone, flesh of my flesh, etc. Employers reason that average looks don't distract co-workers, plus maybe you won't be such a target for a rival-company "takeover," but few people don't line up with the idea you have to try to look as good as you *can,* even if you don't make it all the way to gorgeous. If we had the *choice* of beauty or brains, which we don't, brains are better—truth!—yet I always wonder what it must be *like* to be Catherine Deneuve, Michelle Pfeiffer, Claudia Schiffer. Beauties never tell you. Darling Candice Bergen, one of the prettiest and *best* women—a class act—absolutely hisses if you mention her looks. "Who, me?!" She is glaring over her shoulder to see whom you might be referring to. An early film star, Dolores del Rio, may have started that "beautiful on the inside is all that matters" crap. When reporters remarked her deep Latin beauty, she would always say it came from "drinking weak tea and spending a whole day a week in bed." On *Today,* when Gene Shalit asked Sophia Loren what it was like to be gorgeous, she said, "I have good friends and, finally, peace of mind," paying no attention whatever to what she'd been asked. I was recently chatting with my gorgeous friend Georgette Mosbacher on the subject of beauty and she said, "The most important thing a woman can do if she wants to be beautiful is exude a feeling of confidence." I am pounding my forehead. "Georgette," I scream. "Where are we *getting* this confidence if we aren't beautiful?!" Darling girl didn't *know.* Beauties are frequently well meaning on the subject of looks but full of shit! Great beauties are supposed to suffer *more* as they age and the looks they have so depended on fail. Forget it! We nongreat beauties suffer just as much.

The beauty preoccupation starts early. Richard Lacayo writes in *Vogue,* "Our sense of the matter is wrapped up in teenage traumas. There comes a point in adolescence when you start to imagine that some people are born with every molecule in place. Every high school boasts its elite squad of lookers: sparkling teeth, merciless anatomy, sunny filaments of hair— even their cuticles are kind of interesting. Between classes, they parade down the halls, trooping their supremacies like Clydesdales. Everybody else is supposed to feel like a waste of protoplasm. That sort of thing can complicate your feelings toward physical beauty for the rest of your life." Certainly confidence in your looks comes and goes . . . a shaky business indeed. On a particular day, for no special reason except you got enough sleep, you may just strike yourself as delicious. Another day, looking about the same, you think, Oh, my God, gargoyle! What else to do but *live* with this confidence inconsistency? Confident or not, this is what befalls *all* of us sooner or later.

Skin gets papery.

Spots appear on hands, arms, calves . . . we're no longer one smooth creamy surface.

Hair, moisture, bosom disappear.

We start looking a little neuter in photographs . . . you can't tell the girls from the boys.

A lot of that stuff can be *fixed,* thank God. A sure indicator that it *needs* fixing is when construction workers stop whistling. It was bad enough—well, many women thought it was bad, I never did—when you ran the gauntlet and they said things like "Hey, Big Momma, you lookin' great!" Much worse is walking past now when they say *nothing!* Some men you know do *try* to fill the void. Donald Trump told me the other night at a United Cerebral Palsy gala, "Baby, you look beautiful!" I felt all perked up until three hours later when I made the mistake of looking in the mirror and found I resembled Baby Jane (as in *Whatever Happened to?*) in her terminal stage. (We usually look great going in but I, for one, begin to disintegrate within about forty-five minutes.) Ryan O'Neal greeted me on an airplane: "Helen, you look so *young!*" You know *they* know you aren't and they know you know they know you aren't, so I'd just as soon they pick another compliment. (Is anybody telling Brooke Shields *she* hasn't aged?)

Many intelligent people declare that women should quit *worrying* about looks. Germaine Greer in a *Vogue* article: "You could fight matronliness. You could dye your hair. You could diet until you were as thin as a rail and then get your collapsed jowls hiked up and your crow's feet ironed out. You could get your empty bosom pumped up. And it would all be a dreadful waste of time, money and energy." She goes on. "The great privilege of the middle-aged is to make their own faces; gradually their personality obliterates their physical inheritance, the phenotype prevails over the genotype . . . now, at last, we can escape from the self-consciousness of glamour; we can really listen to what people are saying, without worrying whether we look pretty doing it." Oh, dear, I can listen like a maniac and *still* worry about pretty!

Other abstainers: The wife of a famous politician refuses to dye her hair, take off weight or follow fashion and is the role model for millions of women who also don't want to bother. She is one of the most admirable women who ever lived but not necessarily, in my opinion, for her stand on beauty. (It is said her husband had a mistress of some tenure at the time he last ran for office and the wife refused to help him campaign unless he gave the lady up. He did and she did. Threatening the loss of an election is *one* way to get a man home again but still doesn't convince me letting yourself go gray or portly is the *most* wonderful idea.)

Switching to believers: A CBS cameraman told me that when Margaret Thatcher was interviewed by Diane Sawyer, she told Diane she wanted "exactly the same lighting and flattering angles they're giving *you*." Smart! Even for us who care seriously about our looks and pay close attention, the giant breakthroughs are still to be made, of course. Wish I were to *be* here for them, living to be two hundred wrinkle-free, but meanwhile, I think about Queen Elizabeth I in 1590, with that pocked skin and black teeth and the Marquise de Montespan in the seventeenth century, with those jowls the size of airplane flaps and tubs of baby fat, and think I am lucky to be living *now* with all the stuff we *can* do to look better. There is no comparison between *us* at our age having just come out of New York Hospital after a $15,000 face-lift and a twenty-five-year-old girl just getting out of *bed* in the morning doing *nothing* about her looks. But if we stop acting as though we *could* compete with a junior and stick with our own age group for comparisons, it's really quite gratifying to see how good we *can* look.

I see these nifty women in the streets, stores and restaurants of New York City with their sleek bodies, streaked hair, clothes so *Bazaar* and *Mirabella* and am in *awe*. Probably more beauty paragons exist here than any other place on earth but they *do* exist. Countess Aline de Romanones, an OSS agent in World War II, now in her late sixties, gives me a jump every time I see her. She is stunning and there are lots more like her. One day I was lunching with usually acerbic John Fairchild of *Women's Wear Daily* at La Grenouille, New York's posh French restaurant, and he said of Pauline Trigere (Pauline was born in 1912) across the room, "Look at Pauline . . . doesn't she look great?!" That's what I want them to say about me in a few tiny years from now when I am Pauline's age or even right *now*. In a perfume ad Bill Blass declares, "Looking good is the best revenge." Bet your ass! You need self-discipline to keep up the looks grind and I guess you either have it or you don't. I find it relatively "easy" to do whatever you have to do to keep a job and look okay because the alternatives (unemployment and crone-hood) are unacceptable! *Fear* "self-disciplines" me!

It's good to start at least by your forties to preserve your looks, but if you didn't start then, *any* time is okay. I'm doing stuff now I couldn't be bothered with at thirty. Who tucked her tush against the back of the chair *every* time she sat down?! Or Scotchtaped her forehead lines every morning? I don't think it's smart to pretend to *be* younger. Somebody always has a sister who went to school with you who has a *brother* you can't shut up. ("Jessica couldn't have been born later than 1928 because she and Janice were roommates at Wellesley and Jessica was two years older than Janice who was born in 1930.) But looking sensational at *our* age, oh, yes! Of course, *deep* reality dawns some days . . . like nobody says skiddeldy-boo when you announce at the Delta Shuttle you'd like the senior-citizen rate to Washington ($60 as opposed to $142) and they write it right up without even a lifted *eyebrow?!* I glance carelessly into the floor-to-ceiling bathroom mirror as I am planting a kiss on David's shoulder as he gets out of the shower—he's so pink and cute and all steamed up like a Chinese dumpling—and confront this apparition with sort of fangy yellow teeth and dim eyes (me) and think, who *is* this? I don't recognize this person. The ghastly feeling doesn't last too long, however. It's back to the oatmeal scrub, the face exercises and picking out a pretty dress to erase the mirror image.

On the subject of mirrors, you have to treat them, even at home, like alligators: Don't *surprise* one. Whoever said, if you want to know how you'll look ten years from now, look down in a mirror, has to have been a masochist. It will take you three weeks to recover! The trick is not to be depressed by looking straight *into* a mirror. We've got a killer one just outside the ladies' room at *Cosmo* I ought to have yanked years ago, but the girls like it and I've got my own friendly one with pink lights elsewhere. The mirror by the door of my florist, Macres, at Seventh Avenue and Fifty-seventh Street, you need chloroform to get by (close your eyes and *grope* in and out!). Certain restaurant ladies' rooms are uplifters. At La Grenouille you look sixteen. Frankie and Johnny's steak house on West Forty-fifty Street is a surprise flatterer. Le Cirque, La Côte Basque, "21" are just okay. In some fitting rooms you could take your own life . . . how do they *sell* anything?! I got stuck with a monster three-way job at the Houston Grand Hyatt just before making a talk and nearly couldn't go *on*. Cellulite I couldn't see at home was clear as Lucite and never mind it didn't show during the speech. I was acutely depressed. You probably should have both types of mirror at home—friendly to stay cheerful with, brightly lit *magnifying* for putting on makeup; your audience won't be gazing at you through a silk screen so you need truth. After you finish with the magnifying mirror and look in an ordinary-size one, you look tiny and great! P.S. There are no nonvain people who never *look* into mirrors whatever their age. I see *everybody* gazing surreptitiously in the mirror-lined promenade in the Park Meridien Hotel that goes all the way from Fifty-sixth Street to Fifty-seventh. I just wish they hadn't put so many chairs in front of the mirrors.

So now could I tell you a few thoughts, I hope encouraging, about beauty and older?

I didn't do a cattle call but just asked a few friends who look great—all but two are over fifty—what they do to look that way. Here are their ideas.

Georgette Mosbacher

I tattoo my eyebrows. Mine are colorless and not too thick so I go to a tattoo artist. I read in *Playboy* magazine where the best tattoo people were and went to Gary, Indiana, to have this done. They can now reverse the procedure if you don't like it.

You should brush your teeth in salt and soda once a month. This whitens teeth, but don't do it oftener because it also takes off the enamel.

Alexandra Mayes

(travel-book editor)

A good haircut is the one best thing you can do. If you have good hair to begin with, it will show it off. If you have bad hair, a good cut will improve it. Forget trying to do this yourself—you cannot do the layering and understructure that can be handled by a haircutter—spend the fifty dollars.

I use lip gloss instead of lipstick. You don't need a mirror to put it on, don't need to match shades to your dress or blouse . . . it doesn't run into the corners of your mouth, can't be seen on cups and glasses . . . gloss is efficiency itself!

Shirley Lord

(Vogue *beauty editor*)

When your hair turns gray around the hairline, it looks as though your hair is receding. It *isn't* . . . the pigment has just gone away . . . but you could scare yourself to death! I had remarkable strawberry-blond hair, always took it for granted, but when it went gray I had a totally different look . . . like flatheaded! Reinstate the color around the face and you get a big lift.

Retin-A is the biggest beauty news of the century.

Joan Collins

When I was twenty, newly arrived in Hollywood and a suntanning freak, a friend who had the world's most beautiful skin took me to the Beverly Hills Hotel pool to survey the crocodile-skinned forty-year-olds who were soaking up the sun.

No one was really aware then of long-term damage, but

my friend was and she insisted I stay out of the seductive rays from then on. Well, she was right. Since then I have never let the sun fall directly on my face, although I admit that because I love it so much, I sunbathe my body.

Sun damage doesn't show up immediately—it takes years—and when you see it, it's too late to do anything about it. So my advice is—stay out of the sun or if you must go in it, PROTECT THAT FACE!

Lauren Hutton

Always sleep on your back. Wrinkles melt right down!

Go to a dermatologist and have every single brown spot you've collected from the sun burned off. The procedure is expensive and painful but makes a big difference. Sunspots can turn into cancers so you want them *off*. Your skin also gets to be creamy-smooth and all one color.

Phyllis McGuire

Put warm wet tea bags on top of your eyes for puffiness—not *cold* wet tea bags but warm ones. Leave a wake-up call fifteen minutes earlier than usual and have room service deliver the tea bags. You'll get rid of tired eyes and puffiness like you won't believe. [I assume, Phyllis, those of us minus room service can prepare the tea bags ourselves.]

Polly Bergen

My hair is just this side of Sahara Desert dry . . . always a dull, boring *mess*. It doesn't get dirty . . . it doesn't get *anything* . . . just fine, blowaway hair. Once a month I put on a lot of Best Foods whole-egg mayonnaise. Leave it on under a shower cap for at least three hours—overnight is better. Wash it out—takes two or three soapings. Hair is no longer brittle . . . it has sheen . . . there's something magic about the mayonnaise but it has to be whole-egg. Great treatment after hot rollers, teasing, any kind of hair abuse.

Barbaralee Diamonstein
(author; chairman, New York Landmarks
Preservation Foundation)

I think just plain clean hair is best, so I don't even condition. While the shampoo is still on, I comb my hair with a wide-tooth comb, then wash out all the soap. When you come out your hair will be very combable, without all those tangles.

Someone once said I had pretty lips and I took them seriously. I outline my lips with a pencil, fill in with gloss.

At least once a month slather baby oil all over your body, put on a terry robe and let the oil sink in. Best to do this in a hotel rather than at home as you will get oil all over the bedclothes!

Feet are never paid enough attention and should be babied. Wash them, put on gobs of oil or cream and tuck them into quilted electric booties. They'll be baby-soft and lovely!

Joan Rivers

I drink gallons of water every day. Great for the body, good for the skin.

Robin Chandler Duke

(activist for population control)

I swim against the tide of aging every day—forty laps—breast-stroke, backstroke, and the crawl. At fifty-five, I put myself in the hands of the best plastic surgeon I could find and he did a marvelous job on my sagging face. At sixty-six, I feel healthy and happy. I ski at least thirty days of every winter, and if permitted, would ski three days a week year-round and work four days. That is my ideal. No sunbathing for me. My mother always wore hats and carried a parasol, and like Mother, I am hatted. No smoking— it ages you terribly and also kills you very painfully. My motto is keep working, keep swimming, and keep hoping.

Cecile Zilkha

(socialite; board of Metropolitan Opera)

In the Middle East—Iran, Egypt, Lebanon, Syria—men do not like women to have *any* hair on their bodies, and they take off pubic hair as well. On their wedding day, women have a complete hair removal. This is done with sugar, lemon and water, boiled until the mixture thickens. Spread on legs with hands; pull out hair.

I tried this darling "recipe" without specific amounts or instructions—just boiled up some sugar and water, slapped it on skin and talk about *messes!* I had sticky syrup all over my legs, the kitchen, the walls! Cecile called Paris, where she has this work done, and got exact instructions. Here they are:

Recipe

1 cup sugar

$\frac{1}{4}$ *cup water*

$\frac{1}{2}$ *lemon*

Combine sugar and water in saucepan, boil over medium flame until mixture begins to thicken. Squeeze in half lemon (keeps mixture from caramelizing). Cook some more until mixture is thick like taffy. Let cool to room temperature; start kneading with your hands like taffy. Smooth on skin; let set for a minute and pull off. Hair will come with it. This formula doesn't open pores, so you don't get ingrown hair, just soft-as-velvet skin.

Kitty D'Alessio
(former president, Chanel)

I use a smudgy blue pencil to line the upper lid, also a charcoal-gray regular pencil. The blue gives your eyes, your whole face, a lift.

I figure you can't be all colors in the rainbow—you'd look like a Gypsy—so I concentrate on black, white and pink for my face—blusher for the cheeks, then a tiny touch of blusher on both eyelids.

I plucked my eyebrows when I was young and they never grew back. I now draw them in with a charcoal pencil.

Veronica Hearst
(wife of publisher Randolph A. Hearst)

I curl my eyelashes every day and brush my eyebrows into an arch. My father, thank God, would never let me pluck them.

A few drops of apple-cider vinegar mixed with Mountain Valley bottled water is a wonderful facial spritzer. Spray it on first thing in the morning and clean your face that way. That's all you need. Spritz again possibly an hour later, then put moisturizer on top when you're ready for makeup.

Put fresh avocado puree or olive oil or castor oil on your hair and wear this mix an hour or two or even overnight before you shampoo. Hair comes out luxurious.

Betsy Bloomingdale
(*socialite*)

My best beauty trick is to stand up straight. When I was young, I used to see tall girls trying to be the same height as their dancing partners and their fannies stuck out and looked awful.

The one cosmetic I couldn't do without is mascara. I definitely don't leave home without it.

Aline, Countess of Romanones
(*author*)

My miracle medicine is to have fun working. Do something you love as work and do it intensely. Have lots of physical fun. I take aerobics classes regularly, dance strenuously at least once a week, preferably ballroom dancing, which is sexy and healthy. (I go to Café Society on the corner of Twenty-first Street and Broadway in New York which has a wonderfully wholesome atmosphere with a live band. Yes, you have to bring your own partner.)

Betty Furness

Nothing looks worse on an older woman than little lines of lipstick leaking into tiny lines around the mouth. There are two things to do: 1. Don't wear lipstick at all. That solution is too drastic and unbecoming to me. 2. Use Elizabeth Arden's Lip Fix both under lipstick and on top. This way it's possible to keep a clean lip line (which I do with a lip pencil) all day long. I reapply the Lip Fix after eating. Remarkable product without which I'd look as old as I am . . . not acceptable!

Charlotte Ford

I glue my hair. My sister Anne got the good hair . . . Mother and I both have baby-fine hair, I shampoo every other day or every three days, blow-dry or air-dry, roll up in hot curlers, comb out and spray . . . and *spray!* We are talking major spray here, but the spray makes your hair look and feel thick. I don't think it hurts my hair . . . I use Clinique hair spray that brushes right out.

Pat Bradshaw
(*writer; widow of RCA chief Thornton Bradshaw*)

I love *really* red lipstick . . . go through about a tube a month. Pale lipstick is for people who want to look as though they have tuberculosis! In winter I wear only black and red so it matches my clothes but I like it in summer, too.

Lynn Revson
(*widow of Charles Revson, founder of Revlon*)

People tell me I look natural and fresh. The "trick" is lots of blusher, transparent foundation in the darkest shade by Revlon—nothing else on the skin—mascara, liner and eye-shadow—no skimping there. I use cocoa butter (comes in a tube) night and day on my lips—no lipstick—plenty of lip gloss—Chanel—no color.

Gloria Vanderbilt

I drink Evian all day long—tap water would be just as good—it keeps your weight down. Not sure how this works but probably takes your mind off eating actual food. I have had the same hair-style all my life. Sometimes Kenneth, who's done my hair forever, tells me people compliment him on the cut. That's nice to hear but I think you really can only please yourself. If you do anything because "they" like it, it doesn't work.

Ali MacGraw

I have finally realized that no matter how well cut my hair is, or how well made up my face might be for "an occasion," it is all pretty much of a Band-Aid job if my insides are rattled. So what I really do when I want to look as terrific as I can is take even ten minutes (preferably thirty) to meditate in silence and solitude, with a masque of crushed green papaya on my face. (I get it at Laise Bianco in the Beverly Terrace on Wilshire Boulevard, where I get facials at least three times a month—since forever.) But for *me*, I have to be pretty centered and calm to have a prayer of looking good and these minutes of yoga meditation take down the worry and stress wrinkles and lines and restore me to my own sense of self. I tend then not to go through all that ghastly worry about How-Do-I-Look?—I spend my time being present for the actual event minus a whole lot of my giant ego. Deep and specific breathing and visualization are part of that process, and the whole method of stilling my craziness has totally changed my way of dealing with "occasions." And I look much better.

Dina Merrill

My beauty secret is—fall in love! When Ted [Hartley] came into my life, people began to say, "Gee, you're looking so great these days!" And the comment seems to continue!

I truly believe if you love someone and are happy in all aspects of your life—work, friends, health—you look and feel younger. [Dear Dina—another one who had the bones and skin to begin with and, of course, you have to forgive anybody in love this slightly cliché, old-fashioned, touching recommendation . . . love is love. Maybe Ted Hartley has brothers?]

Andrea Pomerantz Lynn

(Cosmo's *beautiful beauty director*)

I never buy eye shadow that comes in thin pans—too limiting and delicate. These only work with their enclosed brushes, which are lousy. I prefer the single pots that give you a palette of color to work with.

Brush your lips when you brush your teeth to scrape away flakes. Nothing's less alluring than dry, cracked lips. If a toothbrush is too harsh, you can use a washcloth. Next, apply regular moisturizer to lips, then lipstick. Blot with tissue, reapply, then powder through tissue. (Press tissue against lips, dip brush into powder, dust brush over lips.) This method guarantees smooth lips and keeps color on.

Yellow-based makeup works wonders if skin looks pale and tired. I use a gold foundation, banana-toned face powder and light-yellow eye shadow (dust the entire lid and brow area as a base before applying any other shadow). I learned this trick from makeup artists on location. Traditional powders and foundations are pink-based; these make skin appear red and tired. Yellow makeup also works if you tend to look too pink or foundation turns orangy. Prescriptives makes a slew of yellow-toned makeup.

This is the best way I know to add volume to hair. Once dry, you sort of style and crimp with your fingers. Spray hair with hair spray, wait one minute, then tease areas you want voluminized using a vent brush. (This has a row of space between each row of bristles.) Brush hair into place, then spritz again to "set" style. When I go out at night and want *incredible,* even longer-lasting volume, I mist hair with beer or champagne before styling. I find this old trick works better than any mousse/gel/sculpting lotion.

Sounds disgusting, but Preparation H, mixed with moisturizer, plumps up wrinkles, makes skin look baby-fresh! Mix up a jar and apply daily.

Soak hands in milk for twenty minutes a day to fade age spots and reduce wrinkles. Milk contains alpha-hydroxy acids, which have the same effect as Retin-A but won't cause hyperpigmentation.

There's nothing like cold, thinly sliced cucumbers when you're tired or skin is irritated. They should be paper-thin; lie down and cover your face with the slices for ten minutes.

I absolutely avoid caffeine. Not even tea. I drink herbal ones and water. Caffeine makes skin look and feel dirty and old. Smoking is another no-no. There have been actual studies that show when a smoker quits, she looks ten years younger. It's the same with caffeine.

Give your hair and skin a break when possible. On Saturdays, you can dust on a dual-finish (powder combined with foundation) powder eye shadow base if you're going to see people—that's it. On vacations I never blow-dry—just slick my hair back with gel.

So, my darling, the words you've been reading here—the philosophy, tips—are, I suppose you could say, not nearly as important as some other things we should be worried about. The pursuit of beauty once in a while strikes even *me* as absurd. There was the day my hairpiece fell into the john at the Broadmoor Hotel in Colorado Springs—splash!—just as I was getting ready to put it on and go make a talk to the Magazine Distributors of America. On such an occasion you can either lock yourself in the room and let them send a posse to get you or you can say beauty *is* absurd and they're going to *love* me with a flat head. As I was complaining about my thin eyebrows one day to a beautiful friend (not Georgette Mosbacher) she said, "Get them tattooed—Big Joe Kaplan in Mount Vernon, New York, is the place to go." I went, liked huggy-bear Big Joe immediately and assessed him the total pro: Walls and scrapbooks of photographs bespoke his art; motorcycle groups and brassy young women were stacked up all over the place awaiting their turn. After coloring my eyebrows,

Big Joe and I decided to go for a little camouflage at my receding hairline. Tattooing procedure for brows and temple took about three hours . . . mildly uncomfortable from the noise of the drill plus prick, prick, prick of the needle into your skin but nothing terrible. We glob on a tube of Bacitracin to prevent infection; I hotfoot it back to New York. That evening I realize the color is really *brown*, almost black . . . matches the color of my original hair which isn't that color any more but dyed lighter. After you start coloring gray hair, you're supposed to lighten your original shade. Even powdered down, my new eyebrows look like two black crows in flight. . . . I am Vampira's sister!

People *warn* you about bad cosmetic surgery but *it* is often correctable, or the tight look you hate loosens up in time; tattoos are *forever* . . . they tell you that going in. Well, I have been *more* depressed but can't remember more than two times in my life and I did this to *myself* . . . the "accident" isn't a random mugging or being knocked down by a runaway Harley-Davidson. I'm too heartsick to call Big Joe immediately—what can he *say?!* I let the miserable weekend go by and telephone him Monday. "Come on back," says Joe. "I can do something." I went. He did. He injected some white dye into the areas and that took the color down. I'm back on the train . . . choo-choo-choo—beauty doesn't seem absurd again.

Some lovely day perhaps we *will* all be judged strictly by what we are—not one *scrap* of attention paid to creamy thighs, goddess cheekbones, Mona Lisa lips, but that isn't the situation *now* and I'm not sure *we*, the getting-up-there group, are the ones to strike out and demand love and appreciation totally without

artifice. Should we *really* plan to attend the next charity dinner—
or even show up at the office—in a gunnysack, with faces
scrubbed like an Irish potato? You can. I'm not going to. Yes,
there is a lot more important stuff than thinking about your skin
tone, I *know* that, but no apologies . . . you can take the world
seriously, do whatever you can to make it better *and* fit in exfoli-
ation and lip gloss. Truth!

Edith Wharton

The House of Mirth

·ᴗ

S ELDEN PAUSED IN SURPRISE. In the afternoon rush of the Grand Central Station his eyes had been refreshed by the sight of Miss Lily Bart.

It was a Monday in early September, and he was returning to his work from a hurried dip into the country; but what was Miss Bart doing in town at that season? If she had appeared to be catching a train, he might have inferred that he had come on her in the act of transition between one and another of the country-houses which disputed her presence after the close of the Newport season; but her desultory air perplexed him. She stood apart from the crowd, letting it drift by her to the platform or the street, and wearing an air of irresolution which might, as he surmised, be the mask of a very definite purpose. It struck him at once that she was waiting for some one, but

EDITH WHARTON, *an American novelist, wrote of the substantial worries of turn-of-the-century aristocratic New York society. Her cult classics include* Ethan Frome, *and the 1905 satire* The House of Mirth.

he hardly knew why the idea arrested him. There was nothing new about Lily Bart, yet he could never see her without a faint movement of interest: it was characteristic of her that she always roused speculation, that her simplest acts seemed the result of far-reaching intentions.

An impulse of curiosity made him turn out of his direct line to the door, and stroll past her. He knew that if she did not wish to be seen she would contrive to elude him; and it amused him to think of putting her skill to the test.

"Mr. Selden—what good luck!"

She came forward smiling, eager almost, in her resolve to intercept him. One or two persons, in brushing past them, lingered to look; for Miss Bart was a figure to arrest even the suburban traveller rushing to his last train.

Selden had never seen her more radiant. Her vivid head, relieved against the dull tints of the crowd, made her more conspicuous than in a ball-room, and under her dark hat and veil she regained the girlish smoothness, the purity of tint, that she was beginning to lose after eleven years of late hours and indefatigable dancing. Was it really eleven years, Selden found himself wondering, and had she indeed reached the nine-and-twentieth birthday with which her rivals credited her?

"What luck!" she repeated. "How nice of you to come to my rescue!"

He responded joyfully that to do so was his mission in life, and asked what form the rescue was to take.

"Oh, almost any—even to sitting on a bench and talking to me. One sits out a cotillion—why not sit out a train? It isn't a bit hotter here than in Mrs. Van Osburgh's conservatory—and some of the women are not a bit uglier."

She broke off, laughing, to explain that she had come up to town from Tuxedo, on her way to the Gus Trenors' at Bellomont, and had missed the three-fifteen train to Rhinebeck.

"And there isn't another till half-past five." She consulted the little jewelled watch among her laces. "Just two hours to wait. And I don't know what to do with myself. My maid came up this morning to do some shopping for me, and was to go on to Bellomont at one o'clock, and my aunt's house is closed, and I don't know a soul in town." She glanced plaintively about the station. "It *is* hotter than Mrs. Van Osburgh's, after all. If you can spare the time, do take me somewhere for a breath of air."

He declared himself entirely at her disposal: the adventure struck him as diverting. As a spectator, he had always enjoyed Lily Bart; and his course lay so far out of her orbit that it amused him to be drawn for a moment into the sudden intimacy which her proposal implied.

"Shall we go over to Sherry's for a cup of tea?"

She smiled assentingly, and then made a slight grimace.

"So many people come up to town on a Monday—one is sure to meet a lot of bores. I'm as old as the hills, of course, and it ought not to make any difference; but if *I'm* old enough, you're not," she objected gaily. "I'm dying for tea—but isn't there a quieter place?"

He answered her smile, which rested on him vividly. Her discretions interested him almost as much as her imprudences: he was so sure that both were part of the same carefully-elaborated plan. In judging Miss Bart, he had always made use of the "argument from design."

"The resources of New York are rather meagre," he said; "but I'll find a hansom first, and then we'll invent something."

He led her through the throng of returning holiday-makers, past swallow-faced girls in preposterous hats, and flat-chested women struggling with paper bundles and palm-leaf fans. Was it possible that she belonged to the same race? The dinginess, the crudity of this average section of womanhood made him feel how highly specialized she was.

A rapid shower had cooled the air, and clouds still hung refreshingly over the moist street.

"How delicious! Let us walk a little," she said as they emerged from the station.

They turned into Madison Avenue and began to stroll northward. As she moved beside him, with her long light step, Selden was conscious of taking a luxurious pleasure in her near-ness: in the modeling of her little ear, the crisp upward wave of her hair—was it ever so slightly brightened by art?—and the thick planting of her straight black lashes. Everything about her was at once vigorous and exquisite, at once strong and fine. He had a confused sense that she must have cost a great deal to make, that a great many dull and ugly people must, in some mysterious way, have been sacrificed to produce her. He was aware that the qual-ities distinguishing her from the herd of her sex were chiefly external: as though a fine glaze of beauty and fastidiousness had been applied to vulgar clay. Yet the analogy left him unsatisfied, for a coarse texture will not take a high finish; and was it not possible that the material was fine, but that circumstance had fashioned it into a futile shape?

As he reached this point in his speculations the sun came out, and her lifted parasol cut off his enjoyment. A moment or two later she paused with a sigh.

"Oh, dear, I'm so hot and thirsty—and what a hideous place New York is!" She looked despairingly up and down the dreary thoroughfare. "Other cities put on their best clothes in summer, but New York seems to sit in its shirt-sleeves." Her eyes wandered down one of the side-streets. "Some one has had the humanity to plant a few trees over there. Let us go into the shade."

"I am glad my street meets with your approval," said Selden as they turned the corner.

"Your street? Do you live here?"

She glanced with interest along the new brick and limestone housefronts, fantastically varied in obedience to the American craving for novelty, but fresh and inviting with their awnings and flower-boxes.

"Ah, yes—to be sure: *The Benedick*. What a nice looking building! I don't think I've ever seen it before." She looked across at the flathouse with its marble porch and pseudo-Georgian façade. "Which are your windows? Those with the awnings down?"

"On the top floor—yes."

"And that nice little balcony is yours? How cool it looks up there!"

He paused a moment. "Come up and see," he suggested. "I can give you a cup of tea in no time—and you won't meet any bores."

Her colour deepened—she still had the art of blushing at the right time—but she took the suggestion as lightly as it was made.

"Why not? It's too tempting—I'll take the risk," she declared.

"Oh, I'm not dangerous," he said in the same key. In truth, he had never liked her as well as at that moment. He knew she had accepted without afterthought: he could never be a factor in her calculations, and there was a surprise, a refreshment almost, in the spontaneity of her consent.

On the threshold he paused a moment, feeling for his latch-key.

"There's no one here; but I have a servant who is supposed to come in the mornings, and it's just possible he may have put out the tea-things and provided some cake."

He ushered her into a slip of a hall hung with old prints. She noticed the letters and notes heaped on the table among his gloves and sticks; then she found herself in a small library, dark but cheerful, with its walls of books, a pleasantly faded Turkey rug, a littered desk, and, as he had foretold, a tea-tray on a low table near the window. A breeze had sprung up, swaying inward the muslin curtains, and bringing a fresh scent of mignonette and petunias from the flower-box on the balcony.

Lily sank with a sigh into one of the shabby leather chairs.

"How delicious to have a place like this all to one's self! What a miserable thing it is to be a woman." She leaned back in a luxury of discontent.

Selden was rummaging in a cupboard for the cake.

"Even women," he said, "have been known to enjoy the privileges of a flat."

"Oh, governesses—or widows. But not girls—not poor, miserable, marriageable girls!"

"I even know a girl who lives in a flat."

She sat up in surprise. "You do?"

"I do," he assured her, emerging from the cupboard with the sought-for cake.

"Oh, I know—you mean Gerty Farish." She smiled a little unkindly. "But I said *marriageable*—and besides, she has a horrid little place, and no maid, and such queer things to eat. Her cook does the washing and the food tastes of soap. I should hate that, you know."

"You shouldn't dine with her on wash-days," said Selden, cutting the cake.

They both laughed, and he knelt by the table to light the lamp under the kettle, while she measured out the tea into a little tea-pot of green glaze. As he watched her hand, polished as a bit of old ivory, with its slender pink nails, and the sapphire bracelet slipping over her wrist, he was struck with the irony of suggesting to her such a life as his cousin Gertrude Farish had chosen. She was so evidently the victim of the civilization which had produced her, that the links of her bracelet seemed like manacles chaining her to her fate.

She seemed to read his thought. "It was horrid of me to say that of Gerty," she said with charming compunction. "I forgot she was your cousin. But we're so different, you know: she likes being good, and I like being happy. And besides, she is free and I am not. If I were, I daresay I could manage to be happy even in her flat. It must be pure bliss to arrange the furniture just as one likes, and give all the horrors to the ash-man. If I could only do over my aunt's drawing-room I know I should be a better woman."

"Is it so very bad?" he asked sympathetically.

She smiled at him across the tea-pot which she was holding up to be filled.

"That shows how seldom you come there. Why don't you come oftener?"

"When I do come, it's not to look at Mrs. Peniston's furniture."

"Nonsense," she said, "You don't come at all—and yet we get on so well when we meet."

"Perhaps that's the reason," he answered promptly. "I'm afraid I haven't any cream, you know—shall you mind a slice of lemon instead?"

"I shall like it better." She waited while he cut the lemon and dropped a thin disk into her cup. "But that is not the reason," she insisted.

"The reason for what?"

"For your never coming." She leaned forward with a shade of perplexity in her charming eyes. "I wish I knew—I wish I could make you out. Of course I know there are men who don't like me—one can tell that at a glance. And there are others who are afraid of me: they think I want to marry them." She smiled up at him frankly. "But I don't think you dislike me—and you can't possibly think I want to marry you."

"No—I absolve you of that," he agreed.

"Well, then—?"

He had carried his cup to the fireplace, and stood leaning against the chimney-piece and looking down on her with an air of indolent amusement. The provocation in her eyes increased his amusement—he had not supposed she would waste her powder on such small game; but perhaps she was only keeping her hand in; or perhaps a girl of her type had no conversation but of the personal kind. At any rate, she was amazingly pretty, and he had asked her to tea and must live up to his obligations.

"Well, then," he said with a plunge, "perhaps *that's* the reason."

"What?"

"The fact that you don't want to marry me. Perhaps I don't regard it as such a strong inducement to go and see you." He felt a slight shiver down his spine as he ventured this, but her laugh reassured him.

"Dear Mr. Selden, that wasn't worthy of you. It's stupid of you to make love to me, and it isn't like you to be stupid." She leaned back, sipping her tea with an air so enchantingly judicial that, if they had been in her aunt's drawing-room, he might almost have tried to disprove her deduction.

"Don't you see," she continued, "that there are men enough to say pleasant things to me, and that what I want is a friend who won't be afraid to say disagreeable ones when I need them? Sometimes I have fancied you might be that friend—I don't know why, except that you are neither a prig nor a bounder, and that I shouldn't have to pretend with you or be on my guard against you." Her voice had dropped to a note of seriousness, and she sat gazing up at him with the troubled gravity of a child.

"You don't know how much I need such a friend," she said. "My aunt is full of copy-book axioms, but they were all meant to apply to conduct in the early fifties. I always feel that to live up to them would include wearing book-muslin with gigot sleeves. And the other women—my best friends—well, they use me or abuse me; but they don't care a straw what happens to me. I've been about too long—people are getting tired of me; they are beginning to say I ought to marry."

There was a moment's pause, during which Selden meditated one or two replies calculated to add a momentary zest to the situation; but he rejected them in favor of the simple question: "Well, why don't you?"

She colored and laughed. "Ah, I see you *are* a friend after all, and that is one of the disagreeable things I was asking for."

"It wasn't meant to be disagreeable," he returned amicably. "Isn't marriage your vocation? Isn't it what you're all brought up for?"

She sighed. "I suppose so. What else is there?"

"Exactly. And so why not take the plunge and have it over?"

She shrugged her shoulders. "You speak as if I ought to marry the first man who came along."

"I didn't mean to imply that you are as hard put to it as that. But there must be some one with the requisite qualifications."

She shook her head wearily. "I threw away one or two good chances when I first came out—I suppose every girl does;

and you know I am horribly poor—and very expensive. I must have a great deal of money."

Selden had turned to reach for a cigarette-box on the mantelpiece.

"What's become of Dillworth?" he asked.

"Oh, his mother was frightened—she was afraid I should have all the family jewels reset. And she wanted me to promise that I wouldn't do over the drawing-room."

"The very thing you are marrying for!"

"Exactly. So she packed him off to India."

"Hard luck—but you can do better than Dillworth."

He offered the box, and she took out three or four cigarettes, putting one between her lips and slipping the others into a little gold case attached to her long pearl chain.

"Have I time? Just a whiff, then." She leaned forward, holding the tip of her cigarette to his. As she did so, he noted, with a purely impersonal enjoyment, how evenly the black lashes were set in her smooth white lids, and how the purplish shade beneath them melted into the pure pallor of the cheek.

She began to saunter about the room, examining the bookshelves between the puffs of her cigarette-smoke. Some of the volumes had the ripe tints of good tooling and old morocco, and her eyes lingered on them caressingly, not with the appreciation of the expert, but with the pleasure in agreeable tones and textures that was one of her inmost susceptibilities. Suddenly her expression changed from desultory enjoyment to active conjecture, and she turned to Selden with a question.

"You collect, don't you—you know about first editions and things?"

"As much as a man may who has no money to spend. Now and then I pick up something in the rubbish heap; and I go and look on at the big sales."

She had again addressed herself to the shelves, but her eyes now swept them inattentively, and he saw that she was pre-occupied with a new idea.

"And Americana—do you collect Americana?"

Selden stared and laughed.

"No, that's rather out of my line. I'm not really a collec-tor, you see; I simply like to have good editions of the books I am fond of."

She made a slight grimace. "And Americana are horribly dull, I suppose?"

"I should fancy so—except to the historian. But your real collector values a thing for its rarity. I don't suppose the buyers of Americana sit up reading them all night—old Jefferson Gryce certainly didn't."

She was listening with keen attention. "And yet they fetch fabulous prices, don't they? It seems so odd to want to pay a lot for an ugly badly-printed book that one is never going to read! And I suppose most of the owners of Americana are not historians either?"

"No; very few of the historians can afford to buy them. They have to use those in the public libraries or in private collections. It seems to be the mere rarity that attracts the average collector."

He had seated himself on an arm of the chair near which she was standing, and she continued to question him, asking which were the rarest volumes, whether the Jefferson Gryce collection was really considered the finest in the world, and what was the largest price ever fetched by a single volume.

It was so pleasant to sit there looking up at her, as she lifted now one book and then another from the shelves, fluttering the pages between her fingers, while her drooping profile was outlined against the warm background of old bindings, that he talked on without pausing to wonder at her sudden interest in so unsuggestive a subject. But he could never be long with her without trying to find a reason for what she was doing, and as she replaced his first edition of La Bruyère and turned away from the bookcases, he began to ask himself what she had been driving at. Her next question was not of a nature to enlighten him. She paused before him with a smile which seemed at once designed to admit him to her familiarity, and to remind him of the restriction it imposed.

"Don't you ever mind," she asked suddenly, "not being rich enough to buy all the books you want?"

He followed her glance about the room, with its worn furniture and shabby walls.

"Don't I just? Do you take me for a saint on a pillar?"

"And having to work—do you mind that?"

"Oh, the work itself is not so bad—I'm rather fond of the law."

"No; but the being tied down: the routine—don't you ever want to get away, to see new places and people?"

"Horribly—especially when I see all my friends rushing to the steamer."

She drew a sympathetic breath. "But do you mind enough—to marry to get out of it?"

Selden broke into a laugh. "God forbid!" he declared.

She rose with a sigh, tossing her cigarette into the grate.

"Ah, there's the difference—a girl must, a man may if he chooses." She surveyed him critically. "Your coat's a little shabby—but who cares? It doesn't keep people from asking you to dine. If I were shabby no one would have me: a woman is asked out as much for her clothes as for herself. The clothes are the background, the frame, if you like: they don't make success, but they are a part of it. Who wants a dingy woman? We are expected to be pretty and well-dressed till we drop—and if we can't keep it up alone, we have to go into partnership."

Selden glanced at her with amusement: it was impossible, even with her lovely eyes imploring him, to take a sentimental view of her case.

"Ah, well, there must be plenty of capital on the look-out for such an investment. Perhaps you'll meet your fate tonight at the Trenors'."

She returned his look interrogatively.

"I thought you might be going there—oh, not in that capacity! But there are to be a lot of your set—Gwen Van Osburgh, the Wetheralls, Lady Cressida Raith—and the George Dorsets."

She paused a moment before the last name, and shot a query through her lashes; but he remained imperturbable.

"Mrs. Trenor asked me; but I can't get away till the end of the week; and those big parties bore me."

"Ah, so they do me," she exclaimed.

"Then why go?"

"It's part of the business—you forget! And besides, if I didn't, I should be playing bézique with my aunt at Richfield Springs."

"That's almost as bad as marrying Dillworth," he agreed, and they both laughed for pure pleasure in their sudden intimacy.

She glanced at the clock.

"Dear me! I must be off. It's after five."

She paused before the mantelpiece, studying herself in the mirror while she adjusted her veil. The attitude revealed the long slope of her slender sides, which gave a kind of wild-wood grace to her outline—as though she were a captured dryad subdued to the conventions of the drawing-room; and Selden reflected that it was the same streak of sylvan freedom in her nature that lent such savour to her artificiality.

He followed her across the room to the entrance-hall; but on the threshold she held out her hand with a gesture of leave-taking.

"It's been delightful; and now you will have to return my visit."

"But don't you want me to see you to the station?"

"No; good bye here, please."

She let her hand lie in his a moment, smiling up at him adorably.

"Good bye, then—and good luck at Bellomont!" he said, opening the door for her.

On the landing she paused to look about her. There were a thousand chances to one against her meeting anybody, but one could never tell, and she always paid for her rare indiscretions by a violent reaction of prudence. There was no one in sight, however, but a char-woman who was scrubbing the stairs. Her own stout person and its surrounding implements took up so much room that Lily, to pass her, had to gather up her skirts and brush against the wall. As she did so, the woman paused in her work and looked up curiously, resting her clenched red fists on the wet cloth she had just drawn from her pail. She had a broad sallow face, slightly pitted with small-pox, and thin straw-colored hair through which her scalp shone unpleasantly.

"I beg your pardon," said Lily, intending by her politeness to convey a criticism of the other's manner.

The woman, without answering, pushed her pail aside, and continued to stare as Miss Bart swept by with a murmur of silken linings. Lily felt herself flushing under the look. What did the creature suppose? Could one never do the simplest, the most harmless thing, without subjecting one's self to some odious conjecture? Half way down the next flight, she smiled to think that a char-woman's stare should so perturb her. The poor thing was probably dazzled by such an unwonted apparition. But *were* such apparitions unwonted on Selden's stairs? Miss Bart was not familiar with the moral code of bachelors' flat-houses, and her color rose again as it occurred to her that the woman's persistent gaze implied a groping among past associations. But she put aside the thought with a smile at her own fears, and hastened downward, wondering if she should find a cab short of Fifth Avenue.

Under the Georgian porch she paused again, scanning the street for a hansom. None was in sight, but as she reached the sidewalk she ran against a small glossy-looking man with a gardenia in his coat, who raised his hat with a surprised exclamation.

"Miss Bart? Well—of all people! This *is* luck," he declared; and she caught a twinkle of amused curiosity between his screwed-up lids.

"Oh, Mr. Rosedale—how are you?" she said, perceiving that the irrepressible annoyance on her face was reflected in the sudden intimacy of his smile.

Mr. Rosedale stood scanning her with interest and approval. He was a plump rosy man of the blond Jewish type, with smart London clothes fitting him like upholstery, and small sidelong eyes which gave him the air of appraising people as if they were bric-a-brac. He glanced up interrogatively at the porch of the Benedick.

"Been up to town for a little shopping, I suppose?" he said, in a tone which had the familiarity of a touch.

Miss Bart shrank from it slightly, and then flung herself into precipitate explanations.

"Yes—I came up to see my dress-maker. I am just on my way to catch the train to the Trenors'."

"Ah—your dress-maker; just so," he said blandly. "I didn't know there were any dress-makers in the Benedick."

"The Benedick?" She looked gently puzzled. "Is that the name of this building?"

"Yes, that's the name: I believe it's an old word for bachelor, isn't it? I happen to own the building—that's the way I know." His smile deepened as he added with increasing assurance: "But you must let me take you to the station. The Trenors are at Bellomont, of course? You've barely time to catch the five-forty. The dress-maker kept you waiting, I suppose."

Lily stiffened under the pleasantry.

"Oh, thanks," she stammered; and at that moment her eye caught a hansom drifting down Madison Avenue, and she hailed it with a desperate gesture.

"You're very kind; but I couldn't think of troubling you," she said, extending her hand to Mr. Rosedale; and heedless of his protestations, she sprang into the rescuing vehicle, and called out a breathless order to the driver.

Being Beauteous

·◡

S TANDING TALL BEFORE snow, a being of beauty. Death whistles and rings of muffled music cause this worshipped body to rise up, expand, and tremble like a ghost. Scarlet and black wounds break out on the proud flesh. The very colors of life deepen, dance, and stand out from the vision, in the yard. Tremblings rise and threaten, and the persistent taste of these effects combining with the whistle of men and the discordant music which the world, far behind us, throws to our mother of beauty. She draws back and stands up. Our bones are reclothed with a new and amorous body.

All of French Symbolist **ARTHUR RIMBAUD'S** *hallucinogenic poems were written before he turned twenty. During this astonishingly prolific period, he was obsessed by Plato, Buddhism, and the occult. "Being Beauteous" was written in the 1880s.*

Oh! the ashen face, the horsehair emblem, the crystal alms! The cannon on which I must fall, in the medley of trees and light air!

A Pagan World

·ᴗ

I N T H E B R I G H T L I G H T of the Aegean the earliest
known civilization in Europe states clearly what were—and still
are—the hallmarks of beauty: tiny waists, splendid bosoms and
curly hair. Here in Crete at the very beginning of Western history, every artifice known to future ages is used to accentuate
them and the coquetry of the Minoan women appears more
closely akin to the sophisticated eighteenth and nineteenth centuries than to the austere splendor of their contemporaries, the
Egyptians, or to the classic age of Greece which follows them
some thousand years later.

Across the stepping stones of the Greek islands which
lead to the shores of Europe come many Oriental influences:
the Syrian Astarte's cult of the breasts; the accentuated and

---

MADGE GARLAND *has written numerous books on women and fashion. "A*
Pagan World" is from her 1957 study The Changing Face of Beauty:
Four Thousand Years of Beautiful Women.

elongated eye, so typical of the Egyptians; perhaps the enigmatic smiles of the Etruscans; certainly the magnificent and elaborate jewellery which from earliest days decorates the necks and ears.

With the development of Greek art the sculptor creates a type of beauty which has never been excelled: for centuries the measurement and features of the antique Kore and classic Venus are accepted as perfection and ensuing civilizations have created nothing more exquisite than these lovely goddesses, unselfconscious in their nakedness. They have natural figures, firm and well-developed; their waists unlike those of their Minoan forebears are not constricted; their breasts are set high and far apart; and their arms and legs are long, with finely turned wrists and ankles. Feet are now visible, strong and agile—for Greek women walk barefoot or are shod with heelless sandals. Their features are straight, the forehead and nose in one unbroken line, and no maquillage is suggested. The eyes are unaccentuated, the long hair waved but no longer elaborately curled. Few contrivances of fashion are admitted but the simplicity of their garments does not prevent them achieving a variety of exquisite effects, as the charming Tanagra figures effectively illustrate.

Freedom from fashion is equalled by freedom in sex; the pregnant girl could claim that Zeus had seduced her on a mountainside when her partner might have been a youthful shepherd—and what would have been a bastard in other circumstances became the son of a god in ancient Greece. Naked boys and girls run races and take part in outdoor sports together; and the healthy physique and well-developed limbs of the Greek girls, as well as their exiguous garments, bear a striking resemblance to those of the girls of the twentieth century.

Ernest Hemingway

To Have and Have Not

·ᴗ

HIM, LIKE HE WAS, snotty and strong and quick, and like some kind of expensive animal. It would always get me just to watch him move. I was so lucky all that time to have him. His luck went bad first in Cuba. Then it kept right worse and worse until a Cuban killed him.

Cubans are bad luck for Conchs. Cubans are bad luck for anybody. They got too many niggers there too. I remember that time he took me over to Havana when he was making such good money and we were walking in the park and a nigger said something to me and Harry smacked him, and picked up his straw hat that fell off, and sailed it about a half a block and a taxi ran over it. I laughed so it made my belly ache.

ERNEST HEMINGWAY *is equally known for his masterpieces* (The Old Man and the Sea, A Moveable Feast, The Sun Also Rises) *and for his free-wheeling, manly adventures. Some predictable ideas of beauty are found in his 1937 classic,* To Have and Have Not.

That was the first time I ever made my hair blonde that time there in that beauty parlor on the Prado. They were working on it all afternoon and it was naturally so dark they didn't want to do it and I was afraid I'd look terrible, but I kept telling them to see if they couldn't make it a little lighter, and the man would go over it with that orange wood stick with cotton on the end, dipping it in that bowl that had the stuff in it sort of smoky like the way it steamed sort of, and the comb; parting the strands with one end of the stick and the comb and going over them and letting it dry and I was sitting there scared inside my chest of what I was having done and all I'd say was, just see if you can't make it a little lighter.

And finally he said, that's just as light as I can make it safely, Madame, and then he shampooed it, and put a wave in, and I was afraid to look even for fear it would be terrible, and he waved it parted on one side and high behind my ears with little tight curls in back, and it still wet I couldn't tell how it looked except it looked all changed and I looked strange to myself. And he put a net over it wet and put me under the dryer and all the time I was scared about it. And then when I come out from under the dryer he took the net off and the pins out and combed it out and it was just like gold.

And I came out of the place and saw myself in the mirror and it shone so in the sun and was so soft and silky when I put my hand and touched it, and I couldn't believe it was me and I was so excited I was choked with it.

I walked down the Prado to the café where Harry was waiting and I was so excited feeling all funny inside, sort of faint like, and he stood up when he saw me coming and he couldn't take his eyes off me and his voice was thick and funny when he said, "Jesus, Marie, you're beautiful."

And I said, "You like me blonde?"

"Don't talk about it," he said. "Let's go to the hotel."

And I said, "O.K., then. Let's go." I was twenty-six then.

Playing in the Dark

،ـ

M

Y INTEREST IN Ernest Hemingway becomes
heightened when I consider how much apart his work is from
African-Americans. That is, he has no need, desire, or awareness
of them either as readers of his work or as people existing anywhere other than in his imaginative (and imaginatively lived)
world. I find, therefore, his use of African-Americans much more
artless and unselfconscious than Poe's, for example, where social
unease required the servile black bodies in his work.

The serviceability of the Africanist presence I have been
describing becomes even more pronounced when Hemingway
begins to describe male and female relationships. In this same
novel, the last voice we hear is that of Harry's devoted wife,

---

TONI MORRISON *is the author of* Beloved, The Bluest Eye, *and* Song of
Solomon. *Her 1992 collection of essays,* Playing in the Dark, *includes her
thoughts on Ernest Hemingway's* To Have and Have Not.

Marie, listing and celebrating the virtues, the virility and bravery, of her husband, who is now dead. The elements of her reverie can be schematically organized as follows: (1) virile, good, brave Harry; (2) racist views of Cuba; (3) black sexual invasion thwarted; (4) reification of whiteness.

Marie recalls him fondly as "snotty and strong and quick, and like some kind of expensive animal. It would always get me to just watch him move." Immediately following this encomium to sexuality and power and revered (expensive) brutality, she meditates on her hatred of Cubans (the Cubans killed Harry) and says they are "bad luck for Conchs" and "bad luck for anybody. They got too many niggers there too." This judgment is followed by her recollection of a trip she and Harry took to Havana when she was twenty-six years old. Harry had a lot of money then and while they walked in the park a "nigger" (as opposed to a Cuban, though the black man she is referring to is both black and Cuban), "said something" to Marie. Harry smacked him and threw his straw hat into the street where a taxi ran over it.

Marie remembers laughing so hard it made her belly ache. With nothing but a paragraph indentation between them, the next reverie is a further association of Harry with sexuality, power, and protection. "That was the first time I ever made my hair blonde." The two anecdotes are connected in time and place and, significantly, by color as sexual coding. We do not know what the black man said, but the horror is that he said anything at all. It is enough that he spoke, claimed an intimacy perhaps, but certainly claimed a view and inserted his sexual self into their space and their consciousness. By initiating the remark, he was a speaking, therefore aggressive, presence. In Marie's recollection, sexuality, violence, class, and the retribution of an impartial machine are fused into an all-purpose black man.

The couple, Marie and Harry, is young and in love with obviously enough money to feel and be powerful in Cuba. Into that Eden comes the violating black male making impertinent remarks. The disrespect, with its sexual overtones, is punished at once by Harry's violence. He smacks the black man. Further, he picks up the fallen straw hat, violating the black man's property, just as the black man had sullied Harry's property—his wife. When the taxi, inhuman, onrushing, impartial machine, runs over the hat, it is as if the universe were rushing to participate in and validate Harry's response. It is this underscoring that makes Marie laugh—along with her obvious comfort in and adulation of this "strong and quick" husband of hers.

What follows in the beauty parlor is positioned as connected with and dependent on the episode of black invasion of privacy and intimation of sexuality from which Marie must be protected. The urgency to establish difference—a difference within the sexual context—is commanding. Marie tells us how she is transformed from black to white, from dark to blond. It is a painful and difficult process that turns out to be well worth the pain in its sexual, protective, differentiating payout: "They were working on it all afternoon and it was naturally so dark they didn't want to do it . . . but I kept telling them to see if they couldn't make it a little lighter . . . and all I'd say was, just see if you can't make it a little lighter."

When the bleaching and perming are done, Marie's satisfaction is decidedly sensual, if not explicitly sexual: "when I put my hand and touched it, and I couldn't believe it was me and I was so excited I was choked with it . . . I was so excited feeling all funny inside, sort of faint like." It is a genuine transformation. Marie becomes a self she can hardly believe, golden and soft and silky.

Her own sensual reaction to her whitening is echoed by Harry, who sees her and says, "Jesus, Marie, you're beautiful." And when she wants to hear more about her beauty, he tells her not to talk—just "Let's go to the hotel." This enhanced sexuality comes on the heels of a sexual intrusion by a black man.

What could have been the consequence if the insult to Marie had come from a white man? Would the bleaching have followed? If so, would it have been in such lush and sexually heightened language? What does establishing a difference from darkness to lightness accomplish for the concept of a self as sexually alive and potent? Or so powerful and coherent in the world?

These tourists in Havana meet a native of that city and have a privileged status because they are white. But to assure us that this status is both deserved and, by implication, potently generative, they encounter a molesting, physically inferior black male (his inferiority is designated by the fact that Harry does not use his fists, but slaps him) who represents the outlaw sexuality that, by comparison, spurs the narrative on to contemplation of a superior, legal, white counterpart.

Here we see Africanism used as a fundamental fictional technique by which to establish character. Within a milieu that threatens the dissolution of all distinctions of value—the milieu of the working poor, the unemployed, sinister Chinese, terrorist Cubans, violent but cowardly blacks, upper-class castrati, female predators—Harry and Marie (an ex-prostitute) gain potency, a generative sexuality. They solicit our admiration by the comparison that is struck between their claims to fully embodied humanity and a discredited Africanism. The voice of the text is complicit in these formulations: Africanism becomes not only a means of displaying authority but, in fact, constitutes its source.

Personal Beauty and Racial Betterment

H UMAN BEAUTY IS something which is perenni-
ally celebrated in poetry, in song, in romance, and in the petrified conception of the sculptor, but less frequently
considered in the cold analysis of science. We are usually content to leave the topic to the artist and the lover, as one of the
interesting and thrilling, but nonessential, matters of life. I
wish to suggest a different conception of beauty: a conception
of beauty as something which, whatever its importance for the
individual, is for the race and for civilization of such profound
importance that no other fundamental consideration of
human welfare and progress can be divorced from it. I shall
not touch upon the theme with the golden fingers of an artist,
but with the unemotional digits of the psychologist. To some,

---

KNIGHT DUNLAP *wrote on a variety of edifying subjects:* The Dramatic
Personality of Jesus, Habits: Their Making and Unmaking, *and*
Personal Beauty and Racial Betterment *(1920).*

without doubt, this procedure will seem as sacrilegious as the piercing of the anatomist's knife into the dead human form; but where the welfare and progress of humanity are at stake, even these brutal methods must be employed.

Beauty is a term of variable meaning; in fact there is a group of terms—handsome, pretty, attractive, charming, etc.—whose exact relationship is often discussed, and never settled. The way in which I use the term will not be acceptable to many persons, but one may reformulate my conclusions in his own way, using whatever terms he chooses, and the validity of the conclusions will not thereby be affected. I think it will be agreed, when I am through, that I have been discussing something rather definite under the name of beauty, and I hope further, that it will be conceded that, after all, what I have been discussing is that which in the common, and therefore vital, usage is actually designated by the term.

The familiar proverb tells us that "beauty is only skin deep," which nicely exemplifies the mendacity of proverbs; ugliness, it is true, is often skin deep, but beauty, never. Beauty, as I hope to be able to show, is something which depends upon the whole organism.

1. *Stature.* From the point of view of the female, the male must be large, although not a giant, since, as we have seen, too great a deviation from the usual is a negative condition. I have at various times overheard women, who were discussing the relative handsomeness of two or several men, settle the point by such an observation as "*A* is fully an inch taller than *B*." By carefully put questions I have succeeded in eliciting a considerable

amount of information on this point without revealing the actual purpose of the interrogation. For example, if I inquire of a woman concerning the handsomeness of a man who has a general combination of desirable and undesirable characteristics, but who is a trifle below medium height, I very frequently obtain, in her first statement, a criticism of his stature, followed by a consideration of his other attributes; indicating that in her estimation size is of paramount importance. The determining factor is not, of course, mere height but height combined with lateral development not deviating markedly from the average proportion. The tall man of bean-pole build is not considered attractive. Yet, a positive element of height can outweigh a considerable element of disproportion, and a taller man, whose proportions are in themselves worse than those of a shorter man, is usually considered the handsomer.

This preference for stature undoubtedly harks back to more primitive times, when it was above all important that man should be a fighter and hunter, in order to secure food for his wife and children, and protect them against wild beasts and against the designs of other males. Especially was this important during the periods when the woman was pregnant, or nursing a child. It is highly probable that in ancient times the negative rule against abnormal size did not apply, since every increase in physical power, even if it carried to the extreme of gigantic development, was a distinct advantage.

It is sometimes alleged that the woman's preference is not for the *large* man in an absolute sense, but for the man *larger* than herself; either because of a natural wish for a husband to whom she is inferior; to whom she can give a tribute of worship and deference; or else, that it has developed through the necessity of the greater strength on the part of the man in order that he might capture the woman, and carry her away from her parental habitat, to his own dwelling. Both of these suggestions are highly unplausible. Marriage by capture, although a good hypothesis for popular writers, probably never was at any time an institution of any more importance or actuality than it is at the present day. Psychologically, the theory is based on the assumption that woman is naturally opposed to the marital relation, which assumption is a merry jest, to say the least. Historically, there is no evidence for the theory of capture except as a limited and temporary phenomenon. As for the supposition of an unexplained instinct to prefer a dominant partner, I see no support for it, except in so far as the practical consideration I have advanced may itself lead to this preference as a secondary manifestation. It is true that there are women today who openly state that the mates they want are those who can completely dominate them; and that such potential masters are the only men who interest them. These cases (a number have been directly reported to me) are not all to be explained on the same basis, although the primary factor in every case is the admiration for the strong man. In some cases, the preference is distinctly a pathological development; in others, it is pretended by the woman as an explanation for the fact that men are not interested in her. In many cases, however, the preference is the expression of an arbitrary standard which is manifested usually in less egotistical ways. Where a scale of values is accepted, there is commonly a more or less explicit adoption of a minimal acceptable value; the stronger man is the more desirable; a man who measures up to a certain minimum will be acceptable. In most cases, the minimal standard adopted is the father, a brother, or some other impressive individual in real life or in fiction. In the case of a strongly egotistical woman, who sets a high value on her own potentialities, the standard is herself; the man less forceful than herself is below the minimum.

In this, I seem to be confusing physical strength with various sorts of power; perhaps I am; but, as I am trying to point out, the basis of power is muscular, and admiration for physical prowess still retains a primacy when it is a matter of the fundamental attraction of the woman to the man; and all I am trying to establish at this point is that there is no primary desire of the woman for a man who is able to dominate her physically. On the contrary, the woman would prefer, if other considerations did not prevent, the mate whom she can control physically and in every other way, for the *instinct to dominate* is inherent in every normal human being.

2. *Bodily proportions.* In modern civilization there has grown up an immodesty which was lacking in more ancient cultures. We are ashamed of our bodies. Whether the practice of concealing the body is the cause of our uncleanness of mind, or whether our obscenity is rather the cause of the concealment, is a debated question. Whatever may be my general estimate of the Japanese, I cannot but admire their wonderful cleanness of mind, which makes for them clothing a detail which has no bearing on modesty.

Among the Greeks, who, as you know, were in many respects more pure-minded than we are, bodily conformation was an important detail in beauty. And, in fact, it is today amongst us, both in a shame-faced way in daily life, and more creditably when we throw off our prudishness in the presence of plastic and pictorial art, and in the theater. We are skirting here a vital and pressing problem of the present moment, on which I should like to take the time to make you face some problems we all tend to ignore, but I must not digress further.

Our standards of bodily development are still, in the main, Greek. There are certain proportions which are judged both by the artist and the layman to be the ideal of beauty. In this we are of course swayed largely by the limitations of our education, which on these matters is artificial; probably there would be a greater difference in racial ideals, if conditions were more natural.

The simplest explanation for the accepted ideal of form would be that it is the average form of the healthy individual. This explanation, I think, is not supportable. Among the Greeks and Romans, for example, the ideal ankle, for a woman at least, was a *small* ankle, not a medium-sized one. Among us, a small foot has been desirable; so much so that women have been compelled to wear shoes which, by raising the heel several inches, make the ground-base of the shoe about two thirds the real length of the foot. This procedure makes the foot seem shorter, or at least it did until the recent shortening of the skirt brought the artifice out where it cannot be overlooked. One of the most important and desirable effects of the permanent adoption of sensible clothing by women will be the allowing of the foot to retain its natural form. Of body-form, which is by rights the fundamental consideration in beauty, I shall say nothing further, because our standards are so obscure. The subject is in need of thorough investigation by the methods of comparative anatomy, and above all, of social psychology.

3. *The features.* Whatever the cause of our concealment of the body, it has led to an emphasis on the anatomical details of the face which could not be found in more primitive times. Leaving out of consideration the general shape of the face and head, which are probably important mainly as racial signs, we may consider briefly the chin, the nose, the eyes and the ears.

That there is a preference on the part of both sexes, and in the consideration of both sexes, for a well-developed chin, is a matter of common knowledge. The reason for this preference is less evident, and in fact I can here indicate only a strong probability. Racial factors are involved, of course, but there seems to be a more general foundation which is vaguely involved in the commonplace statement, that the possession of a chin is one of the conspicuous points which differentiate man from the beasts. This is obviously true; the vital question is: What are the direct consequences of this structural peculiarity? This question can be answered by reference to comparative anatomy and to the psychology of the thought processes. The projecting chin gives room in the mouth cavity for the human tongue, which is strikingly different from the brute tongue. The tongue of the lower animal is a long thin strip of muscle; the tongue of *homo sapiens* is a thick muscular mass. A somewhat exaggerated comparison is to a leather strap, in one case, and a frog seated in the mouth in the other case. We have now advanced the question one step farther, to ask what may be the advantage, if any, in the form of the human tongue.

The animal tongue is certainly just as well adapted to the purposes of obtaining and preparing food, as the human. In some cases, it is even more efficient. But the human tongue is an important instrument in the production of the most human of all attributes, *language*. Language is not merely the means of communicating thought; it is, as philologists have long known, and as psychologists have been forced somewhat unwillingly to admit, the principal means of thinking. While it is possible to think without language, languageless thought is primitive and inefficient in the complex conditions of civilization, and it is by no means an exaggeration to say that the development of language is a large part of the development of thought.

That both the eyes and ears are beauty marks, and that, in the female especially, they have been selected for especial emphasis by lovers and poets, you are well aware. Both love and poetizing, as most of us well know from our own experience, are conditions of irresponsibility in which the fundamental instincts and habits have large sway; and the first condition usually brings on the second; accordingly the beauty-points which fix the attention of poets demand our attention. But there is little to offer at present in the way of analysis of these. Aside from the indication of physical condition which the eyes afford (and every physician makes use of these indications), the importance of the eye is probably largely racial. The blue or the black, the large or the small, are not in themselves of moment, but they indicate stocks from which we expect certain other characters, mental and physical. The same general consideration is probably involved in ear preferences. This is however by no means the whole story. Anyone who has studied the religious and art symbolism of primitive peoples, and of people not so primitive (I do not refer to the crude and artificial studies of the Freudians) cannot help but see very definite reasons for the fascination of the eye and ear, reasons which are more appropriately discussed amongst psychologists than before a general audience.

Before passing on to the next topic, I wish to protect myself from possible misapprehension by disclaiming any taint of phrenology or blackfordism in the preceding discussion. The significance of cranial and facial characters must be worked out on the lines of physiology and genetics; psychologists have no sympathy with the various systems of so-called character analysis which attempt to decide from a casual examination of an individual what his intellectual and moral peculiarities are in detail.

4. *Hair*. The hair which adorns the human body (or disfigures it, as the case may be), is of two sorts, in regard to its physiological conditions and significance, as well as to its regional distribution. The hair of the head, or *pate-hair*, is the one sort, and the body-hair, including the face-hair, is the other.

The conditions which govern the growth of the pate-hair are not definitely known, but are probably connected with bodily changes which have other important effects. That is to say, the stimulation of the growth of the hair, or the failure of its vitality, are probably due to changes in the internal secretions (hormones) of the organism, although it is not known which of the

secretions are the important ones in this connection. It is probable that another effect of the internal changes which produce
baldness is a lessening of the resistance of the organism, so that
the bald-headed man cannot stand the muscular exertion or the
nervous strain of which the hairy-headed man is capable. At any
rate, baldness is a fatal bar to beauty, both in the male and the
female, although to many persons (men especially) an individual
of the opposite sex whose pate-hair is exceptionally abundant is
repulsive. Another indication of the dependence of the pate-hair
on metabolism in other regions is found in the apparent connection between hair and temperament. It is difficult to conceive of
a baldheaded musical genius or artist; although even to the rule
implied here, exceptions do occur. Temperament, and all emotional factors, as we now know, depend largely on the bodily
metabolism, especially on the functions of the internally secret-
ing glands. The quantitative hair character, therefore, may in all
probability be reduced to an indication of physical vigor; and
physical vigor is far more important, as a beauty asset, than mental ability. Whether the popular belief that the mental ability of a
child is in the inverse proportion to the growth of his hair, has
any foundation, and whether a similar rule holds for adults, I
shall not discuss, as I might be accused of being prejudiced.

The other details of the pate-hair character: fineness or
coarseness, straightness or kinkiness, color and contour of distribution, are largely important as indicators of race or stock; yet
fineness, has a direct sex value in its greater pleasingness to
touch. It may also be true that color has a direct value; that the
masculine preference for red-haired women which is so frequent,

and of which the Elizabethan and pre-Elizabethan erotic writings are so full, is not due solely to the association of the hair color with the ardent temperament which without doubt was a characteristic of the red-haired stocks; but is in part at least due to the direct effect of the visual stimulation.

All parts of the body except the palms of the hands and the soles of the feet, and certain other small areas, are covered with fine hair, which in the pre-adolescent person are usually so fine and so colorless that they are hardly noticeable. With the beginning of puberty, the axillary hair (the hair of the arm pits), and the hair of the pubic region in both sexes begins to develop, increasing in diameter as well as in length and in pigmentation. In the male also, but slightly later, the face hair undergoes similar development, and still later the hair on the chest, abdomen, and limbs of the male develops in manners which differ greatly in different individuals. In the typical, functionally perfect woman, on the other hand, the body-hair, except in the restricted regions mentioned, remains as fine and as colorless as in the child.

This hair development is not associated with sexual ripening in a chance way, but is controlled by the fundamental sex glands. These glands not only produce the germ cells (the egg and the spermatozoön) whose union creates the life of a new individual; they secrete also, into the blood stream, hormones, i.e., substances which profoundly influence the growth of various parts of the organism. The internal secretions of the male glands produce those changes in the vocal organs which are indicated by the voice becoming heavier and lower; stimulate the growth of the body-hair in the manner above indicated; and undoubtedly promote those structural and functional changes which are evidenced in the tendencies of feeling and action distinctive of the male. If the glands are removed in infancy, these changes do not occur. The secretions of the ovaries, on the other hand, seem to inhibit the growth of body hair, to accelerate those structural changes in the muscles, glands and skeleton which differentiate the woman from the man, and promote those functional modifications which make the feelings and emotions of each sex a sealed book to the other.

It may be said of the important races of mankind that, in general, the development of the face- and body-hair in the male, and the absence thereof in the female (except in the three limited areas), are alike an indication of fitness for parenthood. The decline of the sex function in old age is usually marked by significant changes in these details. There are of course many apparently anomalous cases, some of which may be explained by glandular details into which the limitations of time forbid us to go; but in spite of these cases, the social verdict is uniform. The hairlessness of the female face and body, and the hairiness of the male face (or the evidence that hair grows, although shaved off) are important elements of beauty. The male body-hair has little value, because of its irregularity, and the fact of its usual concealment.

There are a number of interesting problems which arise in connection with the body-hair. Theoretically, the pubic hair should be as beautiful, at least, as the pate-hair; yet the Greeks, who set our official standards, did not think so. As to axillary hair, there is lacking information as to its indicatory value. It is an interesting observation, however, and one of no little psychological importance that in recent years when the morbid shame of the body was somewhat lessened, and young women began to expose their arm pits freely in the ball room and theater, some removed the axillary hair, and others did not. A little later, the practice of removing the hair became practically universal, and now the hair is seldom seen. Probably the conflict of opinion in these matters is really between the man's judgment of beauty and the woman's. But we must pass over these details, and hurry on with our main problem.

It is evident now that whether there are other considerations or not, the most important element in the beauty of any individual is the evidence of her (or his) fitness for the function of procreating healthy children of the highest type of efficiency, according to the standards of the race; and ability to protect these children. The positive beauty characters we have already examined are clearly such marks of ability to perpetuate the species in the finest and noblest way, and the characters we shall now consider strengthen the interpretation.

5. *Fat.* Here again there are racial differences, but amongst the European races, no racial indications. We may leave out of consideration the Africans and the South Sea Islanders, with their criteria of beauty-fat which seem so odd to us, but which are quite intelligible when viewed in the light of racial characters, and consider Western conditions and standards.

A certain amount of fatty tissue is normal, and is essential for the health of the individual. Fat constitutes a store of reserve material, which may be drawn on in time of unusual need; and without it endurance is limited. This reserve store is probably not so important at present as it was in primitive times, when man lived in a hand-to-mouth way, uncertain today what the food supply would be day after tomorrow. On the other hand, beyond a certain amount, fat is an encumbrance, impeding the operation of many organs, and thus limiting the efficiency of the individual, and also is in itself a symptom of faulty organic functioning of some kind. We are not surprised therefore to find that beauty demands just the right degree of leanness; just the degree which is found in the most vigorous individual.

The standards are somewhat different for the two sexes, because the anatomical conditions and physiological necessities are different. In the female, especially in the young female, there is a special layer of fatty tissue underlying the skin, which is absent in the male. This gives her the roundness and softness of outline which is essential to the perfection of feminine beauty, and also prevents her from feeling the cold so much as the male does. Possibly also it explains why she swims more easily. (It is a fact that women are as a class far better swimmers; this has been ascribed to the better development of the legs, but this reason is hardly sufficient, since it has been shown that leg action is the least important factor in swimming.)

The softness and roundness of contour of the female is beautiful, because it is the mark of physical fitness. The fatty layer is supposed to be an extra reserve supply of food material, laid up against the heavy demands which are made by child-bearing, and in still another way protects her in that supreme process, of whose splendid fruition beauty is the glorious blossom. When age withers, through the absorption of the adipose tissue, primary beauty is on the decline, and unless it be replaced by the secondary beauty appropriate to advancing years, the drama of life becomes a tragedy. And indeed, the great fact that we all must face at some time, that the strength and vigor of our prime is past, and that the time when the almond tree shall flourish and the grasshopper become a burden advances upon us, is usually announced to a woman in the discovery of wrinkles due to the slipping from her of her subcutaneous robe of office.

6. *Poise.* The consideration of the expression of mental and emotional qualifications leads us over into the general problem of the participation of mental traits in personal beauty. There is no doubt of the value, to the race as well as to the individual, of a high degree of mental development, provided always that the development does not so destroy the physical balance that the individual's chance of survival is impaired. Development in some individuals, by special environment and training, of mental capacity beyond the point of balance, is doubtless of value to the social group of which they are members, but the increase in stock which tends to general overmentalization is a dangerous factor.

The underdevelopment of mental capacity, even at levels far above feeble-mindedness and other obvious mental defects, is a form of inefficiency as positive as the overdevelopment. We can conceive of a world peopled by a race of men and women of splendid physique, from which the common grades of undesirables have been eliminated: a world in which each individual seems admirably constituted for mating and creating children after his kind. Great content and happiness, and joy in the appreciation of the beauty of their mates, might obtain among this people. Nature too would smile on the race which had so far complied with her conditions. But if this race could attain no further than eminence in the traits we have previously considered, it would be a failure. As a matter of fact, a nation on this plan would have a low chance of survival in conflict and competition with nations which had gone beyond it into a richer mental and spiritual flower and fruition.

If it were possible to apply comprehensive and accurate mental tests to candidates for mating, and so to select in accordance with adequate mental standards, racial betterment might be attained along this line: but we have no criteria which are capable of such application, and cannot foresee the time when they may be available. The important question, therefore, is whether there is an element in beauty itself which serves as an index of mental and spiritual potentiality: or whether our selection is indeed blind in this respect.

Sound integrative function: the foundation of sound mental life: is practically recognizable, and is an actual element in human beauty as it is estimated in civilized societies. We call the evidence of this capacity *poise*, and read it in the individual's activities all the way from such commonplace processes as walking and talking, to the most complicated reactions under social conditions. Proper muscular tonicity is of course a necessary condition for poise, although it is but part of the total. In all its details, however, poise takes us over from mere anatomy to action.

Without poise, beauty is the beauty of the marble statue and the painted canvas.

Rita and Marilyn

·

1950: HOLLYWOOD. RITA. Changing her name, weight, age, voice, lips, and eyebrows, she conquered Hollywood. Her hair was transformed from dull black into flaming red. To broaden her brow, they removed hair after hair by painful electrolysis. Over her eyes they put lashes like petals.

Rita Hayworth disguised herself as a goddess, and perhaps was one—for the forties, anyway. Now, the fifties demand something new.

1950: Hollywood. Marilyn. Like Rita, this girl has been improved. She had thick eyelashes and a double chin, a nose round at the tip, and large teeth. Hollywood reduced the fat, suppressed the cartilage, filed the teeth, and turned the mousy

Uruguayan novelist **EDUARDO GALEANO'S** *masterful trilogy,* Memory of Fire, *maps, in brief vignettes, the history of the Americas. His study in contrasts, "Rita and Marilyn," is found in the third volume,* Century of the Wind *(1988).*

chestnut hair into a cascade of gleaming gold. Then the technicians baptized her Marilyn Monroe and invented a pathetic childhood story for her to tell the journalists.

This new Venus manufactured in Hollywood no longer needs to climb into strange beds seeking contracts for second-rate roles in third-rate films. She no longer lives on hot dogs and coffee, or suffers the cold of winter. Now she is a star; or rather a small personage in a mask who would like to remember, but cannot, that moment when she simply wanted to be saved from loneliness.

Lord Byron

She Walks in Beauty

.◞

S HE WALKS in Beauty,
   like the night
Of cloudless climes and starry skies;
And all that's best of dark and bright
Meet in her aspect and her eyes:
Thus mellowed to that tender light
Which Heaven to gaudy day denies.

English poet **LORD BYRON** *wrote of defiant young men and desirable lasses.*
His first poem "Childe Harold" won him international acclaim; he never
slowed down, dying before his masterpiece, Don Juan, was finished. "She
Walks in Beauty" (1814) is from his Collected Poems.

II

One shade the more, one ray the less,

Had half impaired the nameless grace

Which waves in every raven tress,

Or softly lightens o'er her face;

Where thoughts serenely sweet express,

How pure, how dear their dwelling-place.

III

And on that cheek, and o'er that brow,

So soft, so calm, yet eloquent,

The smiles that win, the tints that glow,

But tell of days in goodness spent,

A mind at peace with all below,

A heart whose love is innocent!

This Lunar Beauty

THIS lunar beauty
Has no history
Is complete and early;
If beauty later
Bear any feature
It had a lover
And is another.

This like a dream
Keeps other time
And daytime is
The loss of this;
For time is inches
And the heart's changes

W. H. AUDEN *is considered one of the greatest English poets of the 20th century. "This Lunar Beauty," one of his later works, is from the posthumous* Collected Poems.

Where ghost has
haunted
Lost and wanted.

But this was never
A ghost's endeavour
Nor finished this,
Was ghost at ease;
And till it pass
Love shall not near
The sweetness here
Nor sorrow take
His endless look.

In Ancient Egypt

·ৄ

W

HO CAN IMAGINE the length of fifty-six hundred years? That, roughly speaking, is the span of ancient Egyptian history. It ended in 31 B.C., when the Romans defeated Cleopatra, who, although she was Queen of Egypt, was not an Egyptian. Now, we might expect that over such a tremendous period the Egyptians would have formed many ideals of feminine beauty: but life was then steady, people did not wish it to change, and, let us remember, anything old was also hallowed.

The earliest statuettes have no beauty at all. The men who made them produced, as most primitive men do, simply exaggerated forms of the essentially feminine: very large breasts, immense buttocks; for these primitive men had probably little more sense of beauty than a bull has or a boar. By the time that men delight in

CLIFFORD BAX *is the author of* All the World's a Stage *and* The Beauty of Women *(1946), from which "In Ancient Egypt" is taken.*

anything for its beauty, and not solely for its use, they have grown far away from the level of animals.

Let us realize, then, that Egypt is a hot land, exceedingly hot, and for this reason let us not be upset by the fact that the Egyptians felt no shame of their bodies. Nudity and what we may call transparency were, in fact, the rule. "Boys and girls went about naked," says worthy Dr. Budge, "the former whilst still at school. Men and women worked naked in the field, servants of both sexes went about in the house naked. . . . About 1400 B.C. women wore garments of diaphanous materials, through which every part of their bodies was seen." Female slaves and women of the lower classes went about, according to James Laver, "without any clothes at all, other than a loose girdle resting on the hips." In frescoes and papyrus-pictures we often find this "loose girdle" worn by dancers and parlormaids, and as it hides nothing, it was probably, like the Victorian white apron or cap, a sign of service.

If you imagine a woman of five foot three—that is to say, of sixty-three inches—the Egyptian artist would give only seven inches to her head and neck, but thirty-seven to her body from the top of the shoulders to the top of the knee-cap, and the other nineteen to the length from the knee-cap to the soles of the feet. The head is extraordinarily small, and we need to remember that in art a small head has usually been held to give dignity to a figure. The ideal Egyptian woman possessed long, lustrous and often dark-blue eyes. Women painted their lids with kohl, a black substance, partly as a precaution against the glare of the African sun. They frequently also drew dark formal lines from the outside corner of the eye almost to the ear: and at an early period some women (of the Old Kingdom) used green paint on the underlid. The ears of these earliest of civilised women are usually too long for our liking. The nose most often is small, slightly upturned and a little broad at the tip. The lips are invariably full and sensuous, and as a rule they were painted. The chin is small and round; and the jaw-line curves gracefully from the ear to the chin.

An Egyptian woman's arms are long and slender, but a deficiency of muscle leaves them too straight. Her fingers also are long, and the upper class carefully painted their nails. The wide, handsome shoulders of these women are remarkable. Sloping shoulders seem to be quite unknown. Now, according to Ploss and Bartels in their monumental work called *Woman,* there are four breast-forms—the bowl-shaped, the hemispherical, the conical and the elongated. The Egyptians had so keen an appreciation of the comely breasts that "beautiful breasts and abundant hair" (I am quoting Ebers) "symbolize the supreme loveliness of women in their eyes. Thus, they celebrated not only the face but the breasts of Hathor . . . and when her image was born in procession . . . two acts of the festive ritual were the unveiling of her bosom and its display to the worshippers." Most Egyptian women of the best periods are represented as having bowl-shaped breasts, but later, as in Cleopatra herself, the breasts are "conical," in fact almost pear-shaped.

The waist is naturally slender, alike in women and in men, and only at the very late period do the hips become broad. The legs, like the arms, are long, but they lack the rippling look which muscles give to the skin. It is in their feet, large and squat, that these women are at their worst.

The woman whom we are to remember is one who lived about 1380 B.C. Her name, Nefertiti, meant "the Beautiful One has Come," and she was the wife of the revolutionary Pharaoh, Akhnaton, who vigorously attempted to transform the sacrosanct religion and art of his country. It is interesting also to realise that the now-famous Tut-ankh-amun was his son-in-law.

Now, Nefert was a handsome bourgeoise, but Nefertiti is the perfect example of an aristocrat. Her modern fame is due mostly to a painted limestone head which is in the Berlin Museum. One of the eyes was never inserted, and we may therefore suppose that the head is "the Sculptor's life-study for the Queen's statue." This lady is herself a proof of the high civilisation of what is called the "Middle Kingdom." People of our own time have responded to this face because of its air of poetry, its indications of exquisite sensibility and fine breeding.

Nefertiti had long, languorous eyes, a delicate nose, a fastidious mouth, an out-thrust, pointed chin and a lovely jaw-line which any woman might envy. One authority goes so far as to say that her portraits, "when young, prove her to have been one of the most beautiful women of any period of the world's history," a verdict with which few persons will quarrel.

Artists, during her husband's reign, were suddenly encouraged to break away from four thousand years of stiff tradition and to work "naturalistically." There is, for example, a delightful painting which shows the queen sitting on her husband's knees—a picture which must have been a nine days' wonder; but, remembering her youthful elegance, it is with an ancient sorrow that we come upon a picture of Nefertiti in later life which shows how her graceful figure collapsed.

Although the women of Egypt, during thousands of years, had to content themselves with the simplest of costumes, they could delight in a variety of lovely ornaments. The upper-class woman, when they went to dinner-parties or religious festivals, wore wreaths or coloured ribbons on their heads, anklets and bracelets of copper and gold, and those broad semi-circular bead-collars which illustrate so well the Egyptians' genius for colour and design. They also "used many kinds of perfume, above all one well-known to the Greeks, the *kyphi,* consisting of myrrh, broom, frankincense, buck's-horn and several other ingredients."

Again, Maspéro tells us that "silver and electrum . . . are brought by the Phoenicians and Ethiopians. . . . Emeralds, jasper, olivine, garnets, rubies and cornelians are found in Egypt itself. The lapis-lazuli is imported by Chaldean merchants from the unknown and most fabulous regions bordered by Elam." They had also mirrors of bronze, carved ivory combs, rings, earrings and brilliant necklaces. Moreover, they knew a hundred arts of the toilet. In the British Museum, and no doubt elsewhere, we may find little shallow spoons in the form of a naked swimming girl, who, as it were, offers the paint or the perfume to her mistress. There is also a picture that shows a lady at a dinner-party who holds balanced upon the crown of her black wig a ball which is flattened at the base. It was filled with sweet-smelling oil which percolated slowly on to the wig and so kept it continually fragrant.

In the art of elegant living, the women of ancient Egypt could have held their own with any of the women who were destined to show themselves on the stage of the world during the many centuries which had still to unfold their complicated stories.

The Beauty Myth

·ᴗ

A T LAST, AFTER a long silence, women took to the streets. In the two decades of radical action that followed the rebirth of feminism in the early 1970s, Western women gained legal and reproductive rights, pursued higher education, entered the trades and the professions, and overturned ancient and revered beliefs about their social role. A generation on, do women feel free?

The affluent, educated, liberated women of the First World, who can enjoy freedoms unavailable to any women ever before, do not feel as free as they want to. And they can no longer restrict to the subconscious their sense that this lack of freedom has something to do with—with apparently frivolous issues, things that should not matter. Many are ashamed to admit that such trivial concerns—to do with physical appear-

---

NAOMI WOLF'S *essays describing how images of beauty are used against women are collected in her 1991 book,* The Beauty Myth.

ance, bodies, faces, hair, clothes—matter so much. But in spite of shame, guilt, and denial, more and more women are wondering if it isn't that they are entirely neurotic and alone but rather that something important is indeed at stake that has to do with the relationship between female liberation and female beauty.

The more legal and material hindrances women have broken through, the more strictly and heavily and cruelly images of female beauty have come to weigh upon us. Many women sense that women's collective progress has stalled; compared with the heady momentum of earlier days, there is a dispiriting climate of confusion, division, cynicism, and above all, exhaustion. After years of much struggle and little recognition, many older women feel burned out; after years of taking its light for granted, many younger women show little interest in touching new fire to the torch.

During the past decade, women breached the power structure; meanwhile, eating disorders rose exponentially and cosmetic surgery became the fastest-growing medical specialty. During the past five years, consumer spending doubled, pornography became the main media category, ahead of legitimate films and records combined, and thirty-three thousand American women told researchers that they would rather lose ten to fifteen pounds than achieve any other goal. More women have more money and power and scope and legal recognition than we have ever had before; but in terms of how we feel about ourselves *physically*, we may actually be worse off than our unliberated grandmothers. Recent research consistently shows that inside the majority of the West's controlled, attractive, successful working women, there is a secret "underlife" poisoning our freedom; infused with notions of beauty, it is a dark vein of self-hatred, physical obsessions, terror of aging, and dread of lost control.

It is no accident that so many potentially powerful women feel this way. We are in the midst of a violent backlash against feminism that uses images of female beauty as a political weapon against women's advancement: the beauty myth. It is the modern version of a social reflex that has been in force since the Industrial Revolution. As women released themselves from the feminine mystique of domesticity, the beauty myth took over its lost ground, expanding as it waned to carry on its work of social control.

The contemporary backlash is so violent because the ideology of beauty is the last one remaining of the old feminine ideologies that still has the power to control those women whom second wave feminism would have otherwise made relatively uncontrollable: It has grown stronger to take over the work of social coercion that myths about motherhood, domesticity, chastity, and passivity, no longer can manage. It is seeking right now to undo psychologically and covertly all the good things that feminism did for women materially and overtly.

This counterforce is operating to checkmate the inheritance of feminism on every level in the lives of Western women. Feminism gave us laws against job discrimination based on gender; immediately case law evolved in Britain and the United States that institutionalized job discrimination based on women's appearances. Patriarchal religion declined; new religious dogma, using some of the mind-altering techniques of older cults and sects, arose around age and weight to functionally supplant traditional ritual. Feminists, inspired by Friedan, broke the stranglehold on the women's popular press of advertisers for household products, who were promoting the feminine mystique; at once, the diet and skin care industries became the new cultural censors of women's intellectual space, and because of their pressure, the gaunt, youthful model supplanted the happy housewife as the arbiter of successful womanhood. The sexual revolution promoted the discovery of female sexuality; "beauty pornography"—which for the first time in women's history artificially links a commodified "beauty" directly and explicitly to sexuality— invaded the mainstream to undermine women's new and vulnerable sense of sexual self-worth. Reproductive rights gave Western women control over our own bodies; the weight of fashion models plummeted to 23 percent below that of ordinary women, eating disorders rose exponentially, and a mass neurosis was promoted that used food and weight to strip women of that sense of control. Women insisted on politicizing health; new technologies of invasive, potentially deadly "cosmetic" surgeries developed apace to re-exert old forms of medical control of women.

Every generation since about 1830 has had to fight its version of the beauty myth. "It is very little to me," said the suffragist Lucy Stone in 1855, "to have the right to vote, to own property, etcetera, if I may not keep my body, and its uses, in my absolute right." Eighty years later, after women had won the vote, and the first wave of the organized women's movement had subsided, Virginia Woolf wrote that it would still be decades before women could tell the truth about their bodies. In 1962, Betty Friedan quoted a young woman trapped in the Feminine

Mystique: "Lately, I look in the mirror, and I'm so afraid I'm going to look like my mother." Eight years after that, heralding the cataclysmic second wave of feminism, Germaine Greer described "the Stereotype": "To her belongs all that is beautiful, even the very word beauty itself . . . she is a doll . . . I'm sick of the masquerade." In spite of the great revolution of the second wave, we are not exempt. Now we can look out over ruined barricades: A revolution has come upon us and changed everything in its path, enough time has passed since then for babies to have grown into women, but there still remains a final right not fully claimed.

The beauty myth tells a story: The quality called "beauty" objectively and universally exists. Women must want to embody it and men must want to possess women who embody it. This embodiment is an imperative for women and not for men, which situation is necessary and natural because it is biological, sexual, and evolutionary: Strong men battle for beautiful women, and beautiful women are more reproductively successful. Women's beauty must correlate to their fertility, and since this system is based on sexual selection, it is inevitable and changeless.

None of this is true. "Beauty" is a currency system like the gold standard. Like any economy, it is determined by politics, and in the modern age in the West it is the last, best belief system that keeps male dominance intact. In assigning value to women in a vertical hierarchy according to a culturally imposed physical standard, it is an expression of power relations in which women must unnaturally compete for resources that men have appropriated for themselves.

"Beauty" is not universal or changeless, though the West pretends that all ideals of female beauty stem from one Platonic Ideal Woman; the Maori admire a fat vulva, and the Padung, droopy breasts. Nor is "beauty" a function of evolution: Its ideals change at a pace far more rapid than that of the evolution of species, and Charles Darwin was himself unconvinced by his own explanation that "beauty" resulted from a "sexual selection" that deviated from the rule of natural selection; for women to compete with women through "beauty" is a reversal of the way in which natural selection affects all other mammals. Anthropology has overturned the notion that females must be "beautiful" to be selected to mate: Evelyn Reed, Elaine Morgan, and others have dismissed sociobiological assertions of innate male polygamy and female monogamy. Female higher primates are the sexual initiators; not only do they seek out and enjoy sex with many partners, but "every nonpregnant female takes her turn at being the most desirable of all her troop. And that cycle keeps turning as long as she lives." The inflamed pink sexual organs of primates are often cited by male sociobiologists as analogous to human arrangements relating to female "beauty," when in fact that is a universal, nonhierarchical female primate characteristic.

Nor has the beauty myth always been this way. Though the pairing of the older rich men with young, "beautiful" women is taken to be somehow inevitable, in the matriarchal Goddess religions that dominated the Mediterranean from about 25,000 B.C. to 700 B.C., the situation was reversed: "In every culture, the Goddess has many lovers. . . . The clear pattern is of an older woman with a beautiful but expendable youth—Ishtar and

Tammuz, Venus and Adonis, Cybele and Attis, Isis and Osiris . . . their only function the service of the divine 'womb.' " Nor is it something only women do and only men watch: Among the Nigerian Wodaabes, the women hold economic power and the tribe is obsessed with male beauty; Wodaabe men spend hours together in elaborate makeup sessions, and compete—provocatively painted and dressed, with swaying hips and seductive expressions—in beauty contests judged by women. There is no legitimate historical and biological justification for the beauty myth; what it is doing to women today is a result of nothing more exalted than the need of today's power structure, economy, and culture to mount a counteroffensive against women.

If the beauty myth is not based on evolution, sex, gender, aesthetics, or God, on what is it based? It claims to be about intimacy and sex and life, a celebration of women. It is actually composed of emotional distance, politics, finance, and sexual repression. The beauty myth is not about women at all. It is about men's institutions and institutional power.

The qualities that a given period calls beautiful in women are merely symbols of the female behavior that that period considers desirable: *The beauty myth is always actually prescribing behavior and not appearance.* Competition between women has been made part of the myth so that women will be divided from one another. Youth and (until recently) virginity have always been "beautiful" in women since they stand for experiential and sexual ignorance. Aging in women is "unbeautiful" since women grow more powerful with time, and since the links between generations of women must always be newly broken: Older women fear young ones, young women fear old, and the beauty myth truncates for all the female life span. Most urgently, women's identity must be premised upon our "beauty" so that we will remain vulnerable to outside approval, carrying the vital sensitive organ of self-esteem exposed to the air.

Though there has, of course, been a beauty myth in some form for as long as there has been patriarchy, the beauty myth in its modern form is a fairly recent invention. The myth flourishes when material constraints on women are dangerously loosened. Before the Industrial Revolution, the average woman could not have had the same feelings about "beauty" that modern women do who experience the myth as continual comparison to a mass-disseminated physical ideal. Before the development of technologies of mass production—daguerreotypes, photographs, etc.—an ordinary woman was exposed to few such images outside the Church. Since the family was a productive unit and women's work complemented men's, the value of women who were not aristocrats or prostitutes lay in their work skills, economic shrewdness, physical strength, and fertility. Physical attraction, obviously, played its part; but "beauty" as we understand it was not, for ordinary women, a serious issue in the marriage marketplace. The beauty myth in its modern form gained ground after the upheavals of industrialization, as the work unit of the family was destroyed, and urbanization and the emerging factory system demanded what social engineers of the time termed the "separate sphere" of domesticity, which supported the new labor category of the "breadwinner" who left home for the workplace during the day. The middle class expanded, the standards of living and of literacy rose, the size of families shrank; a new class of literate, idle women developed, on whose submission to enforce domesticity the evolving system of industrial capitalism depended. Most of our assumptions about the way women have always thought of "beauty" date from no earlier than the 1830s, when the cult of domesticity was first consolidated and the beauty index invented.

For the first time new technologies could reproduce—in fashion plates, daguerreotypes, tintypes, and rotogravures—images of how women should look. In the 1840s the first nude photographs of prostitutes were taken; advertisements using images of "beautiful" women first appeared in mid-century. Copies of classical artworks, postcards of society beauties and royal mistresses, Currier and Ives prints, and porcelain figurines flooded the separate sphere to which middle-class women were confined.

Since the Industrial Revolution, middle-class Western women have been controlled by ideals and stereotypes as much as by material constraints. This situation, unique to this group, means that analyzes that trace "cultural conspiracies" are uniquely plausible in relation to them. The rise of the beauty myth was just one of several emerging social fictions that masqueraded as natural components of the feminine sphere, the better to enclose those women inside it. Other such fictions arose contemporaneously: a version of childhood that required continual maternal supervision; a concept of female biology that required middle-class women to act out the roles of hysterics and hypochondriacs; a conviction that respectable women were sexually anasthetic; and a definition of women's work that occupied them with repetitive, time-consuming, and painstaking tasks such as needlepoint and lacemaking. All such Victorian inventions as these served a double function—that is, though they were encouraged as a means to expend female energy and intelligence in harmless ways, women often used them to express genuine creativity and passion.

But in spite of middle-class women's creativity with fashion and embroidery and child rearing, and, a century later, with the role of the suburban housewife that devolved from these social fictions, the fictions' main purpose was served: During a century and a half of unprecedented feminist agitation, they effectively counteracted middle-class women's dangerous new leisure, literacy, and relative freedom from material constraints.

Though these time- and mind-consuming fictions about women's natural role adapted themselves to resurface in the post-war Feminine Mystique, when the second wave of the women's movement took apart what women's magazines had portrayed as the "romance," "science," and "adventure" of homemaking and suburban family life, they temporarily failed. The cloying domestic fiction of "togetherness" lost its meaning and middle-class women walked out of their front doors in masses.

So the fictions simply transformed themselves once more: Since the women's movement had successfully taken apart most other necessary fictions of femininity, all the work of social control once spread out over the whole network of these fictions had to be reassigned to the only strand left intact, which action consequently strengthened it a hundredfold. This reimposed onto liberated women's faces and bodies all the limitations, taboos, and punishments of the repressive laws, religious injunctions and reproductive enslavement that no longer carried sufficient force. Inexhaustible but ephemeral beauty work took over from inexhaustible but ephemeral housework. As the economy, law, religion, sexual mores, education, and culture were forcibly opened up to include women more fairly, a private reality colonized female consciousness. By using ideas about "beauty," it reconstructed an alternative female world with its own laws, economy, religion, sexuality, education, and culture, each element as repressive as any that had gone before.

Since middle-class Western women can best be weakened psychologically now that we are stronger materially, the beauty myth, as it has resurfaced in the last generation, has had to draw on more technological sophistication and reactionary fervor than ever before. The modern arsenal of the myth is a dissemination of millions of images of the current ideal; although this barrage is generally seen as a collective sexual fantasy, there is in fact little that is sexual about it. It is summoned out of political fear on the part of male-dominated institutions threatened by women's freedom, and it exploits female guilt and apprehension about our own liberation—latent fears that we might be going too far. This frantic aggregation of imagery is a collective reactionary hallucination willed into being by both men and women stunned and disoriented by the rapidity with which gender relations have been transformed: a bulwark of reassurance against the flood of change. The mass depiction of the modern woman as a "beauty" is a contradiction: Where modern women are growing, moving, and expressing their individuality, as the myth has it, "beauty" is by definition inert, timeless, and generic. That this hallucination is necessary and deliberate is evident in the way "beauty" so directly contradicts women's real situation.

And the unconscious hallucination grows ever more influential and pervasive because of what is now conscious market manipulation: powerful industries—the $33-billion-a-year diet industry, the $20-billion cosmetics industry, the $300-million cosmetic surgery industry, and the $7-billion pornography industry—have arisen from the capital made out of unconscious anxieties, and are in turn able, through their influence on mass culture, to use, stimulate, and reinforce the hallucination in a rising economic spiral.

This is not a conspiracy theory; it doesn't have to be. Societies tell themselves necessary fictions in the same way that individuals and families do. Henrik Ibsen called them "vital lies," and psychologist Daniel Goleman describes them working the same way on the social level that they do within families: "The collusion is maintained by directing attention away from the fearsome fact, or by repackaging its meaning in an acceptable format." The costs of these social blind spots, he writes, are destructive communal illusions. Possibilities for women have become so open-ended that they threaten to destabilize the institutions on which a male-dominated culture has depended, and a collective panic reaction on the part of both sexes has forced a demand for counterimages.

The resulting hallucination materializes, for women, as something all too real. No longer just an idea, it becomes three-dimensional, incorporating within itself how women live and how they do not live: It becomes the Iron Maiden. The original Iron Maiden was a medieval German instrument of torture, a body-shaped casket painted with the limbs and features of a lovely, smiling young woman. The unlucky victim was slowly enclosed inside her; the lid fell shut to immobilize the victim, who died either of starvation or, less cruelly, of the metal spikes embedded in her interior. The modern hallucination in which women are trapped or trap themselves is similarly rigid, cruel, and euphemistically painted. Contemporary culture directs attention to imagery of the Iron Maiden, while censoring real women's faces and bodies.

Why does the social order feel the need to defend itself by evading the fact of real women, our faces and voices and bodies, and reducing the meaning of women to these formulaic and endlessly reproduced "beautiful" images? Though unconscious personal anxieties can be a powerful force in the creation of a vital lie, economic necessity practically guarantees it. An economy that depends on slavery needs to promote images of slaves that "justify" the institution of slavery. Western economies are absolutely dependent now on the continued underpayment of women. An ideology that makes women feel "worth less" was urgently needed to counteract the way feminism had begun to make us feel worth more. This does not require a conspiracy; merely an atmosphere. The contemporary economy depends right now on the representation of women within the beauty myth. Economist John Kenneth Galbraith offers an economic explanation for "the persistence of the view of homemaking as a 'higher calling'": the concept of women as naturally trapped within the Feminine Mystique, he feels, "has been forced on us by popular sociology, by magazines, and by fiction to disguise the fact that woman in her role of consumer has been essential to the development of our industrial society. . . . Behavior that is essential for economic reasons is transformed into a social virtue." As soon as a woman's primary social value could no longer be defined as the attainment of virtuous domesticity, the beauty myth redefined it was the attainment of virtuous beauty. It did so to substitute both a new consumer imperative and a new justification for economic unfairness in the workplace where the old ones had lost their hold over newly liberated women.

Another hallucination arose to accompany that of the Iron Maiden: The caricature of the Ugly Feminist was resurrected to dog the steps of the women's movement. The caricature is unoriginal; it was coined to ridicule the feminists of the nineteenth century. Lucy Stone herself, whom supporters saw as "a prototype of womanly grace . . . fresh and fair as the morning," was derided by detractors with "the usual report" about Victorian feminists: "a big masculine woman, wearing boots, smoking a cigar, swearing like a trooper." As Betty Friedan put it presciently in 1960, even before the savage revamping of that old caricature: "The unpleasant image of feminists today resembles less the feminists themselves than the image fostered by the interests who so bitterly opposed the vote for women in state after state." Thirty years on, her conclusion is more true than ever: That resurrected caricature, which sought to punish women for their public acts by going after their private sense of self, became the paradigm for new limits placed on aspiring women everywhere. After the success of the women's movement's second wave, the beauty myth was perfected to checkmate power at every level in individual women's lives. The modern neuroses of life in the female body spread to woman after woman at epidemic rates. The myth is undermining—slowly, imperceptibly, without our being aware of the real forces of erosion—the ground women have gained through long, hard, honorable struggle.

The beauty myth of the present is more insidious than any mystique of femininity yet: A century ago, Nora slammed the door of the doll's house; a generation ago, women turned their backs on the consumer heaven of the isolated multiapplianced home; but where women are trapped today, there is no door to slam. The contemporary ravages of the beauty backlash are destroying women physically and depleting us psychologically. If we are to free ourselves from the dead weight that has once again been made out of femaleness, it is not ballots or lobbyists or placards that women will need first; it is a new way to see.

⌣

Beyond the Beauty Myth

Can we bring about another future, in which it is she who is dead and we who are beautifully alive?

The beauty myth countered women's new freedoms by transposing the social limits to women's lives directly onto our faces and bodies. In response, we must now ask the questions about our place in our bodies that women a generation ago asked about their place in society.

What is a woman? Is she what is made of her? Do a woman's life and experience have value? If so, should she be ashamed for them to show? What *is* so great about looking young?

The idea that a woman's body has boundaries that must not be violated is fairly new. We evidently haven't taken it far enough. Can we extend that idea? Or are women the pliable sex, innately adapted to being shaped, cut, and subjected to physical invasion? Does the female body deserve the same notion of integrity as the male body? Is there a difference between fashions in clothing and fashions in women's bodies? Assuming that someday women can be altered cheaply, painlessly, and with no risk, is that to be what we must want? Must the expressiveness of maturity and old age become extinct? Will we lose nothing if it does?

Does a woman's identity count? Must she be made to want to look like someone else? Is there something implicitly gross about the texture of female flesh? The inadequacy of female flesh stands in for the older inadequacy of the female mind. Women asserted that there was nothing inferior about their minds; are our bodies really inferior?

Is "beauty" really sex? Does a woman's sexuality correspond to what she looks like? Does she have the right to sexual pleasure and self-esteem because she's a person, or must she earn that right through "beauty," as she used to through marriage? What is female sexuality—what does it look like? Does it bear any relation to the way in which commercial images represent it? Is it something women need to buy like a product? What really draws men and women together?

Are women beautiful or aren't we?

Of course we are. But we won't really believe it the way we need to until we start to take the first steps beyond the beauty myth.

Does all this mean we can't wear lipstick without feeling guilty?

On the contrary. It means we have to separate from the myth what it has surrounded and held hostage: female sexuality, bonding among women, visual enjoyment, sensual pleasure in fabrics and shapes and colors—female fun, clean and dirty. We can dissolve the myth and survive it with sex, love, attraction, and style not only intact, but flourishing more vibrantly than before. I am not attacking anything that makes women feel good; only what makes us feel bad in the first place. We all like to be desirable and feel beautiful.

But for about 160 years, middle-class, educated Western women have been controlled by various ideals about female perfection; this old and successful tactic has worked by taking the best of female culture and attaching to it the most repressive demands of male-dominated societies. These forms of ransom were imposed on the female orgasm in the 1920s, on home and children in the 1950s, on the culture of beauty in the 1980s. With this tactic, we waste time in every generation debating the symptoms more passionately than the disease.

We see this pattern of *the self-interested promotion of ideals*—eloquently pointed out in the work of Barbara Ehrenreich and Dierdre English—throughout our recent history. We must bring it up to date with the beauty myth, to get it once and for all. If we don't, as soon as we take apart the beauty myth, a new ideology will arise in its place. The beauty myth is not, ultimately, about appearance or dieting or surgery or cosmetics—any more that the Feminine Mystique was about housework. No one who is responsible for the myths of femininity in every generation really cares about the symptoms at all.

The architects of the Feminine Mystique didn't really believe that a floor in which you could see yourself indicated a cardinal virtue in women; in my own lifetime, when the idea of menstrual psychic irregularity was being clumsily resurrected as a last-ditch way to hold off the claims of the women's movement, no one was really vested in the conviction of menstrual incapacity *in itself*. By the same token, the beauty myth could not care less how much women weigh; it doesn't give a damn about the texture of women's hair or the smoothness of our skin. We intuit that, if we were all to go home tomorrow and say we never meant it really—we'll do without the jobs, the autonomy, the orgasms, the money—the beauty myth would slacken at once and grow more comfortable.

This realization makes the real issues behind the symptoms easier to see and analyze: Just as the beauty myth did not really care what women looked like as long as women felt ugly, we must see that it does not matter in the least what women look like as long as we feel beautiful.

The real issue has nothing to do with whether women wear makeup or don't, gain weight or lose it, have surgery or shun it, dress up or down, make our clothing and faces and bodies into works of art or ignore adornment altogether. *The real problem is our lack of choice.*

Under the Feminine Mystique, virtually all middle-class women were condemned to a compulsive attitude toward domesticity, whatever their individual inclinations; now that this idea is largely dismantled, those women who are personally inclined to scrupulous housekeeping pursue it, and those women who couldn't be less interested have a (relatively) greater degree of choice. We got sloppy, and the world didn't end. After we dismantle the beauty myth, a similar situation—so eminently sensible, yet so remote from where we are—will characterize our relationship to beauty culture.

The problem with cosmetics exists only when women feel invisible or inadequate without them. The problem with working out exists only if women hate ourselves when we don't. When a woman is forced to adorn herself to buy a hearing, when she needs her grooming in order to protect her identity, when she goes hungry in order to keep her job, when she must attract a lover so that she can take care of her children, that is exactly what makes "beauty" hurt. Because what hurts women about the beauty myth is not adornment, or expressed sexuality, or time spent grooming, or the desire to attract a lover. Many mammals groom, and every culture uses adornment. "Natural" and "unnatural" are not the terms in question. The actual struggle is between pain and pleasure, freedom and compulsion.

Costumes and disguises will be lighthearted and fun when women are granted rock-solid identities. Clothing that highlights women's sexuality will be casual wear when women's sexuality is under our own control. When female sexuality is fully affirmed as a legitimate passion that arises from within, to be directed without stigma to the chosen object of our desire, the sexually expressive clothes or manner we may assume can no longer be used to shame us, blame us, or target us for beauty myth harassment.

The beauty myth posited to women a false choice: Which will I be, sexual or serious? We must reject that false and forced dilemma. Men's sexuality is taken to be enhanced by their seriousness; to be at the same time a serious person and a sexual being is to be fully human. Let's turn on those who offer this devil's bargain and refuse to believe that in choosing one aspect of the self we must thereby forfeit the other. In a world in which women have real choices, the choices we make about our appearance will be taken at last for what they really are: no big deal.

Women will be able thoughtlessly to adorn ourselves with pretty objects when there is no question that *we* are not objects. Women will be free of the beauty myth when we can choose to use our faces and clothes and bodies as simply one form of self-expression out of a full range of others. We can dress up for our pleasure, but we must speak up for our rights.

Many writers have tried to deal with the problems of fantasy, pleasure, and "glamour" by evicting them from the female Utopia. But "glamour" is merely a demonstration of the human capacity for being enchanted, and is not in itself destructive. We need it, but redefined. We cannot disperse an exploitative religion through asceticism, or bad poetry with none at all. We can combat painful pleasure only with pure pleasure.

But let's not be naive. We are trying to make new meanings for beauty in an environment that doesn't want us to get away with it. To look however we want to look—and to be heard as we deserve to be heard—we will need no less than a feminist third wave.

Speech

The trouble with any debate about the beauty myth is the sophisticated reflex it uses: It punishes virtually any woman who tries to raise these issues by scrutinizing her appearance. It is striking to notice how thoroughly we comprehend this implied punishment. We know well how it works in a typical beauty myth double bind: No matter what a woman's appearance may be, it will be used to undermine what she is saying and taken to individualize—as her personal problem—observations she makes about aspects of the beauty myth in society.

Unfortunately, since the media routinely give accounts of women's appearance in a way that trivializes or discredits what they say, women reading or watching are routinely dissuaded from identifying with women in the public eye—the ultimate antifeminist goal of the beauty myth. Whenever we dismiss or do not hear a woman on television or in print because our attention has been drawn to her size or makeup or clothing or hairstyle, the beauty myth is working with optimum efficiency.

For a woman to go public means she must face being subjected to invasive physical scrutiny, which by definition, as we saw, no woman can pass; for a woman to speak about the beauty myth (as about women's issues in general) means that *there is no right way she can look*. There is no unmarked, or neutral, stance allowed women at those times: They are called either too "ugly" or too "pretty" to be believed. This reflex is working well politically: Often today, when women talk about the reasons they do not engage more with women-centered groups and movements, they often focus on differences not in agenda or worldview but in aesthetics and personal style. By keeping the antifeminist origins and reactionary purpose of this direction of attention always in mind, we can thwart the myth. For us to reject the insistence that a woman's appearance *is her speech*, for us to hear one another out beyond the beauty myth, is itself a political step forward.

Blame

Blame is what fuels the beauty myth; to take it apart, let us refuse forever to blame ourselves and other women for what it, in its great strength, has tried to do. The most important change to aim at is this: When someone tries, in the future, to use the beauty myth against us, we will no longer look in the mirror to see what we have done wrong. Women can organize around discrimination in employment on the basis of appearance only when we examine the usual reactions to such complaints ("Well, why did you wear that tight sweater?" "So, why don't you do something about yourself?") and reject them. We cannot speak up about the myth until we believe in our guts that there is nothing objective about how the myth works—that when women are called too ugly or too pretty to do something we want to do, this has nothing to do with our appearance. Women can summon the courage to talk about the myth in public by keeping in mind that attacks on or flattery of our appearance in public are never at fault. It is all impersonal; it is political.

The reflexive responses that have developed to keep us silent will doubtless increase in intensity: "Easy for you to say." "You're too pretty to be a feminist." "No wonder she's a feminist; look at her." "What does she expect, dressed like that?" "That's what comes of vanity." "What makes you think they were whistling at you?" "What was she wearing?" "Don't you wish." "Don't flatter yourself." "There's no excuse any more for a woman to look her age." "Sour grapes?" "A bimbo." "Brainless." "She's using it for all she can get." Recognizing these reactions for what they are, it may be easier to brave coercive flattery or insults or both, and make some long-overdue scenes.

This will be hard. Talking about the beauty myth strikes a nerve which, for most of us, is on some level very raw. We will need to have compassion for ourselves and other women for our strong feelings about "beauty," and be very gentle with those feelings. If the beauty myth is religion, it is because women still lack rituals that include us; if it is economy, it is because we're still compensated unfairly; if it is sexuality, it is because female sexuality is still a dark continent; if it is warfare, it is because women are denied ways to see ourselves as heroines, daredevils, stoics, and rebels; if it is women's culture, it is because men's culture still resists us. When we recognize that the myth is powerful because it has claimed so much of the best of female consciousness, we can turn from it to look more clearly at all it has tried to stand in for.

A Feminist Third Wave

So here we are. What can we do?

We must dismantle the PBQ; support the unionization of women's jobs; make "beauty" harassment, age discrimination, unsafe working conditions such as enforced surgery, and the double standard for appearance, issues for labor negotiation; women in television and other heavily discriminatory professions must organize for wave after wave of lawsuits; we must insist on equal enforcement of dress codes, take a deep breath, and tell our stories.

It is often said that we must make fashion and advertising images include us, but this is a dangerously optimistic misunderstanding of how the market works. Advertising aimed at women works by lowering our self-esteem. If it flatters our self-esteem, it is not effective. Let's abandon this hope of looking to the index fully to include us. It won't, because if it does, it has lost its function. As long as the definition of "beauty" comes from outside women, we will continue to be manipulated by it.

We claimed the freedom to age and remain sexual, but that rigidified into the condition of aging "youthfully." We began to wear comfortable clothing, but the discomfort settled back onto our bodies. The seventies' "natural" beauty became its own icon; the 1980s' "healthy" beauty brought about an epidemic of new diseases and "strength as beauty" enslaved women to our muscles. This process will continue with every effort women make to reform the index until we change our relationship to the index altogether.

The marketplace is not open to consciousness-raising. It is misplaced energy to attack the market's images themselves: Given recent history, they were bound to develop as they did.

While we cannot directly affect the images, we can drain them of their power. We can turn away from them, look directly at one another, and find alternative images of beauty in a female subculture; seek out the plays, music, films that illuminate women in three dimensions; find the biographies of women, the women's history, the heroines that in each generation are submerged from view; fill in the terrible, "beautiful" blanks. We can lift ourselves and other women out of the myth—but only if we are willing to seek out and support and really look at the alternatives.

Since our imaginary landscape fades to gray when we try to think past the myth, women need cultural help to imagine our way free. For most of our history, the representation of women, our sexuality and our true beauty, has not been in our hands. After just twenty years of the great push forward, during which time women sought to define those things for ourselves, the marketplace, more influential than any solitary artist, has seized the definition of our desire. Shall we let women-hating images claim our sexuality for their royalties? We need to insist on making culture out of our desire: making paintings, novels, plays, and films potent and seductive and authentic enough to undermine and overwhelm the Iron Maiden. Let's expand our culture to separate sex from the Iron Maiden.

We'll need to remember, at the same time, how heavily censored our mass culture is by beauty advertisers: As long as primetime TV and the mainstream press aimed at women are supported by beauty advertisers, the story line of how women are in mass culture will be dictated by the beauty myth. It is understood without directives that stories that center admiringly on an "unprocessed" woman will rarely get made. If we could see a sixty-year-old woman who looks her age read the news, a deep fissure would open in the beauty myth. Meanwhile, let's be clear that the myth rules the airwaves *only* because the products of the process buy the time.

Finally, we can keep our analytical gaze always sharp; being aware of what shapes the Iron Maiden can affect how we see, absorb, and respond to her images. Quickly, with this consciousness, they begin to look like what they are—two-dimensional. They literally fall flat. It is when they become tedious to us that they will evolve to *adapt* to the sea change in women's moods; an advertiser can't influence a story line if there is no audience. Responding to sheer boredom on women's part, creators of culture will be forced to present three-dimensional images of women in order to involve us again. Women can provoke, through our sudden boredom with the Iron Maiden, a mass culture that does in fact treat us like people.

In transforming the cultural environment, women who work in the mainstream media are a crucial inside vanguard. I have heard many women in the media express frustration at the limitations surrounding the treatment of beauty myth issues; many report a sense of isolation in relation to pushing those limits. Perhaps debate renewed in more political terms about the beauty myth in the media, and the seriousness of its consequences, will forge new alliances in support of those women in print and TV and radio journalism who are eager to battle the beauty myth at ground zero.

Quickly, when we put together a personal counterculture of meaningful images of beauty, the Iron Maiden begins to look like an image of unattractive violence; alternative ways to see start to leap out from the background.

"Rosemary Fell was not exactly beautiful. No, you couldn't have called her beautiful. Pretty? Well, if you took her to pieces . . . . But why be so cruel as to take anyone to pieces?" (Katherine Mansfield); "To Lily her beauty seemed a senseless thing, since it gained her nothing in the way of passion, release, kinship, or intimacy. . . ." (Jane Smiley); "She was astonishingly beautiful . . . . Beauty had this penalty—it came too readily, came too completely. It stilled life—froze it. One forgot the little agitations; the flush, the pallor, some queer distortion, some light or shadow, which made the face unrecognizable for a moment and yet added a quality one saw forever after. It was simpler to smooth that all out under the cover of beauty. . . ." (Virginia Woolf); "If there is anything behind a face, that face improves with age. Lines show distinction and character: they show that one has lived, that one may know something." (Karen de Crow); "Though she was now over fifty . . . it was easy to credit all one had heard about the passions she had inspired. People who have been much loved retain even in old age a radiating quality difficult to describe but unmistakable. Even a stone that has been blazed on all day will hold heat after nightfall . . . this warm radiance." (Dame Ethyl Smyth).

The beauty cult attests to a spiritual hunger for female ritual and rites of passage. We need to develop and elaborate better women's rituals to fill in the void. Can we evolve more widely among friends, among networks of friends, fruitful new rites and celebrations for the female life cycle? We have baby showers and bridal showers, but what about purification, confirmation, healing, and renewal ceremonies for childbirth, first menstruation, loss of virginity, graduation, first job, marriage, recovery from heart-break or divorce, the earning of a degree, menopause? Whatever organic form they take, we need new and positive, rather than negative, celebrations to mark the female lifespan.

To protect our sexuality from the beauty myth, we can believe in the importance of cherishing, nurturing, and attending to our sexuality as to an animal or a child. Sexuality is not inert or given but, like a living being, changes with what it feeds upon. We can stay away from gratuitously sexually violent or exploitive images—and when we do encounter them, ask ourselves to feel them as such. We can seek out those dreams and visions that include a sexuality free of exploitation or violence, and try to stay as conscious of what we take into our imaginations as we now are of what enters our bodies.

An eroticism of equality may be hard to visualize now. Critiques of sexuality tend to stop short with the assumption that sexuality cannot evolve. But for most women, fantasies of objec-tification or violence are learned superficially through a patina of images. I believe that they can be as easily unlearned by con-sciously reversing our conditioning—by making the repeated association between pleasure and mutuality. Our ideas of sexual beauty are open to more transformation that we yet realize.

We need, especially for the anorexic/pornographic gener-ations, a radical rapprochement with nakedness. Many women have described the sweeping revelation that follows even one experience of communal all-female nakedness. This is an easy suggestion to mock, but the fastest way to demystify the naked Iron Maiden is to promote retreats, festivals, excursions, that include—whether in swimming or sunning or Turkish baths or random relaxation—communal nakedness. Men's groups, from fraternities to athletic clubs, understand the value, the cohesiveness, and the esteem for one's own gender generated by such moments. A single revelation of the beauty of our infinite variousness is worth more than words; one such experience is strong enough, for a young girl, especially, to give the lie to the Iron Maiden.

When faced with the myth, the questions to ask are not about women's faces and bodies but about the power relations of the situation. Who is this serving? Who says? Who profits? What is the context? When someone discusses a woman's appearance to her face, she can ask herself, Is it that person's business? Are the power relations equal? Would she feel comfortable making the same personal comments in return?

A woman's appearance is more often called to her attention for a political reason than as a constituent of genuine attraction and desire. We can learn to get better at telling the difference—a liberating skill in itself. We need not condemn lust, seduction, or physical attraction—a much more democratic and subjective quality than the market would like us to discover—we need only to reject political manipulation.

The irony is that more beauty promises what only more female solidarity can deliver: The beauty myth can be defeated for good only through an electric resurgence of the woman-centered political activism of the seventies—a feminist third wave—updated to take on the new issues of the nineties. In this decade, for young women in particular, some of the enemies are quieter and cleverer and harder to grasp. To enlist young women, we'll need to define our self-esteem as political: to rank it, along with money, jobs, child care, safety, as a vital resource for women that is *deliberately* kept in inadequate supply.

I don't pretend to have the agenda; I know only that some of the problems have changed. I've become convinced that there are thousands of young women ready and eager to join forces with a peer-driven feminist third wave that would take on, along with the classic feminist agenda, the new problems that have arisen with the shift in *Zeitgeist* and the beauty backlash. The movement would need to deal with the ambiguities of assimilation. Young women express feelings of being scared and isolated "insiders" as opposed to angry and united outsiders, and this distinction makes backlash sense: The best way to stop a revolution is to give people something to lose. It would need to politicize eating disorders, young women's uniquely intense relationship to images, and the effect of those images on their sexuality—it would need to make the point that you don't have much of a right over your own body if you can't eat. It would need to analyze the antifeminist propaganda young women have inherited, and give them tools, including arguments like this one, with which to see through it. While transmitting the previous heritage of feminism intact, it would need to be, as all feminist waves are, peer-driven: No matter how wise a mother's advice is, we listen to our peers. It would have to make joy, rowdiness, and wanton celebration as much a part of its project as hard work and bitter struggle, and it can begin all this by rejecting the pernicious fib that is crippling young women—the fib called postfeminism, the pious hope that the battles have all been won. This scary word is making young women, who face many of the same old problems, once again blame themselves—since it's all been fixed, right? It strips them of the weapon of theory and makes them feel alone once again. We never speak complacently of the post-Democratic era: Democracy, we know, is a living, vulnerable thing that every generation must renew. The same goes for that aspect of democracy represented by feminism. So let's get on with it.

Women learned to crave "beauty" in its contemporary form because we were learning at the same time that the feminist struggle was going to be much harder than we had realized. The ideology of "beauty" was a shortcut promise to agitating women—a historical placebo—that we could be confident, valued, heard out, respected, and make demands without fear. (In fact, it is doubtful whether "beauty" is the real desire at all; women may want "beauty" so that we can get back inside their bodies, and crave perfection so that we can forget about the whole damn thing. Most women, in their guts, would probably rather be, given the choice, a sexual, courageous self than a beautiful generic Other.)

Beauty advertising copy promises that sort of courage and freedom—"Beachwear for the beautiful and brave"; "A fresh, fearless look," "A funky fearlessness"; "Think radical"; "The Freedom Fighters—for the woman who isn't afraid to speak up or stand out." But this courage and confidence will not be real until we are backed by the material gains that we can achieve only by seeing other women as allies rather than as competitors.

The 1980s tried to buy us off with promises of individual

solutions. We have reached the limit of what the individualist, beauty-myth version of female progress can do, and it is not good enough: We will be 2 percent of top management and 5 percent of full professors and 5 percent of senior partners forever if we do not get together for the next great push forward. Higher cheekbones and firmer bustlines clearly won't get us what we need for real confidence and visibility; only a renewed commitment to the basics of female political progress—to child-care programs, effective antidiscrimination laws, parental leave, reproductive choice, fair compensation, and genuine penalties against sexual violence—will do so. We won't have these until we can identify our interests in other women's, and allow our natural solidarity to overcome the organizational obstacles put forward by the competitiveness and rivalry artificially provoked among us by the beauty backlash.

The terrible truth is that though the marketplace promotes the myth, it would be powerless if women didn't enforce it against one another. For any one woman to outgrow the myth, she needs the support of many women. The toughest but most necessary change will come not from men or from the media, but from women, in the way we see and behave toward other women.

Generational Collaboration

The links between generations of women need mending if we are to save one another from the beauty myth, and save women's progress from its past historical fate—the periodic reinvention of the wheel. Gill Hudson, editor of *Company*, reveals the extent to which beauty backlash has propagandized the young: Young women, she says, "absolutely don't want to be known as feminists" because "feminism is not considered sexy." It would be stupid and sad if the women of the near future had to fight the same old battles all over again from the beginning just because of young women's isolation from older women. It would be pathetic if young women had to go back to the beginning because we were taken in by an unoriginal twenty-year campaign to portray the women's movement as "not sexy," a campaign aimed to help young women forget whose battles made sex sexy in the first place.

Since young women will not be encouraged by our institutions to make the connections, we can get past the myth only by actively exploring more useful role models than the glossies give us. We are sorely in need of intergenerational contact: We need to see the faces of the women who made our freedom possible; they need to hear our thanks. Young women are dangerously "unmothered"—unprotected, unguided—institutionally and need role models and mentors. The work and experience of older women gain scope and influence when imparted to students, apprentices, protégés. Yet, both generations will have to resist their externally ingrained impulses against intergenerational collaboration. We are well trained, if young, to shy away from identification with older women; if older, at being a little hard on young women, viewing them with impatience and disdain. The beauty myth is designed artificially to pit the generations of women against one another; our consciously strengthening those links gives back the wholeness of our lifespans that the beauty myth would keep us from discovering.

Divide and Conquer

The fact is, women are not actually dangerous to one another. Outside the myth, other women look a lot like natural allies. In order for women to learn to fear one another, we had to be convinced that our sisters possess some kind of mysterious, potent secret weapon to be used against us—the imaginary weapon being "beauty."

The core of the myth—and the reason it was so useful as a counter to feminism—is its divisiveness. You can see and hear it everywhere: 'Don't hate me because I'm beautiful" (L'Oréal). "I really hate my aerobics instructor—I guess hatred is good motivation." "You'd hate her. She has everything." "Women who get out of bed looking beautiful really annoy me." "Don't you hate women who can eat like that?" "No pores—makes you sick." "Tall, blonde—couldn't you just kill her?" Rivalry, resentment, and hostility provoked by the beauty myth run deep. Sisters commonly remember the grief of one being designated "the pretty one." Mothers often have difficulty with their daughters' blooming. Jealousy among the best of friends is a cruel fact of female love. Even women who are lovers describe beauty competition. It is painful for women to talk about beauty because under the myth, one woman's body is used to hurt another. Our faces and bodies become instruments for punishing other women, often used out of our control and against our will. At present, "beauty" is an economy in which women find the "value" of their faces and bodies impinging, in spite of themselves, on that of other women's.

This constant comparison, in which one woman's worth fluctuates through the presence of another, divides and conquers. It forces women to be acutely critical of the "choices" other women make about how they look. But that economy that pits women against one another is not inevitable.

To get past this divisiveness, women will have to break a lot of taboos against talking about it, including the one that prohibits women from narrating the dark side of being treated as a beautiful object. From the dozens of women to whom I have listened, it is clear that the amount of pain a given woman experiences through the beauty myth bears no relationship at all to what she looks like relative to a cultural ideal. (In the words of a top fashion model, "When I was on the cover of the Italian *Vogue*, everyone told me how great I looked. I just thought, 'I can't believe you can't see all those lines.'") Women who impersonate the Iron Maiden may be no less victimized by the myth than the women subjected to their images. The myth asks women to be at once blindly hostile to and blindly envious of "beauty" in other women. Both the hostility and the envy serve the myth and hurt all women.

While the "beautiful" woman is briefly at the apex of the system, this is, of course, far from the divine state of grace that the myth propagates. The pleasure to be had from turning oneself into a living art object, the roaring in the ears and the fine jetspray of regard on the surface of the skin, is some kind of power, when power is in short supply. But it is not much compared to the pleasure of getting back forever inside the body; the pleasure of discovering sexual pride, a delight in a common female sexuality that overwhelms the divisions of "beauty"; the pleasure of shedding self-consciousness and narcissism and guilt like a chainmail gown; the pleasure of the freedom to forget all about it.

Only then will women be able to talk about what "beauty" really involves: the attention of people we do not know, rewards for things we did not earn, sex from men who reach for us as for a brass ring on a carousel, hostility and skepticism from other women, adolescence extended longer than it ought to be, cruel aging, and a long hard struggle for identity. And we will learn that what is good about "beauty"—the promise of confidence, sexuality, and the self-regard of a healthy individuality—are actually qualities that have nothing to do with "beauty" specifically, but are deserved by and, as the myth is dismantled, available to all women. The best that "beauty" offers belongs to us all by right of femaleness. When we separate "beauty" from sexuality, when we celebrate the individuality of our features and characteristics, women will have access to a pleasure in our bodies that unites us rather than divides us. The beauty myth will be history.

But as long as women censor in one another the truths about our experiences, "beauty" will remain mystified and still most useful to those who wish to control women. The unacceptable reality is that we live under a caste system. It is not innate and permanent; it is not based on sex or God or the Rock of Ages. It can and must be changed. The situation is closing in on us, and there is no long term left to which to postpone the conversation.

When the conversation commences, the artificial barriers of the myth will begin to fall away. We will hear that just because a woman looks "beautiful" doesn't mean she feels it, and she can feel beautiful without looking it at first glance. Thin women may feel fat; young women will grow old. When one woman looks at another, she cannot possibly know the self-image within that woman: Though she appears enviably in control, she may be starving; though she overflow her clothing, she may be enviably satisfied sexually. A woman may be fleshy from high self-esteem or from low; she may cover her face in makeup out of the desire to play around outrageously or the desire to hide. All women have experienced the world treating them better or worse according to where they rate each day: while this experience wreaks havoc with a woman's identity, it does mean that women have access to a far greater range of experience than the snapshots "beauty" takes of us would lead us to believe. We may well discover that the way we now read appearances tells us little, and that we experience, no matter what we look like, the same spectrum of feelings: sometimes lovely, often unlovely, always female, in a commonality that extends across the infinite grids that the beauty myth tries to draw among us.

Women blame men for looking but not listening. But we do it too; perhaps even more so. We have to stop reading each others' appearances as if appearance were language, political allegiance, worthiness, or aggression. The chances are excellent that what a woman mens to say *to other women* is far more complex and sympathetic that the garbled message that her appearance permits her.

Let us start with a reinterpretation of "beauty" that is *noncompetitive, non hierarchical, and nonviolent.* Why must one woman's pleasure and pride have to mean another woman's pain? Men are only in sexual competition when they are competing sexually, but the myth puts women in "sexual" competition in every situation. Competition for a specific sexual partner is rare; since it is not usually a competition "for men," it is not biologically inevitable.

Women compete this way "for other women" partly because we are devotees of the same sect, and partly to fill, if only temporarily, the black hole that the myth created in the first place. Hostile competition can often be proof of what our current sexual arrangements repress: our mutual physical attraction. If women redefine sexuality to affirm our attraction among ourselves, the myth will no longer hurt. Other women's beauty will not be a threat or an insult, but a pleasure and a tribute. Women will be able to costume and adorn ourselves without fear of hurting and betraying other women, or of being accused of false loyalties. We can then dress up in celebration of the shared pleasure of the female body, doing it "for other women" in a positive rather than a negative offering of the self.

And when we let ourselves experience this physical attraction, the marketplace will no longer be able to make a profit out of its representation of men's desires: We, knowing firsthand that attraction to other women comes in many forms, will no longer believe that the qualities that make us desirable are a lucrative mystery.

By changing our prejudgments of one another, we have the means for the beginning of a noncompetitive experience of beauty. The "other woman" is represented through the myth as an unknown danger. "Meet the Other Woman," reads a Wella hair-coloring brochure, referring to the "after" version of the woman targeted. The idea is that "beauty" makes *another* woman—even one's own idealized image—into a being so alien that you need a formal introduction. It is a phrase that suggests threats, mistresses, glamorous destroyers of relationships.

We undo the myth by approaching the unknown Other Woman. Since women's everyday experiences of flirtatious attention derive most often from men reacting to our "beauty," it is no wonder that silent, watching women can be represented to us as antagonists.

We can melt this suspicion and distance: Why should we not be gallant and chivalrous and flirtatious with one another. Let us charm one another with some of that sparkling attention too often held in reserve only for men: compliment one another, show our admiration. We can engage with the Other Woman— catch her eye, give her a lift when she is hitchhiking, open the door when she is struggling. When we approach one another in the street and give, or receive, that wary, defensive shoes-to-hair-cut glance, what if we meet one another's eyes woman to woman; what if we smile.

This movement toward a noncompetitive idea of beauty is already underway. The myth has always denied women honor. Here and there, women are evolving codes of honor to protect us from it. We withhold easy criticism. We shower authentic praise. We bow out of social situations in which our beauty is being used to put other women in the shadows. We refuse to jostle for random male attention. A contestant in the 1989 Miss California Pageant pulls a banner from her swimsuit that reads PAGEANTS HURT ALL WOMEN. A film actress tells me that when she did a nude scene, she refused, as a gesture to women in the audience, to discipline her body first. We are already beginning to find ways in which we won't be rivals and we won't be instruments.

This new perspective changes not how we look but how we see. We begin to see other women's faces and bodies for themselves, the Iron maiden no longer superimposed. We catch our breath when we see a woman laughing. We cheer inside when we see a woman walk proud. We smile in the mirror, watch the lines form at the corners of our eyes, and, pleased with what we are making, smile again.

Though women can give this new perspective to one another, men's participation in overturning the myth is welcome. Some men, certainly, have used the beauty myth abusively against women, the way some men use their fists; but there is a strong consciousness among both sexes that the real agents enforcing the myth today are not men as individual lovers or husbands, but institutions, that depend on male dominance. Both sexes seem to be finding that the full force of the myth derives little from private sexual relations, and much from the cultural and economic megalith "out there" in the public realm. Increasingly, both sexes know they are being cheated.

But helping women to take the myth apart is in men's own interest on an even deeper level: Their turn is next. Advertisers have recently figured out that undermining sexual self-confidence works whatever the targeted gender. According to *The Guardian*, "Men are now looking at mirrors instead of at girls. . . . Beautiful men can now be seen selling everything." Using images from male homosexual subculture, advertising has begun to portray the male body in a beauty myth of its own. As this imagery focuses more closely on male sexuality, it will undermine the sexual self-esteem of men in general. Since men are more conditioned to be separate from their bodies, and to compete to inhuman excess, the male version could conceivably hurt men even more than the female version hurts women.

Psychiatrists are anticipating a rise in male rates of eating diseases. Now that men are being cast as a frontier market to be opened up by self-hatred, images have begun to tell heterosexual men the same half-truths about what women want and how they see that they have traditionally told heterosexual women about men; if they buy it and become trapped themselves, that will be no victory for women. No one will win.

But it is also in men's interest to undo the myth because the survival of the planet depends on it. The earth can no longer afford a consumer ideology based on the insatiable wastefulness of sexual and material discontent. We need to begin to get lasting satisfaction out of the things we consume. We conceived of the planet as female, an all-giving Mother Nature, just as we conceived of the female body, infinitely alterable by and for man; we serve both ourselves and our hopes for the planet by insisting on a new female reality on which to base a new metaphor for the earth: the female body with its own organic integrity that must be respected.

The environmental crisis demands a new way of thinking that is communitarian, collective and not adversarial, and we need it fast. We can pray and hope that male institutions evolve this sophisticated, unfamiliar way of thinking within a few short years; or we can turn to the female tradition, which has perfected it over five millennia, and adapt it to the public sphere. Since the beauty myth blots out the female tradition, we keep a crucial option for the planet open when we resist it.

And we keep options open for ourselves. We do not need to change our bodies, we need to change the rules. Beyond the myth, women will still be blamed for our appearances by whomever needs to blame us. So let's stop blaming ourselves and stop running and stop apologizing, and let's start to please ourselves once and for all. The "beautiful" woman does not win under the myth; neither does anyone else. the woman who is subjected to the continual adulation of strangers does not win, nor does the woman who denies herself attention. The woman who wears a uniform does not win, not does the woman with a designer outfit for every day of the year. You do not win by struggling to the top of a caste system, you win by refusing to be trapped within one at all. The woman wins who calls herself beautiful and challenges the world to change to truly see her.

A woman wins by giving herself and other women permission—to eat; to be sexual; to age; to wear overalls, a paste tiara, a Balenciaga gown, a second-hand opera cloak, or combat boots; to cover up or to go practically naked; to do whatever we choose in following—or ignoring—our own aesthetic. A woman wins when she feels that what each woman does with her own body—unforced, uncoerced—is her own business. When many individual women exempt themselves from the economy, it will begin to dissolve. Institutions, some men, and some women, will continue to try to use women's appearance against us. But we won't bite.

Can there be a pro-woman definition of beauty? Absolutely. What has been missing is play. The beauty myth is harmful and pompous and grave because so much, too much, depends upon it. The pleasure of playfulness is that it doesn't matter. Once you play for stakes of any amount, the game becomes a war game, or compulsive gambling. In the myth, it has been a game for life, for questionable love, for desperate and dishonest sexuality, and without the choice not to play by alien rules. No choice, no free will; no levity, no real game.

But we can imagine, to save ourselves, a life in the body that is not value-laden; a masquerade, a voluntary theatricality that emerges from abundant self-love. A pro-woman redefinition of beauty reflects our redefinitions of what power is. Who says we need a hierarchy? Where I see beauty may not be where you do. Some people look more desirable to me than they do to you. So what? My perception has no authority over yours. Why should beauty be exclusive? Admiration can include so much. Why is rareness impressive? The high value of rareness is a masculine concept, having more to do with capitalism than with lust. What is the fun in wanting the most what cannot be found? Children, in contrast, are common as dirt, but they are highly valued and regarded as beautiful.

How might women act beyond the myth? Who can say? Maybe we will let our bodies wax and wane, enjoying the variations on a theme, and avoid pain because when something hurts us it begins to look ugly to us. Maybe we will adorn ourselves with real delight, with the sense that we are gilding the lily. Maybe the less pain women inflict on our bodies, the more beautiful our bodies will look to us. Perhaps we will forget to elicit admiration from strangers, and find we don't miss it; perhaps we will await our older faces with anticipation, and be unable to see our bodies as a mass of imperfections, since there is nothing on us that is not precious. Maybe we won't want to be the "after" anymore.

How to begin? Let's be shameless. Be greedy. Pursue pleasure. Avoid pain. Wear and touch and eat and drink what we feel like. Tolerate other women's choices. Seek out the sex we want and fight fiercely against the sex we do not want. Choose our own causes. And once we break through and change the rules so our sense of our own beauty cannot be shaken, sing that beauty and dress it up and flaunt it and revel in it: In a sensual politics, female is beautiful.

A woman-loving definition of beauty supplants desperation with play, narcissism with self-love, dismemberment with wholeness, absence with presence, stillness with animation. It admits radiance: light coming out of the face and the body, rather than a spotlight on the body, dimming the self. It is sexual, various, and surprising. We will be able to see it in others and not be frightened, and able at last to see it in ourselves.

A generation ago, Germaine Greer wondered about women: "What *will* you do?" What women did brought about a quarter century of cataclysmic social revolution. The next phase of our movement forward as individual women, as women together, and as tenants of our bodies and this planet, depends now on what we decide to see when we look in the mirror.

What *will* we see?

Beauty

·ᴖ

IN MY EXPERIENCE, an onset of beauty is marked by extremes of stimulation and relaxation. My mind is hyperalert. My body is at ease. Often I am aware of my shoulders coming down, as unconscious muscular tension lets go. My mood soars. I have a conviction of goodness in all things. I feel that everything is going to be all right. Later, I am pleasantly a little tired all over, as after swimming.

Mind and body become indivisible in beauty. Beauty teaches me that my brain is a physical organ and that intelligence is not limited to thought but entails feeling and sensation, the whole organism in concert. Centrally involved is a subtle hormonal excitation in or about the heart—the muscular organ, not the metaphor.

Beauty is a willing loss of mental control, surrendered to an organic process that is momentarily under the direction of an

---

The art critic **PETER SCHJELDAHL'S** *ruminations on the essence of beauty appeared in the January 1984 issue of* Art in America.

exterior object. The object is not thought of or felt, exactly. It seems to use my capacities to think and feel itself.

Beauty is never pure for me. It is always mixed up with something else, some other quality or value—or story, even, in a rudimentary form of allegory, moral, or sentiment. Nothing in itself, beauty may be a mental solvent that dissolves something else, melting it into radiance.

Vladimir Nabokov

A Russian Beauty

⋅⌣

OLGA, OF WHOM WE are about to speak, was born in the year 1900, in a wealthy, carefree family of nobles. A pale little girl in a white sailor suit, with a side parting in her chestnut hair and such merry eyes that everyone kissed her there, she was deemed a beauty since childhood. The purity of her profile, the expression of her closed lips, the silkiness of her tresses that reached to the small of her back—all this was enchanting indeed.

Her childhood passed festively, securely, and gaily, as was the custom in our country since the days of old. A sunbeam falling on the cover of a *Bibliothèque Rose* volume at the family estate, the classical hoarfrost of the Saint Petersburg public gardens. . . . A supply of memories, such as these, comprised her

---

Russian novelist and short story writer **VLADIMIR NABOKOV** *is best known for the monumental success of his novel* Lolita. *"A Russian Beauty" is from his collected stories.*

sole dowry when she left Russia in the spring of 1919. Everything happened in full accord with the style of the period. Her mother died of typhus, her brother was executed by the firing squad. All these are ready-made formulae, of course, the usual dreary small talk, but it all did happen, there is no other way of saying it, and it's no use turning up your nose.

Well, then, in 1919 we have a grown-up young lady, with a pale, broad face that overdid things in terms of the regularity of its features, but just the same very lovely. Tall, with soft breasts, she always wears a black jumper and a scarf around her white neck and holds an English cigarette in her slender-fingered hands with a prominent little bone just above the wrist.

Yet there was a time in her life, at the end of 1916 or so, when at a summer resort near the family estate there was no schoolboy who did not plan to shoot himself because of her, there was no university student who would not . . . In a word, there had been a special magic about her, which, had it lasted, would have caused . . . would have wrecked . . . But somehow, nothing came of it. Things failed to develop, or else happened to no purpose. There were flowers that she was too lazy to put in a vase, there were strolls in the twilight now with this one, now with another, followed by the blind alley of a kiss.

She spoke French fluently, pronouncing *les gens* (the servants) as if rhyming with *agence* and splitting *août* (August) in two syllables (*a-ou*). She naively translated the Russian *grabezhi* (robberies) as *les grabuges* (quarrels) and used some archaic French locutions that had somehow survived in old Russian families, but she rolled her *r*'s most convincingly even though she had never been to France. Over the dresser in her Berlin room a postcard of Serov's portrait of the Tsar was fastened with a pin with a fake turquoise head. She was religious, but at times a fit of giggles would overcome her in church. She wrote verse with that terrifying facility typical of young Russian girls of her generation: patriotic verse, humorous verse, any kind of verse at all.

For about six years, that is until 1926, she resided in a boardinghouse on the Augsburgerstrasse (not far from the clock), together with her father, a broad-shouldered, beetle-browed old man with a yellowish mustache, and with tight, narrow trousers on his spindly legs. He had a job with some optimistic firm, was noted for his decency and kindness, and was never one to turn down a drink.

In Berlin, Olga gradually acquired a large group of friends, all of them young Russians. A certain jaunty tone was established. "Let's go to the cinemonkey," or "That was a heely deely German *Diele*, dance hall." All sorts of popular sayings, cant phrases, imitations of imitations were much in demand. "These cutlets are grim." "I wonder who's kissing her now?" Or, in a hoarse, choking voice: *"Mes-sieurs les officiers . . ."*

At the Zotovs', in their overheated rooms, she languidly danced the fox-trot to the sound of the gramophone, shifting the elongated calf of her leg not without grace and holding away from her the cigarette she had just finished smoking, and when her eyes located the ashtray that revolved with the music she would shove the butt into it, without missing a step. How charmingly, how meaningfully she could raise the wineglass to her lips, secretly drinking to the health of a third party as she looked through her lashes at the one who had confided in her. How she loved to sit in the corner of the sofa, discussing with this person or that somebody else's affairs of the heart, the oscillation of changes, the probability of a declaration—all this indirectly, by hints—and how understandably her eyes would smile, pure, wide-open eyes with barely noticeable freckles on the thin, faintly bluish skin underneath and around them. But as for herself, no one fell in love with her, and this was why she long remembered the boor who pawed her at a charity ball and afterwards wept on her bare shoulder. He was challenged to a duel by the little Baron R., but refused to fight. The word "boor," by the way, was used by Olga on any and every occasion. "Such boors," she would sing out in chest tones, languidly and affectionately. "What a boor . . ." "Aren't they boors?"

But presently her life darkened. Something was finished, people were already getting up to leave. How quickly! Her father died, she moved to another street. She stopped seeing her friends, knitted the little bonnets in fashion, and gave cheap French lessons at some ladies' club or other. In this way her life dragged on to the age of thirty.

She was still the same beauty, with that enchanting slant of the widely spaced eyes and with that rarest line of lips into which the geometry of the smile seems to be already inscribed. Her hair lost its shine and was poorly cut. Her black tailored suit was in its fourth year. Her hands, with their glistening but untidy fingernails, were roped with veins and were shaking from nervousness and from her wretched continuous smoking. And we'd best pass over in silence the state of her stockings. . . .

Now, when the silken insides of her handbag were in tatters (at least there was always the hope of finding a stray coin); now, when she was so tired; now, when putting on her only pair of shoes she had to force herself not to think of their soles, just as when, swallowing her pride, she entered the tobacconist's, she forbade herself to think of how much she already owed there; now that there was no longer the least hope of returning to Russia, and hatred had become so habitual that it almost ceased to be a sin; now that the sun was getting behind the chimney, Olga would occasionally be tormented by the luxury of certain advertisements, written in the saliva of Tantalus, imagining herself wealthy, wearing that dress, sketched with the aid of three or four insolent lines, on that ship-deck, under that palm tree, at the balustrade of that white terrace. And then there was also another thing or two that she missed.

One day, almost knocking her off her feet, her one-time friend Vera rushed like a whirlwind out of a telephone booth, in a hurry as always, loaded with parcels, with a shaggy-eyed terrier whose leash immediately became wound twice in her skirt. She pounced upon Olga, imploring her to come and stay at their summer villa, saying that it was fate itself, that it was wonderful and how have you been and are there many suitors. "No, my dear, I'm no longer that age," answered Olga, "and besides. . ." She added a little detail and Vera burst out laughing, letting her parcels sink almost to the ground. "No, seriously," said Olga, with a smile. Vera continued coaxing her, pulling at the terrier, turning this way and that. Olga, starting all at once to speak through her nose, borrowed some money from her.

Vera adored arranging things, be it a party with punch, a visa or a wedding. Now she avidly took up arranging Olga's fate. "The matchmaker within you has been aroused," joked her husband, an elderly Balt (shaven head, monocle). Olga arrived on a bright August day. She was immediately dressed in one of Vera's frocks, her hairdo and make-up were changed. She swore languidly, but yielded, and how festively the floorboards creaked in the merry little villa! How the little mirrors, suspended in the green orchard to frighten off birds, flashed and sparkled.

A Russified German named Forstmann, a well-off athletic widower, author of books on hunting, came to spend a week. He had long been asking Vera to find him a bride, "a real Russian beauty." He had a massive, strong nose with a fine pink vein on its high bridge. He was polite, silent, at times even morose, but knew how to form, instantly and while no one noticed, an eternal friendship with a dog or with a child. With his arrival Olga became difficult. Listless and irritable, she did all the wrong things and she knew that they were wrong. When the conversation turned to old Russia (Vera tried to make her show off her past), it seemed to her that everything she said was a lie and that everyone understood it was a lie, and therefore she stubbornly refused to say the things that Vera was trying to extract from her and in general would not cooperate in any way.

On the veranda, they would slam their cards down hard. Everyone would go off together for a stroll through the woods, but Forstmann conversed mostly with Vera's husband, and, recalling some pranks of their youth, the two of them would turn red with laughter, lag behind, and collapse on the moss. On the eve of Forstmann's departure they were playing cards on the veranda, as they usually did in the evening. Suddenly, Olga felt an impossible spasm in her throat. She still managed to smile and to leave without undue haste. Vera knocked on her door but she did not open. In the middle of the night, having swatted a multitude of sleepy flies and smoked continuously to the point where she was no longer able to inhale, irritated, depressed, hating herself and everyone, Olga went into the garden. There, the crickets stridulated, the branches swayed, an occasional apple fell with a taut thud, and the moon performed calisthenics on the white-washed wall of the chicken coop.

Early in the morning, she came out again and sat down on the porch step that was already hot. Forstmann, wearing a dark blue bathrobe, sat next to her and, clearing his throat, asked if she would consent to become his spouse—that was the very word he used: "spouse." When they came to breakfast, Vera, her husband, and his maiden cousin, in utter silence, were performing nonexistent dances, each in a different corner, and Olga drawled out in an affectionate voice "What boors!" and next summer she died in childbirth.

That's all. Of course, there may be some sort of sequel, but it is not known to me. In such cases, instead of getting bogged down in guesswork, I repeat the words of the merry king in my favorite fairy tale: Which arrow flies forever? The arrow that has hit its mark.

Romeo and Juliet

I'LL BURY THEE in a triumphant grave;

A grave? O, no! a lantern, slaughter'd youth,

For here lies Juliet, and her beauty makes

This vault a feasting presence full of light.

Death, lie thou there, by a dead man interr'd.

                    [Laying Paris in the tomb.]

How oft when men are at the point of death

Have they been merry! which their keepers call

A lightning before death: O, how may I

Call this a lightning? O my love! my wife!

Death, that hath suck'd the honey of thy breath,

Hath had no power yet upon thy beauty:

Thou art not conquer'd; beauty's ensign yet

Many of **WILLIAM SHAKESPEARE'S** *greatest plays* (King Lear, Hamlet, Othello, Antony and Cleopatra) *concern themselves with the temporalness of beauty. This excerpt is from that most famous of plays,* Romeo and Juliet.

Is crimson in thy lips and in thy cheeks,

And death's pale flag is not advanced there.

Tybalt, liest thou there in thy bloody sheet?

O, what more favor can I do to thee,

Than with that hand that cut thy youth in twain

To sunder his that was thine enemy?

Forgive me, cousin! Ah, dear Juliet,

Why art thou yet so fair? shall I believe

That unsubstantial death is amorous,

And that the lean abhorred monster keeps

Thee here in dark to be his paramour?

For fear of that, I still will stay with thee;

And never from this palace of dim night

Depart again: here, here will I remain

With worms that are thy chamber-maids; O, here

Will I set up my everlasting rest,

And shake the yoke of inauspicious stars

From this world-wearied flesh. Eyes, look your last!

Arms, take your last embrace! and, lips, O you

The doors of breath, seal with a righteous kiss

A dateless bargain to engrossing death!

Come, bitter conduct, come, unsavory guide!

Thou desperate pilot, now at once run on

The dashing rocks thy sea-sick weary bark!

Here's to my love! [*Drinks.*] O true apothecary!

Thy drugs are quick. Thus with a kiss I die.

                                        [*Dies.*]

Immortality

T HE WOMAN MIGHT have been sixty or sixty-
five. I was watching her from a deck chair by the pool of my
health club, on the top floor of a high-rise that provided a
panoramic view of all Paris. I was waiting for Professor
Avenarius, whom I'd occasionally meet here for a chat. But
Professor Avenarius was late and I kept watching the
woman; she was alone in the pool, standing waist-deep in
the water, and she kept looking up at the young lifeguard in
sweat pants who was teaching her to swim. He was giving
her orders: she was to hold on to the edge of the pool and
breathe deeply in and out. She proceeded to do this
earnestly, seriously, and it was as if an old steam engine
were wheezing from the depths of the water (that idyllic
sound, now long forgotten, which to those who never knew

Czech novelist **MILAN KUNDERA** *brilliantly traces the male's ideas of beauty
and love in his novels* The Unbearable Lightness of Being *and* The
Book of Laughter and Forgetting, *and in this excerpt from his novel*
Immortality *(1991).*

it can be described in no better way than the wheezing of an old woman breathing in and out by the edge of a pool). I watched her in fascination. She captivated me by her touchingly comic manner (which the lifeguard also noticed, for the corner of his mouth twitched slightly). Then an acquaintance started talking to me and diverted my attention. When I was ready to observe her once again, the lesson was over. She walked around the pool toward the exit. She passed the lifeguard, and after she had gone some three or four steps beyond him, she turned her head, smiled, and waved to him. At that instant I felt a pang in my heart! That smile and that gesture belonged to a twenty-year-old girl! Her arm rose with bewitching ease. It was as if she were playfully tossing a brightly colored ball to her lover. That smile and that gesture had charm and elegance, while the face and the body no longer had any charm. It was the charm of a gesture drowning in the charmlessness of the body. But the woman, though she must of course have realized that she was no longer beautiful, forgot that for the moment. There is a certain part of all of us that lives outside of time. Perhaps we become aware of our age only at exceptional moments and most of the time we are ageless. In any case, the instant she turned, smiled, and waved to the young lifeguard (who couldn't control himself and burst out laughing), she was unaware of her age. The essence of her charm, independent of time, revealed itself for a second in that gesture and dazzled me. I was strangely moved.

Acknowledgements

Foreword © 1996 by Diane Ackerman. All rights reserved.

"This Lunar Beauty" from *W. H. Auden: Collected Poems* by W. H. Auden, edited by Edward Mendelson. Copyright © 1934 and renewed 1962 by W. H. Auden. Reprinted by permission of Random House, Inc.

Excerpt from The Late Show by Helen Gurley Brown © 1993. Reprinted by permission of William Morrow and Company, Inc.

"Beauty and the Beast" from *Diary of a Film* by Jean Cocteau reprinted with permission of Dover Publications, Inc.

"Beauty-with-the-Seven-Dresses" from *Italian Folktales* by Italo Calvino, © 1956 by Giulio Einaudi editor, s.p.a., English translation © 1980 by Harcourt Brace & Company, reprinted by permission of Harcourt Brace & Company.

Excerpt from *Memory of Fire* by Eduardo Galeano, copyright © 1989 by Eduardo Galeano. Reprinted by permission of W. W. Norton.

"A Pagan World" from *The Changing Face of Beauty: Four Thousand Years of Beautiful Women* by Madge Garland, copyright © 1957 by Madge Garland.

Autobiography of a Face. Copyright © 1994 by Lucy Grealy. Reprinted by permission of Houghton Mifflin Co. All rights reserved.

Excerpt from *To Have and Have Not* by Ernest Hemingway © 1937, copyright renewed © 1965 by Mary Hemingway. Reprinted with permission of Scribner, a division of Simon & Schuster.

Excerpt from *Immortality* by Milan Kundera, translated by Peter Kussi. English translation © 1991 by Grove Press, Inc.

Women and Beauty by Sophia Loren, Arrum Press. Copyright © 1984 by Sophia Loren.